The F

Tina Susedik

Read on my lovely!

Tina Susedik

Table of Contents

Acknowledgements

As always to Linda and Jane for your editing expertise.
To Ginger Ring, Linda Rae Sande, and Randi Alexander for creating the wonderful "Wild Deadwood Reads" event in Deadwood, South Dakota. Without this event, I never would have been on the 1880s train ride that ended in Keystone where I read a sign incorrectly and instantly got the idea for "The Balcony Girl." The sign actually read: "The Balcony Grill." Oops.
To my husband, Al. Without you, life wouldn't be as interesting and fun.

Author's Notes

As I mentioned in the acknowledgements, the idea for *The Balcony Girl* came to me when I was on the bus after an 1880s train ride caught a sign in Keystone that read: "The Balcony Grill." I read it as "The Balcony Girl," and instantly had the idea of a woman who goes to Deadwood in 1879 with her sister. I had intended the story to be a short one for the anthology, *Wild Deadwood Tales*. Instead the story ended up being about the sister in *The School Marm*, which will be my next book in *The Darlings of Deadwood* series.

In 1879, when Julia and Suzanna arrive in Deadwood, the town is only three years old and as wild and rowdy as ever, and divided into "The Badlands" (the bad side of Main Street) and the good side, which for some reason wasn't named. While the main characters in the story are fictional, I used real Deadwood characters. Al Swearingen and Molly Johnson did own brothels and were as bad as described in the book. The "Bottle Fiend" also existed. Hattie's brothel didn't. Although there were shops and stores in the Badlands, Haywood's is fictious.

The fire of September 1879 destroyed the downtown, one of several times the town was destroyed by fires or floods. It is true that the fire of 1879 started in a bakery. The fire department's equipment (such as it was) burned before they could do anything to stop the raging flames. Gunpowder exploded at a hardware store making the fire even worse. People headed up the hills to safety, and, surprisingly, only one person died as a result of the fire.

5

I hope you enjoy *The Balcony Girl* as much as I did writing and re-searching it. If you ever get the chance to attend Wild Deadwood Reads, you won't be disappointed. Go to their website to find about up-coming events: www.wilddeadwoodreads.com[1]

---

1. http://www.wilddeadwoodreads.com

Chapter One

June 1879
Deadwood, Dakota Territory

Julia Lindstrom let the door of King's Restaurant and Hotel slam behind her and trailed her sister, Suzanna, along with school board member, Mr. Ogden. The wooden walkway was so uneven, if she took her eyes from it, she'd trip and break something.

Back ramrod straight, nose stuck in the air as if she were one of those princesses in foreign lands they'd read about, Suzanna paid little mind to the short, bald, stocky man. If her sister was wise, and Julia had had her doubts over the past weeks traveling from Iowa to Deadwood, Suzanna would let the man lead. After all, he was one of the men who'd hired her to be the town's new schoolteacher. Having arrived in the town only yesterday, they had no idea where the schoolhouse and new lodgings were located.

A few splashes of mud dotted Suzanna's shoes from her encounter with a man the day before. Julia clapped a gloved hand over her mouth, holding back a giggle at the memory of her sister being propelled into the muddy street. She'd hoped her haughty sister would have been knocked down a peg or two. Julia had no idea where her sister had acquired her lofty attitude.

"C'mon, Julia," Suzanna called over her shoulder, the excitement in her voice unmistakable. "Mr. Ogden says we're almost there."

Reaching the end of the boardwalk, Julia lifted the edge of her skirt and gingerly set her foot in the thick, gooey mud seeming to pervade the entire town. Would she end up like her sister, lying flat on her back surrounded by snickering townsfolk? She stepped around hundreds of mud encrusted bottles, dung, and other refuse to catch up. Holding up her skirt and carpet bag with one hand and, using the other to wave away swarms of flies, moving through the muck was precarious. The least Mr. Ogden could have done was offered to carry both their bags, but then, as a representative of the school board, he only had the new schoolteacher to impress, not her sister.

Julia shook her head at Suzanna's back. Had her sister forgotten their humble background in the weeks since they'd left the family farm outside the booming town of Drakesville, Iowa, population two hundred? Leaving their family had been difficult, but necessary. With too many mouths to feed and not enough food to go around, they'd left home to make a new life in Deadwood. At least Suzanna had a job waiting for her.

Julia nodded to a man who tipped his hat. Even though he appeared not to have washed nor changed clothes in a month of Sundays, he acted like a gentleman. Hopefully, he wouldn't get any ideas about Suz or her. They'd read about these western towns where the men outnumbered the woman ten to one. No matter how desperate she might get in finding work, there was no way she'd offer up her body for money as her parents had warned her about.

Like Suzanna, she could have attained a job as a schoolteacher somewhere, since she had as much schooling. As the eldest, after helping take care of her younger siblings, she had no desire to spend her days reining in a bunch of ragamuffins. Besides, their parents wouldn't let either of their daughters go to an unknown territory unchaperoned.

During a family meeting, it was decided she would use her one talent to earn a living: sewing. With her mother taking care of so many kids, the task of mending and making clothing for the family fell to her. So now her goal was to find work sewing for the rich women in town—if there were any. From the looks of the ramshackle buildings, crooked boardwalks, and drunks in the streets, it was highly unlikely any existed.

With the school board supplying housing for Suzanna and allowing Julia to live with her, they wouldn't have the expense of paying rent. According to the letter they'd received, a small cottage had been erected behind the schoolhouse, making it easy for the new teacher to go to school. Thankfully, Suzanna didn't have to board with families, or Julia would have had to find other accommodations. After spending their precious coin on breakfast this morning, Julia figured they had barely enough to money left to purchase the bare necessities until money started coming in.

Suzanna stopped and clapped her hands. "Oh, Julia. Hurry, you won't believe this."

For all her lofty ways, Suzanna loved teaching. Once she'd finished her own schooling, she'd taken it upon herself to teach their younger siblings. With her help, most could read, write, and cipher before they were old enough to attend the local one-room school.

"I'm coming," Julia yelled back. A two-story, yellow clapboard building, complete with a bell tower stood on a small knoll, keeping it safe from spring flooding. Instead of being mired in mud, the land around it was lush and green. A set of wooden stairs rose on the outside of the building, leading to the second level. She'd never seen a school this large.

Julia stopped at the edge of the schoolyard and shaded a hand over her eyes. A fresh coat of paint made the walls gleam like pearls in the sunlight. The long bell rope swayed in the morning breeze, setting the clapper pinging against the insides. The double doors stood open as if waiting to greet its new teacher. Without screens, sheer white curtains flapped through the opened windows giving the impression of ghosts escaping.

"Oh, my." Suzanna's face turned a shade paler than her normal Swedish skin. "Two stories? Am I expected to teach children on two different levels?"

Ogden shook his head and grinned. "No, Miss Lindstrom. The way this town is growing, the businessmen who cared to become involved, decided that we should think ahead. We built a school to accommodate future children. The upper story will be for older students. For now, you'll be using only the first floor. As there are more students, we'll add another teacher."

Suzanna let out a breath. If she were in her sister's shoes, Julia would be relieved, too. Imagine the chaos of having younger children on one floor while running upstairs to work with older children on the top floor.

"Shall we go inside?" Mr. Ogden swept a hand toward the entrance. "We've been trying to get the whitewash to dry." He led them up the three steps. "Some idiot thought he needed to use two coats because he didn't care for the color. Now it is taking forever to dry."

"Suz, you can investigate by yourself. I'll wait out here. After all, it's your domain."

While waiting for her sister, she checked out her surroundings. To the left, set off a bit from the schoolhouse, was a stable for students who arrived at school by horseback and have a place to house the horses during the day. Another shed stood beside it. If she had to venture a guess, it was a woodshed. To the left were two smaller buildings, each with a moon carved into the doors. The necessaries: one for the girls, and one for the boys.

As much as she wanted to peek at their new home, she refrained from going any further. This was something she wanted to do with her sister. Mr. Ogden and Suzanna's voices came from a door at the back of the school building. There was a front and back door? How convenient for Suzanna.

Mr. Ogden and Suzanna took the wooden, tree-lined path toward her. "C'mon, Julia, we're going to see the house." She took Julia's elbow and squeezed it against her side. "Isn't this exciting?"

Nothing could have prepared her for their new home nestled in a grove of trees. Instead of a sod structure where their family of twelve had been crammed, this was a one story, pale-yellow house with green trim. The green front door stood between two tall windows. White curtains, similar those in the schoolhouse, fluttered through open windows. The building was as close to a cottage as a newborn calf was to her father's prized bull.

Julia blinked at the tears in her eyes. Was this someone else's house? Was Mr. Ogden toying with their emotions? Still too exhausted from their bone-jarring trip to put up with a joke, she clenched her fists at her sides and opened her mouth to give the man a piece of her mind.

"Welcome home, Misses Lindstrom," he said, bowing at the waist. "The parents of your students along with the school board hope you'll be comfortable here. I'll leave you to settle in." Slapping his hat onto his bald pate, he strode down the sidewalk toward town.

"Julia, come here." Suzanna stood in the doorway, waving her into the structure. "This is a palace."

She followed her sister into the house, holding her breath in trepidation. This had to be a dream. Mr. Ogden was certain to come back or send someone else to take them to their real abode and tell them this was the home of the banker or a business owner, not two girls from a dirt-poor farm.

"Can you believe this?" Suzanna whispered, interrupting Julia's thoughts. "After seeing the awful streets and haphazard buildings in town, I expected to be living in a hovel." Giggling, arms stretched wide, she spun in a circle.

Julia pinched her arm to make sure she wasn't dreaming. The front door opened to a large, fully furnished room. Two high-backed, dark green, padded chairs book-ended a sofa in the same color and fabric. A rocking chair sat in a corner near a tall window. A black stove with shining metal trim stood in the corner, a ribbed, black bucket of coal beside it. A multi-colored, braided rug covered the center of the room, edged by gray painted wooden floors.

Suzanna disappeared through the first door to the left, while Julia flopped onto the nearest chair before she fainted. Three doors led from the main room. The open door to the right revealed a large bed covered in a patchwork quilt. From her vantage point, she couldn't tell if there was a bureau, or only typical hooks to hang clothing. Through the crack in the next door, a similar bed was visible. They wouldn't have to share a bed? As the eldest, the only time in her twenty-one years she'd slept alone was the first two years of her life. That was only because when Suzanna was born a short ten months later, she'd slept in the cradle their father had fashioned.

Would she even be able to sleep by herself? Well, she was darn well willing to try. The idea of not having to spend the night fighting her sister for covers or being kicked as Suzanna flipped and flopped around made her giggle. A room of her own. Who would have thought?

"You have to come see this kitchen. You won't believe it," Suzanna called from the room closest to the front door.

Julia opened the swinging door, her heart pounding like she'd spent an afternoon chasing after her youngest siblings to keep them from killing each other. Standing in the doorway, she pressed her hand to her mouth. This was their future. One she'd never dreamed possible. A future that held great things for them. Anyway, that's what she prayed for.

Chapter Two

The pounding of boots on the wooden stairs leading to his law office above Stebbin's Post and Company Bank took Daniel Iverson's attention from the report he was reading. No doubt another Chinaman being accused of selling opium. When would these men be left alone? They weren't harming anyone by selling the drug to their own people. Even though opium wasn't for him, in his opinion, if any of the miners wanted to waste their hard-earned money on easing their loneliness with drugs, let them. What was the difference between that and drowning their sorrows in booze?

The door creaked open, revealing the short, stout form of Oliver Ogden, a sometime friend.

"So, what did they think?" Daniel asked.

Ogden sat on a wooden chair on the other side of the desk and mopped his red face with a white hanky. Dan tossed the paper aside then propped his feet on the wooden surface, hooking his hands behind his head.

"Miss Suzanna was in awe of the school building. I didn't stick around to see what they thought of the house. If the older sister's wide eyes were any indication, I believe they loved it."

"Well, they should. It cost a pretty penny to build and furnish both buildings. I'm glad the school board listened to us."

Ogden puffed out his chest. "Yes, it was a good idea, if I do say so myself."

Daniel held back a snort. As if the idea of making the accommodations nice enough to entice a teacher to the rough and tumble town and stay longer than it took to find either a husband or gold, was Ogden's idea. Hell. When Daniel first proposed the idea to the school board, Ogden's voice had been louder than any of the other men when they turned him down. When given the choice of boarding with families in already crowded conditions or living in a new, clean place of her own, they hoped a woman would choose to fulfill her contract to teach one year before marrying.

And when he suggested paying more for a teacher than they'd offered in the past, the voices rose enough to rouse old Mr. Olson, who was deaf as a post.

"Pay a woman forty dollars a month?"

"Women aren't worth it."

"That's preposterous. A waste of money."

It had taken more than a large amount of reasoning with the men to convince them Deadwood could afford to pay a woman to travel to an unknown, still rather lawless town. The last three teachers hadn't worked out. The first teacher never taught one day before disappearing. A year ago, the next teacher, the wife of a miner, Minnie Callison, was found murdered in her bed. It was doubtful, but he hoped the new teacher wouldn't hear about the unsolved incident.

The following teacher decided to introduce pocket novels to her students. Teaching contemporary pulp fiction to their children nearly caused an uprising by the parents. Needless to say, the teacher quickly found a husband to support her. According to her, it was love at first sight.

Personally, he didn't understand this 'love at first sight' crap. A couple needed to spend time together, let their feelings grow and mature before making the leap into marriage. Hell, marriage was nothing more than a trap set by women to have someone take care of them for free.

Dan fingered his pristine, brown cowboy hat, resting brim side up on the desk. He wished this new schoolmarm would stick it out.

His reputation was on the line. He wasn't close to being the only lawyer in town but garnered the majority of the work. If his idea failed, his career in Deadwood would be . . . well, dead.

When he'd first followed the gold to Deadwood three years ago, he was simply another man in a long line of men dreaming of striking it rich. No one had paid attention to him. It took helping convict Jack McCall of murdering Bill Hickock to bring him to the notice of the town leaders. Work was sent his way, including helping to set up city ordinances.

Daniel dropped his feet to the floor and leaned his elbows on a desk filled with three piles of neatly stacked papers. "Did you let Miss Lindstrom know when school would start?"

"I told her the kids would arrive Monday morning. That should give them time to get settled and for us to let the families know school will be in session again."

He huffed a breath. "Think they'll believe us this time?"

Ogden shrugged. "I'm sure there will be those that'll wait to see if this one pans out."

Daniel laughed at Ogden's use of the word *pan*, even if the man didn't seem to get the pun. "Did you show them where to buy supplies?"

Ogden shook his head. "Didn't have time. I wanted to let you know I'd delivered girls safely to their house." He slapped his knees and stood. "I'd best be getting back to . . ."

The front door of his small office opened. "Off to where?" Kingston Winson, 'King' to his friends, asked.

"The wife is whining about coming to town. She claims the bottoms of two of her cooking pots are ready to drop off. I promised her I'd take her to the tinsmith to see if they can be repaired. If not, I'll have to take her to Jensen and Bliss' Hardware to get new ones. If'n I don't do it today, she says I'll be eating my supper raw."

Daniel rose, tugged down the edges of his dark blue, brocade vest, slipped on a black dress jacket, and plopped his hat on his head. He followed Ogden to the door and attempted to open it. "Damn doorknob."

"When the hell is your landlord going to fix that thing?" King asked.

"I don't know," Daniel said, turning the loose knob left then right. "I've asked him about a dozen times to repair it. I even offered to do it myself, but he won't let me."

When Daniel finally finagled the doorknob and opened the door, Ogden stopped and slapped the doorframe. "Jumpin' Jeehosofat. I'll be losin' my mind if I'm not careful. Mary said to let everyone know about the party at the schoolhouse Saturday night to welcome the new teacher. The women are making food and such. Starts at five o'clock. Clyde is bringing his fiddle, George his guitar. I hear Zeb is playing the washboard."

"Sounds fun. Has anyone told the Lindstrom sisters about it?" Daniel asked.

Ogden scratched his head. "I didn't, but someone should." Ogden followed his friends down the stairs.

"Where're you headed, Dan?" Kingston asked, nearly falling over as he reversed directions to trail after Dan when he left the building.

"Ogden took the new schoolmarm and her sister to the school and their house but didn't bother to tell them where to buy supplies." Daniel stopped at the edge of the boardwalk waiting for a wagon pulled by two oxen to pass, their heads down as they forced their legs through the mud. "I thought I'd stop by and escort the ladies to Haywood's Dry Goods and tell them about the dance. Why don't you come along?"

Daniel held back a chuckle when King hesitated before stepping into the mud to cross the street. After yesterday's fiasco, he didn't blame the guy.

"Um, sure."

"You're not afraid to see the new schoolmarm again, are you?"

When they safely reached the other side, they stomped the mud from their boots. Since they'd have to cross several other streets, it was a crazy, futile thing to do.

King chuckled. "She sure is a feisty one."

"Which one? The teacher or her sister?"

They moved to the side then tipped their hats to the banker, J.W. Woods, and his wife, Bertha.

"Heard about your little encounter with the new teacher, King," Woods said, rolling back on his heels and smirking. "Poor woman. But then what could we expect from our illustrious hotel owner? Good thing you didn't drown her."

Daniel seized his friend's arm when King took a step toward the banker. It was well known there was no love lost between the two men. Woods was a pompous jackass believing the town should bow and kiss his boots because he owned a bank. There was more to the animosity between the two than simple personality clashes. From the time King bought up the land where his business and several others stood and purchased a large parcel of land outside of town that Woods coveted, there was tension between the two. Also, King was known as a kind, hard-working man, whereas the banker seemed to grow richer without lifting a finger.

Many times, over drinks, they had discussed Woods' rise in fortune. They both believed there were some under-handed dealings going on between him and Al Swearingen and other brothel owners but were never able to pinpoint what they were.

As if she were a coquette thirty years younger, Mrs. Woods flicked open her fan, waved it in front of her face, and giggled. "I want to thank you again, Mr. Iverson, for escorting me to my husband's bank. J.W. appreciates it, too, don't you, James?"

J.W. ran a hand over his face. "Uh, yeah, sure, dumplin'."

Daniel held back a snort. As if the banker would ever appreciate or thank anyone for doing anything for him. Like an emperor staring down at his subjects, he expected them to do his bidding. Plus, it was well known that the man had frequented the upstairs rooms of several brothels before his wife arrived on the scene. Whether he kept it up or not wasn't for Dan to worry about.

Mrs. Woods tugged on her husband's arm. "James, you promised to take me to lunch at the hotel. I'm famished."

Daniel bit back a grin. With her wide hips, bosom large enough to hold a plate without falling, and wobbling neck, Woods' wife looked about as famished as a mountain lion after gorging himself on his latest kill. "Going to King's?"

Woods tugged at his lapel and puffed out his chest. "Not likely. I wouldn't want my precious to be poisoned."

Once again Daniel held King back. "He's not worth it, King," he whispered to his friend. "Let him go to Oyster Bay." He turned to the couple. "Have a good lunch. Ma'am, Woods." With a tug on King's arm, they headed down the boardwalk, their boots thudding on the worn wood.

"Watch out for mud puddles and dogs, King," Woods called out behind them.

King's jaw muscles clenched. "Bastard."

"You got that right, but don't give him the satisfaction of seeing you angry. All he cares about is himself." Daniel stepped behind King to let a couple of the women who worked at the Gem Theater pass. Not that he frequented the establishment much. He never partook in the pleasures of the flesh.

They tipped their hats to the ladies. He and King were unlike most of the men in this town, who made snide comments about the women who made their living on their backs. Men like Woods who paid for the women at night then acted all high and mighty during the day and refused to acknowledge the women they'd tumbled. But come dark, they scuttled from one side of the street to the other through the underground tunnel, then up the stairs to the establishments.

King moved beside Daniel, then hesitated before stepping into another muddy street, an action Daniel couldn't ignore. He chuckled, slapping his friend on the back. "Afraid?" He didn't blame the guy after yesterday's fiasco. Knowing how easy-going King was, though, it wouldn't be long before he'd be laughing about the incident.

"Hell. Wouldn't you be?" Nothing more was said while they maneuvered through the muck. "Do you know how many buckets of ice-cold water it took to clean myself off?" he asked when they safely reached the other side.

They walked past wooden buildings looking as though they'd been constructed by one-eyed drunks. "Why didn't you order a hot bath in your room?"

"Are you kidding? Leona would have shot me if I'd tracked mud into her—I mean my hotel. You know how particular she is about the place."

Leona was King's younger sister. A spinster who took it upon herself to crack the whip and make sure King's Inn was the best-kept place in Deadwood. When she'd first arrived to help King, Daniel had harbored thoughts of courting the woman. She wasn't unattractive—until she opened her mouth to give orders, expecting everyone to obey immediately. He enjoyed a more docile woman, one who catered to her man. He had a feeling there wasn't a man in all of Deadwood who'd put up with the woman.

Anxious to see how Miss Lindstrom liked the schoolhouse and lodging, Daniel picked up speed. "What the hell are you dragging your heels for?" he asked King when the buildings came into view. "You're not afraid that little filly will call you names again, are you?" He faced King, who had stopped at the edge of the boardwalk, and wiped away his smile. Judging from King's scowl fierce enough to scare away the most violent man in the town's jail, something was up. "You reckon where the women stayed last night?"

King stomped from foot to foot shucking away the mud from his boots. "I . . . Um . . ."

"Spit it out man, the day's not getting any longer, you know."

"They stayed at my hotel."

"So, why does that have your spurs rubbing your ass?"

"Well . . . Um . . . Remember all those buckets of water I said it took to wash away the mud?"

"Yeah?"

"Well, I might have accidentally on purpose dumped a bucket over the teacher's head."

Daniel stopped in his tracks and gaped at his friend. "You what? Why the hell would you do that?" He held up a hand. "Wait, I don't think I want to know."

"Thanks. But she got her comeuppance this morning."

"What did you do?"

"I didn't do anything except show up at their table and introduce myself as the owner." King's eyes twinkled. "She barely said a word before scurrying out the door to meet Ogden."

Daniel shook his head. Something told him that wouldn't be the end of the story between Miss Lindstrom and King. It was going to be interesting to watch how they reacted to one another this morning. "Well, let's get going so we can get them to the store before lunch."

King's sigh was strong enough to knock over a young child. "When you suggested it, I thought coming along would be a good idea. Now, I'm not so sure."

"You're a big, brave man." Daniel slapped King on the back. "Hell, you've been known to wrestle with a bear. I'm sure you can handle one tiny schoolteacher." Did King's snort mean he didn't agree?

Chapter Three

"What are we going to eat?" Suzanna called from the kitchen. "There are a lot of cakes and some loaves of bread probably left by parents, but I don't see anything else."

Julia hung the last of her four blouses beside three skirts and one dress on the wall hooks behind her bedroom door. She bit back a giggle. A room of her own. No sharing a bed with Suzanna and their younger sister, Rosie, in the loft that was freezing in the winter and sweltering in the summer. No little ones jumping on top of her to get her up in the wee hours of the morning. What was it going to be like rolling over in the double bed without getting yelled at for accidentally touching someone's leg?

Fingering a woolen wrap that never seemed to keep out the cold of winter, she sighed. If she hoped to sew for the society ladies of the town, she was going to have to make a few more stylish outfits. The stagecoach stops in towns and way stations showed them how out-of-date their clothes were. By the shabby way most of the men in town were dressed, maybe it wouldn't make any difference to them, but it might to the women. And, even though this house came free, they couldn't rely on Suzanna's salary alone. From what she'd heard on the trip here, the cost of goods in mining towns was immense.

She picked up her small, blue, fabric coin purse, left her bedroom, and sat on one of the parlor chairs. "How much money do we have in our funds?" Julia pulled open the strings and poured her coins on the side table.

Suzanna came through the kitchen door, carrying her pale yellow purse. Both pouches were made from leftover blouse material. Suzanna knelt on the floor beside Julia's legs and dumped out her purse.

"I have a grand total of fifteen dollars and . . . thirty cents." Suzanna said, resting back on her legs. "How much do you have?"

Julia sighed. "A bit more. Remember how I patched some clothes and made that quilt for old Mr. Robinson back home? He was so happy, he paid me extra, so I have twenty-two dollars and eleven cents."

"That gives us thirty-seven dollars and forty-one cents." Suzanna bit her bottom lip. "Do you think that will be enough? I don't get paid for an entire month."

"Didn't I see pots, pans and dishes in the kitchen?"

Suzanna nodded. "And, except for food, nearly anything else we'll need to cook."

"We have sheets, pillows, blankets, coal, and more furniture than we've had our entire lives." Julia returned her money to her purse. "That means we'll only have to purchase food."

"Do you think we can buy some material? When we stopped at the way stations, I noticed how outdated and backcountry our clothes are."

Julia pulled the purse strings tight. "You saw that, too? We'll have to see what the stores in town have for fabric. I want to dress up a bit more, too, to impress women like Mrs. Woods. I imagine she has some influence in this town and could help me get some work."

Suzanna ran a hand down her dark blue skirt. "I'm sure my skirts and blouses will be fine for teaching, but we both need something a bit more special for church and social functions. If we let the women know you made the clothes you should get some orders."

"Let's come up with a shopping list, so we don't buy what we don't need. Did you happen to see a general store when we came into town?"

"No. I was too busy trying to keep Mr. Silverstone's hands to himself and observing all the riffraff roaming around."

"Not to mention taking a spill in the mud."

Suzanna wrinkled her nose. "Please, don't remind me. If I ever see that brute again, it'll be too soon."

"Just remember he owns a hotel and eatery."

"That doesn't make him a gentleman," Suzanna said, her nose stuck in the air. "Is there anything to write with?"

Julia stood and nodded toward a small desk in one corner of the room. "Maybe there's something on this desk." On the top were paper and an item resembling a pen, but without the quill. A tan cork stood out on a familiar bottle of black ink. Back home, they were still using quills. "What's this?"

"Oh, that's one of those fountain pens. I saw one in the store in Drakesville when I went to town with Pa."

"How does it work?" Julia asked, fingering the black pen with a pointed tip.

"Sit and watch," Suzanna said, taking the pen from Julia. "See this little lever on the side? You put the tip of the pen in the inkwell and lift the lever, which sucks the ink into the pen. Then . . ." She wrote her name on a piece of paper. "Ta-da. It holds quite a bit of ink, so you don't have to keep dipping the tip into the inkwell all the time."

"What'll they think of next?" She took the pen from Suzanna and tapped the end to her lips. "Let's see. What do we need?"

"Flour, sugar, eggs, milk, spices, lard, beans, rice," Suzanna suggested.

"And saleratus to make bread and rolls." Julia tapped the pen against her lips. "Bacon, some beef and chicken. Cheese."

"Vegetables, some fruit."

"If they have them."

"I wonder if we'll have time to plant a garden for food for the winter."

Julia held back a shudder. If there was one thing she'd hated on the farm, it was planting a garden, pulling weeds all summer long. In the fall, harvesting the crops and putting it all up for the winter was as bad. She'd heard winters in Deadwood were rough. If they wanted to stretch their money, she'd have to bite the bullet and do her part. "I'll put seeds on my list."

Suzanna rose, pulled aside the sheer curtains, and peered out the window. "We'll have to ask, but it looks as if there is enough space in the yard to put in a garden. Maybe a few flowers, too."

It wasn't the first time since they'd left Iowa that she wished she'd had more of an interest in the preparation and preservation of food, but as the oldest, she was in charge of the little ones, leaving Suzanna in the kitchen with their mother. At least one of them knew what to do. Other than her sister wanting to live above their station in life, they were a nice mix. She was better at money than Suzanna, while Suzanna was better at planning, keeping house, and cooking. The garden would come under her charge, since she'd wrangled with it back home. They both loved books, checkers, and card games. If Suzanna could keep her nose out of the air, they'd get along perfectly fine.

Suzanna dropped the curtain and settled onto the other chair. "How are we going to get to the store?" She frowned. "I don't relish the idea of trudging through that mud again, nor coming into contact with some of those men. Who knows what they'd do to us?"

"I can't imagine anyone accosting us in broad daylight."

"After yesterday, I'm not so sure."

"The biggest question is how we'd get our purchases back here. It's quite a list."

"Do you think they deliver?"

"I don't know, but it would be nice. It's not like we're miles from town. But we still have to get to the stores and don't even know which one to use."

Suzanna checked a clock sitting on the desk. "It's nearly lunchtime. Maybe we should venture out. If we have enough coin left, we could stop somewhere and eat."

"At King's? Hoping to run into the owner again?"

"Certainly not!" Suzanna's cheeks turned pink as her voice rose to a screech. "If I ever see that clod again, it'll be too soon."

"The lady doth protest too much, methinks."

Suzanna stomped to the kitchen. "Oh, hush up."

A loud rap on the front door halted Julia from following her sister. Who could be visiting them? They didn't know anyone in town. Parents? Mr. Ogden again? Someone hoping to steal from them, or worse, thinking two single women on the edge of town were fair game? Fear skittered across her skin. Was there a lock on the door? If so, they should have used it, but she'd been too excited about their new home to take notice.

Instead of opening the door, she peered out a side window. Even though the images were blurry, it was obvious two men waited for her to answer. She eased an edge of the curtain back. She could hardly wait to tell Suzanna that one of their guests was Mr. Winson. The other she recognized from yesterday but couldn't place him.

Another knock reverberated through the room.

"Is someone at the door?" Suzanna asked, wiping her hands on a towel as she came from the kitchen. "Why don't you answer it?"

"Um . . . Because . . ."

"Oh, for heaven's sake, Julia." Suzanna pursed her lips. "Open the door. What if it's Mrs. Woods or one of the other important ladies from town coming to meet me?" Without giving Julia a chance to speak, Suzanna yanked open the door then slammed it shut. "It's . . .

It's . . ." She pointed a shaking finger at the door. "That man. That oaf. That defiler of women."

Julia rolled her eyes at her sister's theatrics. "He didn't defile you any more than he did me. And he was a perfect gentleman this morning."

Suzanna crossed her arms over her chest. "I don't care. Don't you dare open that door."

"Since you've already opened it, it would be rude to leave them standing on our front step." She took a deep breath and pulled the door open. "Mr. Winson. What a nice surprise."

"Obviously your sister doesn't think so." He glanced over her shoulder, his eyes twinkling with laughter.

Julia stood to the side. If the man was smart, he'd hide his amusement. "Please come in. We were discussing what we need from the general store." She closed the door and stood beside her sister.

A tall, slim man wore a dark blue brocade vest, the kind she imagined a gambler would wear, beneath a dark dress coat. A black string tie was wrapped around the stiff collar of his white shirt. As Mr. Winson had, the man removed his cowboy hat and rolled the brim in his hands.

From his hat, she turned her attention to his face. Her breath caught. Something fluttered in the vicinity of her heart. Oh my. Dark, thick, wavy hair hung to his shoulders while several strands curled over his forehead. A bump on his nose meant he'd broken it at one time. A fistfight in a saloon brawl? His grin revealed twin dimples on either side of a thick mustache. Then her eyes met ones as blue as a clear Iowa summer sky. Her stomach flipped like the time she'd fallen from the haymow door to her father's wagon below.

Only this time, instead of being a frightened flutter, it was . . . What was it? She pressed a hand to her stomach. Was she getting sick? She didn't feel sick, maybe a bit warm, but . . . Now wasn't the time to figure out what she was feeling. The man continued to gaze into her eyes. Coming from an area of Iowa settled predominantly by blonde, blue-eyed Swedes and the French, she'd never encountered someone with such dark hair combined with brilliant blue eyes. Usually black hair meant brown eyes. The combination of his hair and eyes, made him look . . . dangerous?

Taking a step back, Julia broke eye contact. They'd only officially met Mr. Winson this morning, but the other man was a stranger. Were they here to harm them? Her stomach clenched. Men were known to not be able to control their baser instincts, and although they were strong from all the farm work they'd done, they were no match for two tall, well-built men.

"Misses Lindstrom." Mr. Winson said. "You may remember me from this morning." His lips twitched as if he were trying not to smile. "And this is my good friend, Daniel Iverson. We came to escort you to town."

Mr. Iverson bowed as if he were in the presence of royalty, and not a schoolteacher and her sister. Between his clothing and manners, she pictured him sitting at a table, cigar in his mouth, dealing cards, while fleecing unsuspecting miners out of their hard-earned gold.

Julia tipped her head at the men. "Mr. Iverson. Mr. Winson."

Mr. Winson kept his eyes on Suzanna. "Please, call me King. We don't hold with Eastern society rules out here in the West."

"And call me Daniel."

That was good to know, since back home they'd never called anyone close to their own ages Mister. "I'm Julia and this is my sister, Suzanna. Thank you for your offer but I'm sure you have other things to do. We can manage ourselves."

"Excuse me, Julia," Mr. Iverson said, his deep voice reverberating through her system, "But you're new here to Deadwood and . . ."

The man paused and stared at her as if he didn't know what he'd been saying. Was he addled in the brain? "And what?" she prodded.

Daniel's face turned red. Men blushed? She thought only women did.

"Um." He slapped his hat against his leg. "You aren't aware of the riffraff in town."

Julia visualized the muddy streets. Buildings were seemingly built by drunken brawlers, dogs and other animals ran wild, and men dressed as if their clothing hadn't been washed in months. She'd even seen a few hogs roaming about. "Based on what we saw yesterday coming through town, I believe we have a good idea of what Deadwood is like."

King rolled back on his heels. "Seeing is different than experiencing Deadwood. Yesterday, you barely had a chance to take in the, uh . . ." He licked his lips. "Uh, scenery before you were escorted to the hotel. While Deadwood is settling down some and this side of town is quiet, no woman walking alone downtown is completely safe."

"Ladies, I agree with King." Daniel's chest heaved as he took a deep breath. "Please let us escort you. We can either carry your purchases back here or help secure delivery."

Julia pinched Suzanna's fingers when her sister mumbled under her breath, "I don't want to go with them." She knew how Suzanna felt about King but these jolts of energy snaking their way through her at not only Daniel's deep, rasping voice, but also his good looks, were scaring her. Was she any safer with him than the riffraff he mentioned? The two men may look like gentlemen, but the girls' mother had warned them about wolves in sheep's clothing.

King bowed his head. "I assure you we only have your best interests at heart. We want to make sure you get to the store and home safely. We'll also," he winked at Suzanna who sucked in a breath, "make sure you navigate our muddy streets undamaged."

Julia recalled the man on the stage who'd given Suzanna a bit of trouble. Her sister wasn't aware she knew of the man's attempts to enjoy what wasn't his to enjoy, but she'd been ready to push the man from the conveyance if he'd become more persistent. If he was roaming the streets, maybe they'd be safer with these two men, even if Daniel was a gambler more than likely visiting the houses of ill repute she'd read about.

Taking Suzanna's arm, she tugged her to the other side of the room. "I think we should accept their offer."

"Are you crazy? I don't want to have anything to do with Mr. Winson."

"So you've said a million times. But remember Mr. Silverstone from the stage? What if he accosts you? Remember the drunks we saw yesterday and the noises coming from the saloons on the way to the hotel? What if someone does something to us? I think we're better off with these men than wandering around on our own."

Suzanna glanced over her shoulder and tapped a finger against her lips. "I suppose you're right, but you're walking with Mr. Winson."

With the way her body reacted to Daniel Iverson, that would be for the best. A shudder went through her. If the man touched her, she'd most likely fall off the boardwalk and end up landing in the mud as Suzanna had. Deadwood could call them 'The Mud Sisters.' Since she had a feeling there was more to Suzanna's dislike of Mr. Winson than yesterday's incident, it would be interesting to have the two walk together, but then that would put her beside the intriguing Mr. Iverson. She didn't care for the way he looked at her or the way she felt when he looked at her. Not one bit. Oh, heck, why were things so complicated?

"Why don't we walk side-by-side and let the gentlemen walk behind us?" Julia suggested. "That way we wouldn't have to walk with either of them."

"Or talk to them. Or look at them."

"Ladies." Daniel pulled out his pocket watch. "If we hurry along, you can shop, take lunch at King's restaurant, and we'd have plenty of time to escort you back home."

"All right, gentlemen," Julia nodded, hoping they weren't making a mistake. "Let us gather our bonnets and purses and you may show us the way to the store."

Chapter Four

"**S**o, what do you think?" King whispered as they followed the two sisters down the boardwalk.

Daniel nearly tripped on a loose board. The sway of Julia's hips was distracting. He needed to pay attention to where he was walking or land flat on his face. "About what?"

"About the women."

"Other than the fact that the teacher cleaned up nicely, I haven't thought anything." Which was an out and out lie. The minute he laid eyes on the older sister his heart nearly pounded out of his chest. When he tried to talk, it was as if a rattler was in his mouth, shaking its tail against his tongue and teeth, making him spit and sputter.

He never had problems talking to women, so why the hell did he blush like some ignoramus? For heaven's sake, he was a grown man, not a young pup coming face-to-face with a girl after figuring out they weren't so bad. So why did looking at the older Miss Lindstrom turn his insides into something resembling the muddy goo filling Deadwood's streets?

King slapped him on the arm. "Are you kidding me? Are you blind? They're both pretty and have nice figures. Even though the teacher seems a bit prickly, I think I'm in love."

Daniel stopped, making King change directions again. "Have you lost your mind? You only met the woman yesterday and, may I remind you, under rather unfavorable conditions."

"Yeah, well. There was something about her that," King placed a hand over his heart, "set my heart on fire."

With a grunt, Daniel double-stepped to catch up to the women. "*Set your heart on fire?* Jeez. Have you been reading Lord Byron again?" Shaking his head at his friend, he strode beside the women. "Ladies, we're getting closer to downtown. It would be safer if we were to walk beside you, so the men in town know you're with us."

Julia stuck her nose in the air. "We'll be fine, Mr. Iverson," she said, hooking her arm through her sister's.

Before she'd taken a few steps, Daniel took Julia by the arm and spun her around to face him.

Her nostrils flared. "Mr. Iverson, unhand me this instant."

Daniel's fingers burned at her touch. His heart raced while his stomach did a jig. Damn. What was happening to him? "As much as I want to, I'll not release you until you and your sister listen to me."

King stood behind Suzanna, folded his arms over his chest, and grinned.

What? Did King believe he didn't have the guts to chastise the women? Well, he'd come against angrier men in his life and survived. Two young women from back East certainly couldn't do any harm to him. Could they?

"Mr. Iverson, if you don't let go of my arm, I'm going to scream so loud and so long, some gentleman in this town will surely come to our rescue."

"And I'll join her," Suzanna added.

Over the younger sister's shoulder, King shrugged as if to say they should let the women go. Not a chance. He'd seen what some of the men in town did to women. If that no good, slippery dance hall owner of the Gem Theater, Al Swearingen, ever got his hands on them, they'd never see the outside of his brothel again. Swearingen's trips to towns back East to recruit women to work for him as 'actresses' and 'waiters' were well known. With promises of a better life, they were in for a big surprise when their jobs were as dance hall girls and worse. So it didn't matter that Suzanna was the new schoolteacher.

Julia and her sister would disappear into the bowels of the Gem The-ater, never to be seen again.

Daniel ground his teeth together. "Both of you listen to me. Life back in Iowa is significantly more civilized than here. There are too many men in this town who don't care that you're genteel women. With so many more men than women, there are some who will see you for only one thing. How can I make you understand that you're not safe on the streets alone, or together for that matter?"

Julia paled. Good, maybe she was going to take his words to heart.

"Must you walk alongside us? Can't you simply walk behind where you can keep an eye on us?"

Daniel removed his hat and raked his fingers through his hair. Hope that she'd listen disappeared like a leaf in a spring tornado. "Miss Julia."

"Oh, for heaven's sake, Mr. Iverson. Let's go so we can get our shopping done. My sister has a lot of work to do to get ready for the children on Monday." She glanced over her shoulder at him. "You do want her to be prepared, don't you?"

King nudged him in the side. "Let them have their way, or we'll never get to Haywood's. We can only hope no one accosts them."

"I hate to say this, but maybe it would be a good thing if someone did. Teach the teacher and her sister a lesson."

"Maybe." King shrugged and swept his hand toward the sisters. "Ladies, lead on."

KEEPING ONE EYE ON the men passing by and one on Julia's swaying hips was difficult. Too bad he didn't have a third eye, or eyes in the back of his head. With King keeping his focus on the teacher, he wouldn't be much help in an emergency.

As they approached the "Badlands" of Deadwood, the number of men milling in front of buildings, mostly saloons, increased. Daniel's heart rate doubled. He placed his hand on his gun. It never ceased to amaze him how rapidly the town had grown since he'd arrived three years ago. In a matter of a few weeks, more than ten thousand men and a few women descended on Deadwood Gulch.

From the tents and shanties that had sprung up by the first arrivals, to hastily constructed wooden saloons, brothels, and businesses, the area was a mix of Chinamen, Negroes, Irish, and men from all walks of life. Deadwood was a melting pot of people hoping to strike it rich.

Even though the streets were muddy and many of the buildings were haphazardly built wherever the businessman wanted to put up a few boards, the town was becoming a bit more civilized. There was a move to organize the town. Unfortunately, the best places to purchase goods, Haywood's Dry Goods and John Wallace Groceries were in the "Badlands," making it more dangerous for the sisters to venture there, even if they were being escorted. But they had no choice. Until the city leaders decided to clean up the town, the riffraff and good citizens had to mix.

They crossed Wall Street, the imaginary line between the good and bad sides of Deadwood. Daniel moved closer to Julia, nearly stepping on the back of her skirts.

"Would you please back off, Mr. Iverson," she called over her shoulder.

Damned if he would. The noise increased three-fold when they stepped onto the boardwalk as every other establishment was a dance hall, saloon, brothel, or all three combined. It didn't matter that it was still morning. Music blared, women laughed, men argued, and the scent of unwashed bodies, cigars, and liquor permeated the air.

Daniel held his breath as they passed the Gem Theater. Four men stood outside the door, smoking their rolled cigarettes.

"Well, look what we have here." One of the men pushed away from the wall and staggered toward them. "Two new ladies coming to work at ol' Ed's. I've a hanker'n for some fresh meat."

The man tipped his hat but the gleam in his eyes sent chills down Daniel's spine. "Joe, you're drunk. These ladies are not what you think." Daniel knew Joe might act polite, but there was only one thing on his mind. Thankfully, the sisters caught on fast. He tugged Julia to his side. King put himself between the other men and Suzanna.

"What does he mean?" Julia whispered behind him.

Didn't she have any idea what these men wanted? What type of sheltered life had they led? "Let me do the talking. Now Joe, you and your buddies go back into the Gem." He reached into his vest pocket and pulled out a small coin. "I'll even spring for a round of drinks."

Behind him Julia screamed. "Let go of me, you brute."

Damn. Somehow, while he was dealing with Joe, Mingus Thoreson had snuck up and made a grab for her. "C'mon, sweetheart. How's about a little kiss?"

Daniel pulled out his gun. Keeping it trained on Joe and his buddies, he glanced over his shoulder ready to come to her rescue. "Mingus, remove your hands from the lady."

Before Daniel had a chance to react, Mingus grunted, clutched his crotch, fell to his knees, and then to his side, rolling into a ball like an armadillo. Tears streaming down his face, he rocked from side to side. "I'll. Get. You. For. This. Bitch."

"Don't you dare ever touch me again, you brute." Julia faced her attacker, fingers clenched in fists, arms held in a boxer's pose.

"What did you do?"

"What my mother taught me to do when a man tries something. Kicked him where it'll hurt the worst."

Daniel swore his own privates shrunk and buried themselves deep inside his drawers. There was nothing worse for a man than getting his privates struck. He had to give the woman credit for handling Mingus, but all she succeeded in doing was making him angry, almost certainly angry enough for him to retaliate at some point in the future.

Giving each man a glare, Suzanna moved to her sister's side. "And that's not all Ma and Pa taught us, so if you baboons get any more ideas about accosting us, you'd better think twice if you know what's good for you." She took Julia by the elbow. "C'mon, sister, let's go."

Still in shock at Julia's actions, Daniel scrambled to catch up with them. "Ladies, wait. I'm impressed by what you did back there, but only a few men saw you in action, so you still need protection. It's one thing to be face-to-face with your attacker, but what if they came up from behind you? What would you do then?"

Julia narrowed her eyes. "Want me to demonstrate what I could do?"

His privates clenched. "Uh. No."

"Thought so." She wove through a crowd of men, ignoring their catcalls and whistles.

Momentarily struck with enjoying Julia's feistiness, Daniel let out a sigh of relief that King had the presence of mind to stay with the ladies. When he gathered his thoughts, he had to race through the press of men to overtake them before they entered the store.

After all the noise outside, the relative quiet of the Haywood's Dry Goods Store was a welcome relief. The bell over the store's door had barely stopped ringing before the sisters moved to the fabric piled in shelves along an inner wall.

King leaned against a table filled with mining equipment, ankles crossed, arms folded across his chest, and grinned. "I guess Julia gave you a what-for, didn't she?"

"Shut up, King." Daniel copied King's stance. "And you shouldn't talk so smart. I don't see Suzanna treating you any better."

"That's true. But I'm not one to give up. There's something about the schoolteacher that interests me. She cleans up right nice."

Daniel knew what King meant, except he had his eyes on the older sister. He swiped a hand down his face. Hell, she wasn't even his type. He'd always been attracted to dark-haired, full-breasted women with a bit of padding on their hips. Julia was tall and willowy, with slim hips and not much on top. Not that he was staring at her or anything. So why did his heart skip a beat and his stomach feel as if he'd eaten one of those awful oysters from the Oyster Bay Restaurant, the ones that caught in his throat and made his stomach roll? He heaved a sigh. What would she do if she found out she made his stomach pitch as if he were on a ship in a hurricane? Possibly bean him over the head with her coin bag.

Suzanna held a piece of lavender fabric printed with pale yellow flowers to her sister's face. The color made Julia's blue eyes darker. Her blonde hair seemed to sparkle. If the woman wore something in that shade, the men in town would swarm to her like bears to honeycomb.

"Do you know what Suzanna's sister is going to do?" King asked, taking a cigar from his breast pocket.

Nodding at several women perusing the shelves, Daniel nudged his friend in the side. "Better not let Sadie see you with that thing. She'll go after you with a broom."

King slipped the cigar back into his pocket. "For a moment I forgot where we were."

"I don't know what Julia will do." To his chagrin, Suzanna put down the lavender fabric, while Julia picked up a brown piece that reminded him of the street muck. She wasn't going to make something from that horrid-looking color, was she? Hell, if she ever landed in the street, she'd blend in so well, they'd never find her.

"Lord, I hope they don't buy that dreadful material," King said, reading his mind.

"Me, either." He bit back a curse when Julia said something to Sadie Haywood as the woman spread the fabric on a table, picked up a pair of scissors, and cut a large piece. Daniel didn't know much about sewing clothes, in fact he knew nothing, but it seemed to him there was enough there to make several dresses and a few skirts to boot. "Let's go see what Colin is up to," Daniel said, turning his back on the ladies and the god-awful fabric.

Chapter Five

Since their family farm lay so far from the nearest town, opportunities to wander through a store had been rare. On those occasions when she'd accompanied her father to town for necessary goods, she had to rush to complete her shopping before her father was ready to leave. So they took their time checking out the goods piled on shelves reaching to the ceiling.

Ignoring other shoppers, they picked through ready-made shoes, gloves, hats, dishes, silverware, and cleaning supplies.

"Do you recall if there was a broom in the house?" she asked Suzanna.

"I saw one in the schoolhouse, but I don't recall there being one in our house." Suzanna wandered to a table stacked with fabric. "Maybe we should wait," she said over her shoulder. "We can use the school's for now."

"Good idea." One less thing they'd have to spend their money on.

The shop bell rang. Julia ignored the newcomers. Probably more uncouth miners, anyway. One-by-one, voices of other customers came to a halt until a strand of broom straw falling to the floor could be heard. Julia glanced up.

Three women had entered the store. Was it their presence bringing conversations to a halt? Granted, their high-necked, long-sleeved dresses in bright yellow, pink, and green would stop anyone in their tracks. But it was more than people not talking. The women shoppers sniffed, stuck their noses in the air, and gave the three women a wide berth. Some of the men chuckled. The women ignored everyone as they moved to the back of the store.

Sadie slapped her hands to her waist. "The nerve of those ladies."

"Who are they?" Suzanna asked.

"Hmph. Some of Hattie McDougal's girls. Women you don't want to associate with."

Julia glanced at the other shoppers, some of whom were leaving the store. "Her daughters?"

"Daughters?" Sadie's laugh held an edge. "Not hardly. Hattie McDougal is the madam of a house of ill repute." She glared at the three women. "Although I'd have to say Hattie is not as bad as some of the other women who run brothels, like Maggie Johnson."

They were prostitutes? Julia had only heard whispered rumors about some of the women in Drakesville, but as far as she knew, she'd never encountered one before. Other than the bold color of their clothes, they didn't appear different from any of the other women.

What circumstances had these women found themselves in that they gave their bodies to men for money? Were they forced to do what they did? Were they so poor that letting men do such disgusting things was their only option? Did they enjoy it? What made a madam good or bad? Weren't all prostitutes bad?

She bit her bottom lip. To be set aside by "polite society" had to be particularly difficult. She didn't know anything about their lives, but shouldn't they be more pitied than scorned? Heaven forbid if either she or Suzanna found herself in that predicament. Unless Suzanna did something horribly wrong while teaching, at least she had a solid job, but if she didn't get enough people to sew for, she might end up working in a brothel.

"Julia?" Suzanna tugged on her sleeve.

"What?"

"We need to keep shopping if we want to get done some time today."

Julia drew her mind from the women and patted a bolt of dark brown fabric Suzanna had pulled from the bottom of a pile of material. Her sister's suggestion of making smocks for the students to wear when they did art projects was a good one. Even though the price per yard was ridiculously cheap, the amount she needed would cut deeply into their funds. Sadie must have noticed her hesitation.

"Is something wrong, Miss Lindstrom?"

"Um . . ." If Deadwood was anything like her hometown, if she said they were low on cash, it would be spread around the town as quickly as it took a lightning bug to blink on and off. She had no choice. "I want to make smocks for the schoolchildren to wear, but it's more fabric than I can afford."

"Well, goodness, Miss Lindstrom. Why didn't you say so?" Mrs. Haywood rolled out the fabric along a yardstick nailed to the edge of the table. "Colin purchased this stuff without my knowledge. Why he thought this drab brown would sell is beyond me. No self-respecting woman would use this god-awful mess, so it's been sitting on the shelf for nearly a year and a half." She paused, looked around the store, then rolled the fabric back up. "I'll tell you what. Take it all. No charge."

No charge? Was the woman mad? "I can't let you do that, Mrs. Haywood."

Suzanna set the lavender fabric they'd been admiring on the counter. "I agree. We can't let you give us this material."

"Oh, please, call me Sadie. We don't hold with that stuffy nonsense from the East." She put the brown material on a piece of heavy paper nearly the same color and wrapped it up. "You'll be doing me a favor by getting it out of the store." She leaned across the counter and winked. "Just don't let Colin know," she whispered.

"Thank you, Sadie. That's very kind of you."

Sadie flicked her hand. "It's nothing." She snipped the string she used to hold the paper together. "And to let you know, Colin is on the school board, so I know they have money to purchase what you need for your school."

That was good to know. It would make their lives easier not having to spend their own money on materials for the students.

"I love this print," Sadie said, taking the bolt of lavender. "What are you going to use it for?"

"I'm going to make a dress for myself."

"Are you a seamstress, Julia?"

Here was an opportunity to let the women in Deadwood know she was ready to make their clothing, for if there was one person who was good at spreading news, it was usually the owner of a local store. "Yes, I am. My goal is to take orders from the women in town. Maybe open my own shop. I hope there is a need for one."

"There certainly is." Sadie added the lavender to a stack of yellow, blue, green, and pink fabrics. Do you design your own patterns?"

Most poor people did. They were nothing fancy. She'd torn apart dresses, pants, shirts, and nightgowns as they wore out to use as patterns. It was easy to make the clothing larger as the children grew. Adding a bit of ribbon and bows to the girls' clothing made them less boring. But what she dreamed of was creating fancier clothing, ones that society ladies could wear to dances and balls, if they had such things in Deadwood.

"I do. I can make anything anyone wants." She swallowed around the lie. While she hoped she could, she'd never made anything fancy.

"Would you be willing to do repairs, too? The men in this town are hard-pressed to have someone fix their damaged clothing. There's so much of it, even Hong Kee at the laundry can't keep up."

Julia grit her teeth. Mending clothes was the worst job. It seemed all she'd done was fix her siblings' rips and tears. But if it brought in money while she grew her clothing business, so be it. "I'd love to do that."

Suzanna shook her head behind Sadie's back. Was she going to say out loud how Julia hated the tedium of mending clothes and ruin any chances of getting work? Thankfully, Suzanna kept her mouth closed.

"That's wonderful," Sadie said, moving to the front counter. "I'll get the word out. Can they reach you at your home?"

Having strange men coming to their house wasn't appealing and certainly not safe. Then there were the three prostitutes watching them. Did they abduct other women to work in the brothel? If that was the case, they would have to worry about trouble coming from all directions. "Is there somewhere they could leave their clothes? I'd hate to have them go all the way out to the school."

Sadie grinned. "Good idea. Let me think about it. Now, is there anything else you'll be buying?"

Suzanna handed over their list. "I believe this is what we need."

"Just give me a minute while I gather everything."

"Thank you for putting out the word, Sadie."

"Putting out the word for what?" Daniel's voice came from over her left shoulder.

A shiver ran down her spine. Not like the creepy shivers Jimmy Olson back home gave her when he tried to hold her too close while they danced, but warm, delicious shivers. She shook away the warmth. No way was she going to fall for a man on their second day in town.

Sadie put a bag of flour and one of sugar on the counter. "Julia has agreed to mend clothes."

"You're going to do what?"

She didn't care for Daniel's tone. Did he think she couldn't do it? Or maybe that she shouldn't? Either way, it wasn't his business.

"She's a seamstress, Daniel. While she gets orders for dresses and such, she's going to take up the mending slack for the Chinese."

Daniel crossed his arms over his chest. "Is that so?"

"Is what so?" King stood beside his friend, took a strand of licorice from a jar, and chewed on the end.

"Julia is going into the mending business."

"Minding business?" King asked around the licorice. "What's she going to mind?"

"Not mind, you moron, *mend*." Daniel slapped King on the shoulder. "You know, like clothes."

Sadie added a few jars of spices and a bag of potatoes to the growing pile of goods. "The only problem is getting the clothes to her. It wouldn't be a good idea having men traipsing out to their place."

"They can drop their belongings off at the hotel, then I can take them to her."

Had they forgotten she was standing right there? Were they ever going to let her talk? "I wouldn't want to put you out, Mr. Winson."

Before King could answer, Daniel glanced at his pocket watch. "Sadie, can you finish this while we take the ladies to lunch?"

"Sure. You want us to deliver, too? I can send a bill along with Colin. They can pay him."

"That would be great." Daniel tipped his hat and took Julia's elbow, guiding her toward the door. "Could you have it there around three?"

Julia dug in her heels, making Suzanna and King nearly run them over. "Wait."

Daniel stopped midway through the door. "What?"

"Maybe Suzanna and I don't want to wait for our things. Maybe we're not ready to eat." Darn if her stomach didn't choose that moment to let out an angry growl.

With a raised eyebrow, Daniel tipped back his hat, then nodded at the growing pile of goods on the counter. "Are you going to carry all of that home yourselves?"

She hated to admit he was right. There was a lot to get home. Carrying it around the throngs of men on the boardwalks while trying to get through the mud would be a challenge. But still, he didn't need to take over. "I could have procured our own transportation."

"Do you know anyone who has a cart?"

Once again, he had a point, which only served to make her more irritated.

"Why don't you simply accept our help?" He took hold of her elbow again. "Besides, your stomach growled so loud, I'm surprised you didn't start a tunnel cave-in."

"Tunnel cave-in?" Suzanna said, walking beside King. "What do you mean by that?"

King chuckled and tucked her hand in the crook of his arm. "There are so many mining tunnels beneath town, there is always a chance of one collapsing."

Suzanna shuddered, searching the ground as if a hole would open right before them. "Oh, my," she sighed, glancing up at King, then batting her eyelashes at him.

Julia rolled her eyes at Suzanna's back. What had happened between the two from the time they'd left the store and now? Going from calling the man all sorts of names to making cow eyes at him was quite a switch. A stern talking to her was in the near future. They couldn't afford to have Suzanna lose her job over a man. No man was worth it.

"Don't let King worry you. There hasn't been a tunnel collapse in town in a good year," Daniel said, leading them down the boardwalk. "Except for a few on the edges of town, most of the tunnels have been filled in."

"What about . . ." King hesitated. "Never mind."

Julia didn't miss the glare Daniel gave King's back. What was that all about? She knew King owned a hotel and eatery, but what did Daniel do? Was he a miner? With his clothes making him look as if he'd stepped from a haberdasher's, she doubted it. His nails were neatly trimmed and clean. A gambler? Her knowledge of gamblers wouldn't fit through the eye of a needle, but she imagined one would look like Daniel—handsome, dapper, self-important.

But what were two women, new to a town filled with wild and boisterous men, to do? She'd hidden it well, but it hadn't taken long after kicking that man between the legs, for her legs to grow weak, and her heart to race like a prong-horned antelope charging across the field. If it hadn't been for Daniel's holding onto her elbow as they walked to the store, she would have collapsed right in the midst of all those obnoxious men.

It was one thing to have the men's protection, which, she loathed to admit, was welcomed. It was another to have them take over their lives. Heck, they'd made it across the country to Deadwood on their own, they didn't need a man telling them what to do.

"Julia?"

She pulled her mind from his high-handedness. Daniel held open a door. She stepped back and read the sign hanging above it. They were at the hotel already? How had that happened? Suzanna and King's murmured voices had come from behind her, but she'd had no idea what they'd been saying. How long had Daniel been standing there holding the door?

"Welcome, Daniel," a tall, willowy woman said. "King and Miss Lindstrom are already seated."

With his hand at her back, Julia followed the woman as she wove her way through diners to a table seated beneath sheer-covered windows.

"Glad you finally decided to join us," Suzanna said, smirking as she looked between Julia and Daniel. "I thought you were going to stand outside all day."

"Sorry. I guess I was lost in my own thoughts." Daniel held a chair for her. "Thank you, Mr. Iverson."

Daniel hung his hat on a hook then took a chair across from her. "You're welcome. And it's Daniel. Remember?"

"Daniel," she replied, not bothering to hide a tinge of sarcasm in her voice. What was wrong with her? She didn't know this man, yet she was treating him as if he'd been the one to attack her, rather than the one who had tried to protect her. He'd been nothing but a gentleman so far while she was acting like a shrew.

"Did I do something to offend you, Julia?"

"Oh." Suzanna set down her menu. "Don't mind her. She always acts as if she's in charge. It bothers her to have someone else take over."

What? She never did. Well, maybe not too often. But after being the oldest for so long, it was hard to give up the reins to someone else. "Suzanna Marie Lindstrom. I do not."

"Well, then, what did I do to upset you?" Daniel frowned at her.

Julia swallowed around the lump in her throat. Why was she being a hag when all he was trying to do was help? But she'd be darned if she'd let him off the hook for being so boorish. Julia set down her menu. "I don't care to have a man, especially someone I don't know, take over my affairs without consulting me." She sent him what she hoped was a scathing look. "I don't mind you keeping the riffraff from us, but while we were in Haywood's store, you never gave me a chance to say what I wanted to do with our goods. You never asked if I was done shopping. Never asked if I wanted our things delivered."

"But there's no way you could cart all that back to your place."

Julia picked up her menu and snapped it open. "I'm aware of that, Mr. Iverson, but you and Sadie decided everything without asking. That, Mr. Iverson, is why I'm peeved at you." There. That should put him in his place. Her heart pounded for standing up for herself.

Suzanna blushed. Mr. Winson's mouth hung open. Oh, fiddlesticks, now she'd embarrassed both her sister and the owner of the hotel.

"I'm sorry, Mr. Iverson." His grin, with its twin dimples, set her heart racing. Then he placed his hand on hers. Tingling heat rose up her arm down her chest and settled—she didn't realize a woman could feel something in her breasts. Something scary, yet exciting. What was happening to her?

"No, Julia. I'm the one who should apologize." Thankfully, he removed his hand, picked up his napkin, and put it on his lap. "I did run rough-shod over what should have been your decisions. My concern was only for your welfare. Don't forget to call me Daniel."

Suzanna leaned toward her and glared. "We accept your apology, don't we, Julia?"

"Yes, we do."

King slapped his hands together. "Good, now that we're all friends, let's order lunch. I highly recommend the roast beef and gravy, with mashed potatoes, and beans."

Julia's mouth watered. "Oh, my, that does sound delicious. We haven't had a meal like that since we left home."

The same woman who greeted them at the door, came to the table and rested a hand on King's shoulder. Julia didn't miss Suzanna's glower at the gesture.

"What can I get everyone?" the woman asked.

"Ah, Leona." King grinned over his shoulder and patted the woman's hand. "I believe we all want the special today." He paused, then grinned at Julia. "I mean, if that's all right with you."

Julia couldn't help smiling at his wide eyes. Was he afraid she'd rant again because he chose to order for everyone? "That's fine, King."

"By the way, this is my sister, Leona," King said. "While I own this place, she runs it like a drill sergeant. Leona, this is the new schoolteacher, Suzanna Lindstrom, and her sister, Julia."

Leona smiled at the women. "Nice to meet you, but I must get back to keeping the troops in order for the lunch crowd. Coffee will be right out."

Julia didn't miss her sister's sigh of relief. King whispered something in Suzanna's ear, bringing a blush to her face. When had she changed her mind about the restaurant owner? This wasn't good. "Suzanna, what do you have to do to get ready for the students on Monday?"

Suzanna faced Julia, blinking a few times as if to bring herself back from wherever her mind was. What had King said to her? "Uh. I need to make sure the school is clean."

"It is," King said.

Julia poured a good amount of cream and several spoons of sugar into her coffee. Tea was more to her liking, but again, she hadn't been asked what she wanted. "Remember Mr. Ogden said it had recently been painted?"

Suzanna wrinkled her nose. "That's right. I need to see a list of students, where they are in their studies, make name tags for their desks, do some lesson plans, make sure the slates are clean."

"You're going to be quite busy, my dear," King said, giving Suzanna a big grin. "If you need any help, let me know."

'My dear?' Who called a woman that endearment after less than twenty-four hours, and part of that spent covered in mud and angry at each other? "That's all right, King. I'll help her."

"But, Julia, you'll be busy making smocks for the children."

"I'll never get them done in time for the first day of school, anyway, so I might as well give you a hand."

King leaned to one side when their meals arrived. "At least let me come over and help you move books and desks."

Suzanna smiled. "That would be lovely, King."

Yesterday her sister had been calling the man every name in the book. Today she was batting her eyes and grinning as if he were a god or something. Fickle woman.

Daniel sat back in his chair. "Oh, my gosh, I'm as bad as Odgen. I almost forgot."

King set down his fork. "What did you forget, Dan?"

"Remember Ogden told us about the dance Saturday night?"

King angled his body toward Suzanna. "The families of the school children are hosting a party in your honor at the schoolhouse Saturday night."

Suzanna turned pale and held her fingers to her mouth. "They're what?"

"They want to properly welcome you to Deadwood," King answered, taking hold of her free hand. "It'll also be a chance to meet the children before Monday morning."

"But . . . But . . ." Suzanna's fingers shook. "I'm not sure I can do that. I thought I'd meet the parents one at a time, like when they brought their children to school or picked them up. Oh, my."

"Don't worry, my dear. We'll be there to help you."

"King's right. Counting Ogden, you know three people. You remember Mrs. Woods? You came in on the stage with her yesterday? She'll be there, so that makes four. The women will bring food, the men drinks. There will be music. If the weather holds out, it will be held outside."

Suzanna turned panicked eyes to Julia.

"Do you have a choice? You're the schoolteacher. Everyone will want to meet you." Since she was only the sister, she'd hopefully be left alone.

"But what will I wear?"

That was an issue. Neither had dresses fit for a dance. "With the material we purchased today, I can get something made for you before Saturday night."

Daniel set down his fork and took a sip of coffee. "Sadie said you can do more than mend clothes."

"Oh, my goodness, yes, Daniel," Suzanna said, her eyes lighting up. "Julia is quite adept with a needle and can make most anything."

Heat rose to Julia's face at her sister's glowing testimonial. "I try my best." Like in the store, conversations faltered, then stopped altogether. Chairs scraped across the wooden floor as diners stood and headed to the door. What was going on this time? She glanced over her shoulder. The same three women from Haywood's store stood just inside the restaurant while people gave them a wide berth.

One woman settled her gaze on Julia. Had they been looking for her? She clutched her napkin. She wasn't sure why. It wasn't as if they'd steal her and Suzanna right from under Daniel and King's noses, would they?

When they approached the table, Daniel stood. "Dorrie, Ivy, Franny, can I help you?"

The tallest one kept her eyes on Julia. "Not you. Her."

Julia's heart sank. Daniel knew these ladies? While he looked like a gambler, he didn't seem the type to frequent one of those establishments. But then, what did she know of men? Other than her father and a few of the boys back home, basically nothing. What on Earth could they want with her?

"And what would you ladies want with Miss Lindstrom?"

"We heard she is a seamstress." The tall one must be the spokesperson for the group. "The gal that sewed for us up and . . ." She didn't finish the sentence, but tears filled her eyes. "None of the rest of us know how to thread a needle."

King rose and tossed his napkin on his plate. "Ladies, I'm sure Miss Lindstrom would not take kindly to making the type of clothing you require for your line of work."

"I agree with King," Daniel said. "I believe you should all leave before you chase away the rest of his diners."

Here they went again, making decisions for her. "What if I want to sew for them?"

Suzanna squeezed Julia's hand. "Julia, you can't. You know darn well what those women do. It would ruin your reputation. Because you're my sister, mine, too."

They were right, but darn it, she needed the work.

"I'm Dorrie," the tall one said. "These are my sisters, Ivy and Franny."

"I'm sorry, Dorrie, but I can't take the chance of harming my sister's reputation. You see, she's the new schoolteacher."

"That's what I figured, but it don't hurt none to ask." Dorrie lifted her downcast eyes. "Well, thank you for listening. We won't take up any more of your time."

King swept an arm toward the entrance. "Ladies, if you'll please leave. I can ill afford to lose any more money."

With their heads held high, and without a backward glance, the three left.

It must be hard to be treated as if you were evil, wicked, and the lowest of the low. A flicker of pity washed through her. She understood what it was like to be treated poorly simply because you didn't meet other people's expectations. Her entire life had been spent trying to ignore comments about her family being poor farmers and how her parents should stop having children they couldn't afford. At least the prostitutes seemed to have each other.

"I'm sorry about that," Daniel said, retaking his seat.

Julia hated to ask what his relationships with the women were. It was none of her business. "You knew their names. Are they friends of yours?"

Daniel frowned. "Are you asking me if I know them from frequenting their establishment?"

The irritated tone in his voice said her question was out of order. "I shouldn't have asked that. It's none of my business. I apologize.

Chapter Six

Daniel leaned back in his chair. Damn. There had been no reason for him to snap at Julia. Hell, most men he knew, whether married or not, visited the fallen women. He and, as far as he knew, King also valued his health and stayed away from the brothels.

Not that he didn't go into a saloon to partake in a drink or two, but he left the women alone. Taking a chance on getting the pox from a few minutes of pleasure didn't fit into his idea of a good time.

Did he owe Julia an answer as to why he knew the women's names? Yes, she was pretty, but beauty was only skin deep. So far, she'd been rather prickly toward him. Was this her true nature, or were she and Suzanna simply trying to protect themselves from men they didn't know?

What would she think if she found out he'd represented some of Hattie's girls in cases against their employers or former employers? Since working for Hattie, the girls hadn't had any more problems with the men they serviced. Hattie ran a tight ship.

"Are you going to sit there all day and stare at your coffee," King asked, raising an eyebrow, "or are you going to answer Julia's question about those women?"

Daniel blinked and refocused his attention on the room. Many of the patrons had come back after the prostitutes had left. Those that had remained resumed their conversations. Only his table was silent. King and Suzanna stared at him expectantly and Julia kept her eyes on her lap.

He toyed with his coffee cup. Julia glanced at him. "I'm a lawyer. A lawyer who believes in the law that says everyone should have representation in a court of law. With that being said, I'll represent anyone except for murderers, wife beaters, swindlers, and anyone who deceives or harms women and children."

Julia tipped her head to one side as if she liked what he was saying.

"Those three women, and several like them, had been working for the worst brothels. They were cheated of money, beaten, accused of stealing, starved, forced to take drugs to handle more customers. Since they are prostitutes, no one would stand up for them against their employers or the men who were too rough with them."

"Until you," Julia whispered.

"I couldn't stand by and see the women being treated as though they were slaves." Daniel sighed. "Someone had to help them."

"Why do they work in those places?" Suzanna asked, a frown marring her face.

King shrugged. "There are many reasons. Lured by the prospect of being on their own, without a job or a man to take care of them, they end up where they least want to be. Sometimes they've lost their entire families and have no other recourse."

"And," Daniel added, "there are unscrupulous men who tempt them with what seems a good job but is really a position in their brothel." He tossed his napkin on the table, the reminder of what men like Swearingen did making him lose his appetite.

Julia shuddered. "Why would men do that?"

"Money. It's always about money," King answered.

"Do any of the women ever get out of that life?" Suzanna asked, fiddling with the ribbons on her bonnet.

"I have no idea, but I'd guess not many," King answered. "Most men I know wouldn't marry a woman who'd been with too many men to count. They want their women pure."

Daniel tugged at a tie that grew tighter. "Unfortunately, many die from disease before they have a chance to make a new life. Every once in a while, a man will come along, see the value in a woman other than her trade, fall in love, and marry her, but that's rare."

Suzanna folded her arms over her chest. "Why is it all right for men to sow their wild oats as much as they want, but a woman has to be pure on her wedding day? I don't think that's quite fair."

"I agree with my sister. Not that either of us plan to do anything before we find the right man, but the standard between men and women is simply unfair."

Even though he'd wish his wife to be a virgin when they married, the ladies had a point. Look at how much less the school board wanted to pay a woman teacher than they were willing to pay for a man. Until they married, women had to support themselves somehow.

King patted Suzanna's hand. "I agree it's not fair, but that's the way of it."

"Dorrie called Ivy and Franny her sisters," Julia said. "They don't look anything alike."

"They're not sisters like in being related." King said, eyeing Daniel across the table.

Daniel didn't care for this line of questioning. "Why the interest in bordellos?"

"I feel sorry for them."

Even though he tended to agree, he'd never known a woman to feel that way. "How so?"

"I do, too," Suzanna said. "Having to resort to pleasuring men for money." She shuddered. "Not to mention with dirty, smelly men. Women should be given more choices in life than to be a teacher or a prostitute until the right man comes along to take care of her."

"So, why did she call them her sisters if they're not related? Do all the women who work in those places treat each other like sisters?"

Julia leaned her elbows on the table. "Do all the women from different houses get along?"

Daniel sighed. "I don't know how they treat each other within the bordellos, since I've never visited one." Besides, if he ever had, he'd be too busy getting 'serviced' to notice how the women treated each other. "But I do know the bordellos are in competition with each other, so the women don't always get along."

"There have been a few fights between the madams," King added. "You'll probably see a few."

"Especially between Mollie Johnson and Hattie McDougal," Daniel said, shaking his head. Most of the fights he'd come across were between the two madams. "I had to help break one up once when they nearly pulled out each other's hair."

Julia frowned. "Why?"

King lifted his shoulders. "Who knows, but it's been going on since Hattie arrived in Deadwood. Mollie hassles all the prostitutes who don't work for her, but she gives Hattie's girls the most grief."

Suzanna chewed on her bottom lip and shook her head, obviously upset about the women. Julia, on the other hand, kept her features passive, as if she was trying to decide what to think.

He patted Julia's hand. "But you won't have to worry about coming into contact with those types of women."

THE VISION OF THE THREE women leaving the restaurant, heads held high, stuck in Julia's brain. What a horrible way to make a living. Having to do what they did with the unwashed, ill-kempt men they'd passed on the street had to be disgusting and then to be ostracized by the other people in town, degrading. Well, there was nothing she could do about it.

"Food's here," Daniel said, interrupting her thoughts.

Julia's mouth watered. They hadn't seen such a meal since their going-away party. Brown gravy, filling a hollow created in a mound of mashed potatoes, spilled over the side, oozing into several pieces of roast beef. The only part of the meal that didn't appeal to her was the green beans. She loathed them to the point where she'd refused to help plant the beans in the family garden.

Suzanna cut a small piece of meat, slipped it into her mouth, closed her eyes, and sighed. "This is heavenly."

How was it possible for her sister to eat so daintily? But she was right, it was heavenly. All Julia wanted to do was tuck into the meal like a wolf over a new kill. Slurp up every bite then lick the plate clean. Well, except for the horrid green beans. No one spoke for a few minutes as they worked through their food.

"How is your food?" Leona asked, placing a hand on her brother's shoulder.

King glanced over his shoulder as he swallowed. "Delicious as always."

"Why, Miss Julia," Leona said, slapping her hands at her waist, "you haven't touched your beans."

"Julia hates beans," her sister said. "Ma and Pa never could get her to eat them, even after threatening her with having to clean out the chicken coop for a year unless she did."

It wouldn't be gracious of her to reach across the table to wipe the smirk from Suzanna's face. Would it?

Daniel chuckled then gave an exaggerated shudder. "I'm that way with beets. But you should try the beans. Leona does something special to them."

While they watched, Julia took a small bite of the dreaded green vegetable. Expecting to have the usual reaction of gagging, she was pleasantly surprised when a flavor she'd never encountered before teased her taste buds. She raised an eyebrow at Leona. "What did you put in these? They're delicious."

Leona's smile was worth tasting the beans. "Something I learned out East when I worked under a chef. Louie calls it garlic. I also add some onion along with crumbled bacon."

Garlic. She'd never heard of it. "Delicious. Can you get it out here?"

"I have to order it from Louie, who sends it to Cheyenne, then it gets shipped here." Leona took a step back. "Now if you'll excuse me, I have other meals to prepare. I'll be back with your pie in a bit."

"I wonder if we can grow garlic in our garden," Suzanna said, stabbing the last bean on her plate. "This is amazing."

Julia nodded. "Much better than simply adding salt."

King set down his fork and wiped his lips with his napkin. "You plan on having a garden?"

Suzanna shrugged. "May we? Would the school board give us permission to dig up a piece of the yard?"

"We're so used to growing our own food and putting it up for the winter, we can't imagine having to buy from the store all the time," Julia added, setting her fork across the plate.

"Let me talk to the board," Daniel said, sitting back in his chair and patting his stomach. "I'm not sure I have room for pie."

"Me, neither." If it was proper, Julia would loosen her stays.

King grinned. "Well, Leona's pies are not to be missed. In fact, I'll ask her to bring a couple to the shindig on Saturday."

Julia didn't miss her sister's pale face. "We never did finish talking about that. Are you certain it's necessary?"

"Of course, it is," King said, patting Suzanna's hand.

What was it with men and patting women's hands as if that would placate them? Treating them as little children and not the intelligent, worthy people they were? Why, she'd met men back home who couldn't read or write, didn't work, lost themselves in the bottle, yet still thought they were superior to women, stronger than women, smarter than women. Well, chicken feathers. She'd seen her father nearly pass out with the birth of her younger siblings, while her mother popped them out and was back on her feet in a few days. But today was not the time to set the men straight. She'd wait until they had settled themselves into Deadwood before getting on her soapbox about women's rights.

She brought her thoughts back to Saturday. "Suzanna, I think it's a good idea to meet the parents and children before school starts. What do we have to do to get ready?"

Daniel set down his coffee cup. "Nothing. Saturday morning a bunch of the men will come to the schoolhouse, set up tables for food, and chairs for seating."

"There are several people who play instruments, so there will be dancing," King added.

"What if it rains?" Julia pictured people trekking into their small house, creating havoc, leaving a mess for her and Suzanna to clean up.

"We'll use the schoolhouse." Daniel leaned his elbows on the table and toyed with his mustache. "The desks can be hauled out to the woodshed and stable so there'll be plenty of room inside for tables of food and dancing."

Julia silently prayed for good weather, recalling how hot the schoolhouse back home became when filled with food, dancers, and those who had taken too much to drink. "What should we bring?"

"Nothing." King smiled at Suzanna. "This is in honor of you. The women will provide all the food and lemonade. The men will bring. . ."

"Liquor?" Suzanna asked.

King nodded.

So, things weren't any different here than they were in Iowa. Hopefully the party didn't get out of hand like they often did when men got into the spirits.

A young girl, no more than thirteen, gathered up their dirty plates. Was she one of Suzanna's students or a girl who wasn't allowed to go to school? Leona followed, carrying a tray with four plates. "Anyone ready for pie?"

Daniel patted his stomach. "After that delicious meal, I'm not sure I could eat another bite." He winked at Julia. "But there's always room for a piece of Leona's pies."

Julia had to agree with being too stuffed for desert, but not wanting to hurt Leona's feelings, took a plate from the woman. Steam rose from the plate. Not only was it apple, but warm apple pie. Even though her mother had been a good cook, making pies was not one of her accomplishments. Based on Suzanna's and her attempts, they'd inherited her mother's lack of baking skills. If Leona's tasted as good as it smelled, they were in for a real treat. She might break down and lick her plate.

The young girl returned with a black metal coffee pot. "This is Lucy, the daughter of a friend," Leona explained. "She's helping out until school starts next week."

Suzanna smiled at the girl. "So, you'll be one of my students. I look forward to having you in my classroom."

Lucy's eyes widened. "You're my new teacher?" She moved around the table, topping off their coffee cups. "Will you be staying?"

"I signed a contract for a year, and I have no intentions of breaking that contract."

"I sure hope so. I've missed going to school so much." With a short curtsy, Lucy went back to the kitchen.

"See, Suzanna," King said. "The students are anxious to get back to their book learning. Having a pretty teacher will keep the boys coming back."

Lowering her eyes to her plate, Suzanna blushed. Oh boy, Julia smelled trouble. In her opinion, it would take more than a pretty face to keep the older boys coming back and ready to learn. But Suzanna had a knack for making learning fun and interesting.

The pie called to her. Heavenly days, it was every bit as delicious as Daniel proclaimed. She closed her eyes, holding back a moan of delight. A mixture of cinnamon, nutmeg, and something she couldn't identify rolled across her tongue. The second bite revealed light, flaky crust, not like the crust her mother made that took both knife and fork to cut through.

"See what I mean?"

She opened her eyes to Daniel's smile.

"I told you her pies were amazing. She also makes mincemeat, pumpkin, and cherry, when she can get the fruit for them."

Julia hated to eat the last bite, mainly because it meant the delectable dessert was gone. Without thinking she put her hands on either side of the plate, preparing to pick it up and lick it clean.

"Julia," Suzanna whispered across the table, a hint of panic in her voice. "Stop. We're not at home anymore."

In an apple pie daze, she glanced at her sister, then at her hands. The plate was halfway to her mouth. "I . . . Uh . . ."

Daniel laughed. "I know how you feel. I'd love to lick my plate, too."

Suzanna peeked around the room. "Don't you two dare. As much as I'd love to join you, it would be unseemly for the new schoolmarm to be seen licking her plate in public."

With a sigh, Julia set down the plate, nearly weeping over the crumbs and juice left behind. "Sorry, Suz. It's just so good."

King pulled a pocket watch from his vest pocket. "We'd better get you ladies home and back to work."

Secretly, Julia jingled the coins in her purse. How much was this meal going to cost? Certainly, more than breakfast had. She wasn't sure what the bill from the store would be, but they'd be broke before Suzanna got her first pay and she stitched one stitch. She opened her bag, but before she had a chance to withdraw a coin, Daniel put a hand on hers. At least he hadn't patted it.

"The food is on King and me."

"Oh, but we can't have you buy us lunch," Suzanna said, once again searching the room in case anyone was observing them. "It's not right."

"We invited you ladies to lunch," King said, rising from his chair. "And as owner of this fine establishment, it's my decision on who pays and who doesn't."

Would they expect something in return? There were men in her hometown that thought if they paid for a meal or bought a trinket for a woman, they deserved something in return. What they wanted was generally what a woman was not willing to give—unless there were a ring and marriage vows involved.

Julia stood. "Well, then, I thank you for the wonderful meal. We should be heading home before Colin delivers our goods."

Daniel grasped her elbow as she headed toward the door.

"Hold on. We're escorting you home."

Julia tugged her elbow away from him. "That isn't necessary. We know the way now."

King pulled out Suzanna's chair. "It is necessary. Didn't you learn anything on the way to the mercantile?"

That gave her pause. How could she have been so stupid as to forget those awful men? While she was able to take care of herself that time, what if they were accosted by more than one? What if someone jumped out from behind a building? As much as she didn't want to rely on anyone, it would be foolhardy to ignore the offer of assistance.

"Thank you for your offer." She took a deep breath. "We accept."

Daniel grinned down at her as he opened the restaurant door. "Now, was that so hard?"

Once on the boardwalk, she was doubly glad. It must have rained while they were eating. The walks were darkened with moisture, the mud in the street thicker. Where had all these men come from?

Horses charged down the street, flinging mud on anyone who walked too close to the edge. If not for Daniel and King walking on the street side, she and Suzanna would be covered in the stuff.

Suzanna and King led the way, weaving between the throngs of people, her arm tucked in the crook of King's elbow. Even though Julia wanted to, she didn't have the nerve to touch Daniel. "Why is it so busy?" she asked, keeping her eyes averted from the men who called out and whistled as they passed by.

"I don't know what's going on," Daniel said, taking her elbow, guiding her around two men staggering from a saloon. "Sunday is usually the day when the prospectors come into town, get their gold weighed, and buy supplies, not a Thursday. Some might bathe at the bath house, have their whiskers scraped, and their clothes cleaned."

They stopped at a corner and let two horses charge past, the men whooping, waving their hats and splattering mud in the air. "I would venture to guess they visit the saloons, too." She wasn't about to mention the women who worked upstairs. A vision of the three prostitutes came to mind. She didn't know how much money they made, but it couldn't be enough to put up with the dirty, smelly, rowdy men coming into town.

"Sometimes when a prospector strikes it rich, they celebrate by buying drinks for everyone," Daniel said, brushing a spatter of mud from his coat. "That could be what all the hollering is about."

A yelp from her sister turned her attention back to what was going on. King, with Suzanna in his arms, strode across the muddy intersection. Before she had a chance to yell at the man for accosting her sister, Daniel swept her up in his arms. "What do you think you're doing?" She kicked her legs to get him to put her down.

"This is safer, quicker, and cleaner." His voice vibrated against her chest. "And if you don't stay still, you'll end up on your backside in the street."

He was right. Even though the journey to other side of the street was short, since she'd never have a chance to touch him again, she might as well enjoy it. Julia hooked her arms around his neck, taking in his clean scent. He obviously visited the bathhouse more often than Sundays. The warmth of his arms seeped through her dress, making certain parts of her body tingle in response. Their parents would be appalled. Young, single women did not let young, single men carry them around, no matter how chivalrous their actions might be. Especially not young, single, handsome men.

All too soon, they were on the other side. Was the high color in her sister's face from embarrassment or the thrill of being in King's arms? While she needed to have a talk with her sister about King, was she any different than Suzanna? Her cheeks burned as she unraveled her arms from around Daniel's neck and touched her toes to the wooden surface. She was surely going to hell.

IT WAS WITH GREAT RELUCTANCE that Daniel set Julia down. Her breasts had pressed against his chest when she wrapped her arms around his neck, nearly burning a hole clear through his coat, vest, and shirt. The edge of her bonnet nearly took out an eye, but the arm beneath her legs sent his system into overdrive. He may have even accidentally touched her rear end. Shoot, he needed to quit thinking about how good it was having her in his arms. It certainly wouldn't be wise to become aroused in public.

Thankfully, he hadn't dumped her in the mud before making it to the other side of the street and setting her on the boardwalk. To hide his burning face, he tipped his hat lower. If his face was as red as the sisters', he looked like some of the prospectors after spending a day in the sun without a hat or a night hitting the bottle. At least they didn't seem to notice, but King's wink meant he would later be teased unmercifully.

"Shall we?" King held out his arm for Suzanna.

He didn't dare touch Julia again, but stayed by her side. Too many men leered. Had word gotten out of two new women in town? He took a deep breath. It would be best if he took Julia's arm to show everyone she wasn't on the market.

Before they reached the end of the next block, a group of men from across the street yelled and jeered at a feeble-looking man carrying a burlap sack and slogging through the mud in the middle of the street. While so many men were in various stages of being dirty and unkempt, this man took it to the new level.

"Who is that man?" Julia asked, wrinkling her nose.

Hell, he wanted to do more than wrinkle his nose at the stench emanating from the decrepit character. Pinch his nose closed would be more like it.

"That's Justin Cachlin," King answered, standing beside them. "Otherwise known as the Bottle Fiend."

"Good heavens," Suzanna whispered. "His clothes are nothing but rags. What is he doing in the street?"

Daniel sighed and shook his head. "He's collecting bottles and cigar butts people tossed away."

"But why?" Julia asked, waving a hand in front of her face.

He nudged her arm to continue walking. "No one knows for sure. He was here when I arrived. In that time, he's amassed thousands of bottles he stores in barrels around his cabin along with other junk he collects."

"Doesn't he ever take a bath or change clothes?"

King laughed. "He doesn't have the money for either one. A few people, including myself, have paid for a trip to the bathhouse and given him clean clothes, but he prefers his dirty, smelly ways."

Thankfully, someone had placed boards across the next intersection, saving him from having to carry her again. He kept close to Julia as she inched her way across the boards. In order to be ready to catch her if necessary, he kept a hand at the small of her back, making his fingers burn.

"One time I had to take some papers out to his cabin," Daniel said, breathing a sigh of relief when they'd made it safely to the other side. "I smelled the place long before I saw it. From the doorway I couldn't miss the piles of old rags, clothes, codfish boxes, and so many gunnysacks, I couldn't begin to count them. He'd covered the roof with hundreds of rusty kerosene cans."

Suzanna glanced at him over her shoulder. "Sounds like a real fire trap."

"At least the roof doesn't leak," King added.

Daniel grinned. "Not that we know of."

Julia was silent on the remainder of the walk. What was she thinking? Worrying about her safety? Wondering about the shindig Saturday night? Thinking of ways to trap a man into marriage?

Who was he to say she wasn't looking for a man? Maybe that was why she came with her sister, to find a man with money. While most of the prospectors never struck it rich, there were several who had, and some who'd given up wading in cold water to start successful businesses in town.

One block to go. He could manage one block without touching her again, couldn't he? Maybe he needed to visit one of the brothels to relieve the tension building in his groin. A picture of the multitude of men each woman serviced entered his mind. Nope. No way. He'd have to use his hand tonight to take care of the need burning inside him.

"Daniel, Suzanna asked you a question," King wriggled his eyebrows as if he knew what Daniel had been thinking.

Daniel took in his surroundings. How had they arrived at the schoolhouse already? "I'm sorry, Suzanna. I was wool-gathering."

King snorted, then covered it with a cough. *Ass.*

Suzanna stopped by the front door of the school. "I asked what time the party was set for on Saturday."

Good question. "I don't rightly know, but perhaps later in the afternoon. I'll find out and give you a call."

Julia frowned. "Call? You mean you'll send someone over with a message."

Daniel swept out a hand to tell the women to precede him to the house. "No, I mean I'll call on the telephone." Maybe they didn't have phones in Iowa, yet. But if Deadwood had had them for two years, the sisters would certainly know about them in Iowa.

Julia unlocked the door and entered the front room. Daniel followed with Suzanna and King bringing up the rear. She set her small bag on a table.

"Um. Of course, we heard of them, but we didn't know anyone who had one. I wouldn't know a telephone if it came over and introduced itself."

Daniel grinned. "Well, turn around. Meet the Deadwood telephone."

Suzanna removed her bonnet and tipped her head to the side. "Where? I don't see anything."

Julia bit her bottom lip and moved in a circle. "I agree with Suz."

IN A FEW STRIDES, DANIEL crossed the room and pointed to a brown box on the wall. A black piece of metal, reminding her of Old-Man Jackson's overly large nose, protruded from the front. With its two circular, silver things at the top, a handle on one side, and a long black thing on the other, if she looked at it straight on, it reminded her of a face.

"That's a telephone?" Daniel's grin set her heart pinging. "Why do we have one? More importantly, how do we use it?"

"With two women living on the edge of town, the school board was concerned about your safety if someone should try to break in." King sat on the arm of the sofa. Daniel picked up the thing hanging from a rope. "We thought you'd be safer if you were able to contact the sheriff or someone for help. We installed one in the schoolhouse, too."

Sounded like a good idea—if they knew how to use it.

"This is the receiver," he said, holding out the black thing. "You put it up to your ear and give this crank a turn. It'll get you to the operator."

"Not that many people in town have a telephone," King added. "All you have to do is talk into the mouthpiece and tell Miranda who you want to speak with. She'll connect you."

"Let me show you." Daniel turned the handle. After a moment, he spoke into the mouthpiece. "Hi, Miranda. This is Daniel Iverson. I'm at the schoolteacher's house showing the sisters how to use the telephone. Can you get me the restaurant?"

Julia held her breath. He wouldn't be able to talk with Leona, would he?

"Hi, Leona. It's Daniel."

He paused. Was Leona talking back?

"Yeah, we enjoyed the food. Fantastic as always. Listen, King and I are showing," he glanced over his shoulder and winked, "Julia and Suzanna how to use the telephone. Could you call me back? Thanks." He put the earpiece back on the hook.

In a few seconds the silver things chimed, making her jump. Suzanna, her eyes wide, slapped her fingers over her lips.

"When the telephone rings, you pick up the receiver, and say hello into the speaker." Daniel did as he said. "Hi again, Leona. Do you have a minute to help us out? I'm going to have each one of the girls try this on their own. Thanks." He hung up the receiver again.

Julia put her hands behind her back. "I can't . . . can't do that."

Daniel tugged her to the telephone. "Of course, you can. It's simple."

"Are you sure?" She wrinkled her brow.

He nodded.

With a deep breath and shaking fingers, Julia took the receiver. The cold metal was a surprise, as was the weight. It was heavier than it appeared.

"Now put the receiver to your ear and turn the crank once."

She hovered her hand over the crank. "I'm nervous."

"Here, I'll help you."

The warmth of his hand over hers was unexpected. Instead of being soft as she thought a lawyer's would be, his fingers were calloused, as if he did more than work behind a desk all day. Did he pan gold when not lawyering? His touch sent tingles, rather like goose bumps, over her skin.

Even with his help, the crank was hard to turn. Daniel had made it look so easy, but with his help she managed to rotate it once. In a matter of seconds, a female voice came through the receiver.

"Operator. Who can I connect you to?"

Julia pulled the receiver from her ear and stared at it. "Where is she talking from?"

"How does it work?" Suzanna asked from behind her at the same time.

Daniel put the receiver back to her ear. "Tell Miranda you want King's Restaurant."

"Um." She bit her bottom lip, then stood on her tiptoes. The metal was cold against her lips.

"Not so close, or she won't be able to understand you," Daniel said, moving her back a step.

"Uh, Miranda? This is Julia Lindstrom," she yelled.

Daniel smiled. "You don't have to talk so loud. Use your normal voice."

Julia nodded. "Can you please get me King's Restaurant?" She jumped when, in a few seconds, Leona answered. Julia released the receiver and hugged Suzanna. "It worked!"

Daniel laughed, picked up the receiver swinging on the cord, then handed it to her. "You need to talk."

"Oh, that's right. Hello, Leona," she said in as prim and proper a voice as she could find. "This is Julia Lindstrom. I loved your lunch today." How amazing to hear someone talking who wasn't in the same room, but clear across town.

"Now tell her goodbye."

"I'm sorry, Leona, Daniel says I have to say goodbye." She paused, listening to Leona. "Yes, I'll see you on Saturday."

"Now all you have to do is hang the receiver on its hook."

Her hands shook as she replaced the receiver. "That was absolutely the most amazing thing I've ever done."

Suzanna nudged her to the side. "My turn."

"I'll help you," King said, changing places with Daniel.

"I forgot to tell you something," Daniel said, leaning against the doorframe to the kitchen.

Oh my. There was more? As it was, she'd be a nervous wreck using the telephone when Daniel wasn't here. She tugged on her bottom lip with her teeth. If there were more, she'd never remember it all. "What's that?"

"The front opens so you can put paper and pen in there. The bottom board is to give you a place to write down messages. Of course, you can put other things in there if you want. I keep a list of everyone, which isn't many, who has a telephone in mine."

Julia stuck her hands in the hidden pockets in her skirt, wrapped a fist around her grandmother's metal thimble, and kept an eye on the couple at the telephone, making sure they didn't stand too close. Unlike her voice when she'd first talked into the mouthpiece, Suzanna's was so quiet, King had to tell her to speak up.

Removing her hand from a pocket, she put the thimble on her little finger. Heavier and smaller than her own, light gray instead of silver, it had a dent in one side. Had Granny Jo rapped someone on the head with it as she was known to do? From decades of use, the rows of etched dots going from the bottom to the top were barely visible. Somehow Grandpa Jack had managed to etch Granny Jo's initials, JL, on the inside. With fingers crooked from arthritis, Granny Jo no longer sewed, but had taught Julia everything she knew about making and repairing clothes.

Her eyes had filled with tears when Granny Jo had presented it to her as a parting gift. It would always be a treasured object.

"What's that you have on your finger?"

Daniels words jerked her from memories of her favored grandmother. She blinked away tears pooling in her eyes. Would she ever see her again? "My Granny Jo's thimble. She gave it to me before I left home."

"Can I see it?"

Why would a man want to look at something as simple and feminine as a thimble? "Why?"

"My grandmother did so much sewing, there were times she'd forget to take it off before cooking." Daniel took the thimble from her. "One time, my brother, Sam, found it in his bowl of soup. He almost swallowed it." Their fingers touched, sending prickles over her skin.

"One of our other brothers gave him the name 'thimble head.'" Suzanna added.

With a raised eyebrow and a chuckle, Daniel studied the thimble. "Except for the initials inside, it looks similar to my mother's. Do you use it when you sew?"

Julia shook her head. "Granny Jo was a tiny woman, so it's too small for me. I just like to carry it in my pocket to remember her by."

Daniel returned the thimble. "Aren't you afraid you'll lose it?"

"I'd be devastated if I lost it, so I'm careful. I'll leave it in the house when I'm working in the garden or doing other chores." She tucked the thimble back into her pocket. Maybe inside the telephone would be a good place to put it. She couldn't imagine keeping anything else in there. After all, the phone was only for emergencies, so there would be no reason to have a list of people who had one. Who would she call?

"She did well," King said, beaming at Suzanna. "She'll have no trouble if she needs to call from the schoolhouse." He pointed a finger at her. "But only for emergencies, like to the jail, fire station, Daniel, or me. Right?"

Suzanna nodded. "I'll remember." If it were evening, the beaming smile she gave King could have lit the room.

King slapped on his brown bowler hat. "We'd best get going so these lovely ladies can get settled."

The sounds of creaking wheels and a horse whinnying came through an open window.

"That must be Colin with your supplies," Daniel said, replacing his hat on his head. "We'll help him unload, then take our leave."

As soon as the wagon was empty, a block of ice put in the icebox, and Colin was gone, Daniel tipped his hat. "We'll see you on Saturday. Be sure to save a dance for me."

King placed a kiss on the back of Suzanna's hand and winked. "Until Saturday. Will you save a couple dances for me?"

Chapter Seven

"Suzanna Marie Lindstrom," Julia said, pulling her sister away from the window.

Suzanna jerked her arm away. "What's wrong with you?"

"Wrong with me? There's nothing wrong with me. You've been making cow eyes at King all day." Julia pushed her sister into the kitchen. "Remember the contract? The one you signed to teach for a year? The one where you can't be seen alone with a man?"

With a dismissive flick of her wrist, Suzanna entered the kitchen. "I was not making cow eyes. I was simply being nice." As if she was a little girl again, she stuck out her tongue. "And I was never alone with him. Was I?"

Julia pulled open the yellow gingham curtains covering a cupboard. "For a woman who, only a day ago, was angry enough to call him all sorts of names, you sure seemed taken by him today." After stacking some canned goods and spices on the shelf, she slapped a hand at her waist and pointed a finger at her sister. "I'm warning you. If you do anything to break this contract and we have to vacate this amazing house, not only will I kill you, but we'll both find ourselves flat on our backs servicing men in one of the brothels."

"Don't worry, I'm not going to do anything to break the contract."

"And don't forget it." Julia picked up the packages of fabric and stomped to the living room. "Put away the rest of the supplies," she called over her shoulder. "I'm going to start cutting out a dress for you so I can have it done by Saturday."

"Don't be so bossy," Suzanna yelled after her.

"I'm the oldest. I can be bossy if I want to," she called back. She cut the string on the brown paper, removed a light blue fabric decorated with darker blue flowers, and set it on the sofa. "And don't argue with me or I'll make the stitches so loose the seams will come apart while you're dancing."

She shook her head at the choice of rather unladylike words Suzanna shouted from the kitchen. Living alone with her sister was either going to be a joy or a royal pain in the backside. In her bedroom, she gathered a pattern, scissors, pins, and needles then returned to the parlor.

"I didn't see you ignoring Daniel, either," came Suzanna's next retort.

"I'm not sure how you noticed, with most of your attention on King." She unfolded the fabric on the floor and knelt beside it. "What was I supposed to do, be rude and ignore the man?" There was no way she was going to admit how he'd made her heart race. "Besides, I don't have to worry about losing my job."

Suzanna stood in the kitchen doorway. "Rather hard to do when you don't have one."

Tempted to cut a chunk of her sister's hair, Julia held up a pair of scissors. "If I were you, I wouldn't be so sarcastic. I'm about to cut out your dress."

"I'm sorry. That wasn't nice of me." Suzanna knelt beside Julia helping place the pattern pieces to get the most out of the fabric. "I guess I'm nervous about this dance. King makes me feel . . ."

"Well, you need to bury those feelings for one year, then you can do what you want."

Suzanna sighed. "I know. I know. But he's so handsome and kind."

"You didn't think so yesterday or this morning."

"Yesterday he was covered in mud and threw water on me." Suzanna flattened the bodice pattern and placed it beside a sleeve. "When I saw him this morning, something happened. My heart raced so fast, I thought it would jump out of my chest. I swear the world spun faster."

Julia sat back on her haunches and stared at the layout of the pattern pieces. "If you move that piece a bit, I should be able to make a matching bag." When she was satisfied with the arrangement, she pinned the first piece down. "What was he whispering to you?"

Suzanna puffed out a breath. "None of your business."

"Ouch." Julia sucked her finger. She hadn't pricked her finger in ages. It was Suzanna's fault. All the talk about the world spinning faster made her think of how her reactions to Daniel had been the same. "It is my business."

"Actually, it's not." Suzanna handed Julia a scrap of material. "Don't get blood on the fabric. Press this on your finger.

"I won't." When it had stopped bleeding, she pinned down the next pattern piece. "Are you done putting the supplies away?"

"Almost." Suzanna rose and shook out her skirt. "I'll finish, then head over to the schoolhouse to take inventory. There's supposed to be a list of students with their ages in the teacher's desk. I'm hoping there is also something about where they were in their studies."

"What if there isn't?" Julia asked around the pins held between her lips.

"Then I'll be spending some time learning their skills before I can actually teach them something."

"Best get moving then."

A FEW HOURS LATER, Julia used her toe to keep the rocking chair in motion. Located nearest the window, it was the best place to sew. Once she had the material cut and Suzanna was out of the house, sewing the pieces together was a breeze—if she hadn't had to remove the stitches she'd made in error while thinking about one Daniel Iverson. She'd been using long basting stitches to make adjusting the dress to Suzanna's form easier, so removing them had been quick. She'd made so many garments for her family she could sew in her sleep. But it was Daniel's handsome face playing in her mind that had made her sew the bodice to the skirt backward and stitch the cuff part of the sleeve to the top's shoulder.

Her stomach rumbled as she checked the wall clock. Five-thirty already? With a sigh, she set the dress aside. She had all day tomorrow to work on it.

The house was quiet. Had Suzanna been at the school all this time? Knowing how she got lost in lesson plans, books, chalk, and all the other accoutrements needed for teaching, it wouldn't be surprising. Since it had been a while since their noon meal, she should put something together for supper.

Julia rose, stretched her back, rubbed her scratchy eyes, went into the kitchen, and stared at the mess. "Darn her. She hardly put anything away." Donning an apron, she put the flour and sugar on a shelf above the counter. Thankfully her sister had had enough sense to put the bacon, milk, cheese, eggs, and butter in the icebox. If Suzanna weren't the sole bread winner, she'd be more upset. Yes, the dress was for the new teacher, but she wasn't getting paid for it, so it didn't count.

She shook her head, put some wood into the stove, and struck a match to the kindling. While she waited for the stove to heat up, she took out a cast-iron skillet from a low shelf, cut strips from the slab of bacon, and put them in the skillet. Then she cracked several eggs into a bowl, added milk, and beat them with a fork. Sliced bread would go on the grate to toast as the bacon and eggs cooked.

"What's for supper?"

Julia jumped at Suzanna's voice. "Breakfast."

"I don't care what we have, I'm starving." Suzanna took two plates from an upper shelf and set them on the wooden table sitting in the middle of the room. "You're cooking, so I'll set the table and clean up."

"Sounds fair to me." It was strange breaking only four eggs instead of the dozen and a half needed for their family. A pang of homesickness hit her. By now, chores would be done, kids cleaned up, and everyone sitting around the table waiting for Pa to say grace.

It didn't take long for the meal to finish cooking. Her mouth watered as she sat across the table from her sister. With their heads bowed, Julia recited the meal prayer she'd said ever since she could utter the words.

Suzanna sniffled. "Cleaning up should be a breeze with only two of us."

Julia put scrambled eggs, bacon, and two slices of toast on her plate. "You homesick?"

Suzanna shrugged and wiped her cheek. "A bit. It's so quiet." She took the rest of the food then stared at her plate. "It's strange not having to grab my share before Bobby and Simon took more than theirs."

"Then Ma would make them put some back for the younger ones." She sprinkled salt on her eggs. "With the way those two are growing and always hungry, I imagine Ma won't be making any less food with us gone."

"I thought that was the point of us leaving—having more food for the rest."

Julia pushed her food around on her plate. As hungry as she was, it was difficult getting the food down around the lump in her throat. For someone who'd been anxious to leave home, it was surprising how much she missed everyone. "Ma may have to cook the same amount of food, but it means more for everyone else."

"Aren't you hungry?" Suzanna asked, biting into a piece of bacon.

"I am. Just missing everyone."

"Yeah, me too."

They remained quiet for a few minutes, the only sound the scrape of forks against their plates. "I imagine we'll get over it once we make friends here," Julia said, hoping it wouldn't take long.

"Will you have my dress ready by Saturday?"

Julia drained her glass of milk. "I'm sure I'll have it ready for you to try on by lunch tomorrow. All I'll have to do is resew it with smaller stitches, add some trim, and hem it. Barring any interruptions, it should be done by supper."

She removed her empty plate. With a ladle, she took water from a pot heating on the stove then poured it into one of the pans in the sink. "I can't believe we have a hand-pump inside the house. No more hauling water." With a few pumps on the handle, cold water met hot until the temperature was perfect. A few scrapes of soap into the wash water, and she was ready to do dishes. "There's a drain in the sink, too, so we don't have to toss the dirty water in the yard."

"Wouldn't Ma love it?" Suzanna set her dirty dishes next to Julia's and hip-bumped her to the side. "I said I'd clean up. If you want, you can dry."

Folded dishtowels were stacked neatly under the counter. "Whoever set up this house knew what they were doing. I'm glad we didn't have to buy anything more than food."

"I'll make sure to tell Ma about it when we write her."

Julia wiped a clean glass and put it upside down on a shelf. "Good idea. Both she and Pa will be glad to know we didn't have to spend a lot of money setting up house."

Suzanna dropped silverware into the rinse pan. "After we're done with the dishes, we can write letters to the family."

SINCE THE DAYS WERE longer, it wasn't necessary to light candles right after supper. It was difficult to describe everything that had happened in one letter, so Suzanna's suggestion that they each write something different was excellent. No sense in duplicating their news. After deciding who would write what, they sat at the kitchen table.

Dear Ma, Pa, and Imps, I hope all is well with you. Our trip to Deadwood was at times exciting and other times, boring. The stagecoach made our bones feel as if they'd been through a battle. Some of the stopping places were nice. Others I wouldn't put our pigs in. Suzanna and I stayed together as some of the people we met were a bit menacing. Nothing unpleasant happened. On the last leg of the trip, we met the wife of one of Deadwood's bankers, Mrs. Woods. She is a lovely lady. I'm hoping to make better acquaintance with her to drum up some business.

Today we went shopping downtown and got the supplies we needed. You won't believe how well set up the house we're living in is. With the exception of food and material for clothing, what we need has been supplied. Mrs. Sadie Haywood and her husband own the mercantile we went to. When she found out I was a seamstress and was willing to do repairs as well as other sewing, she promised to get the word out. There are a lot of miners here in Deadwood that are in need of clothing repairs, not to mention a body washing more than once a month!!!

Suzanna is writing about our house and the school. I'll try to write as often as I can. After all, postage is three cents. We'll send our letters together to save our coins. Give my love to Robby, Simon, Josie, Ella, Tommy, Ben, Susie, and baby Anna. Make sure they write so they practice their letters. The little ones can draw a picture. Missing you, love, Julia.

They had agreed before penning their letters not to mention King or Daniel, lest their parents worry Suzanna wouldn't fulfill her contract. They also decided not to mention being accosted in the street, Suzanna's tumble in the mud, nor the fallen women they'd met. Pa would yank them home in two seconds if he found out.

Leaving Daniel out of the letter was best, too. There was no way she could tell them about her reactions to the man. How her heart sped up and cheeks heated. How her stomach flipped like she'd rolled down the steep hill behind their soddy. How something happened to her lower regions. How she wished she had someone to talk to about her feelings. She certainly couldn't and didn't want to share them with her younger sister. What if Suzanna had had the same reactions to King? Something she definitely didn't want to think about, let alone hear.

Leaving the letter on the table to let the ink dry, Julia went into the parlor to fold the dress she'd carelessly tossed on the sofa. Good thing she'd found a flatiron on the back of the stove or she'd be heading back to town to purchase one. There was no way she'd be able to get the wrinkles out by hand-pressing it.

Suzanna followed her into the room and planted herself on one of the chairs. "What are you going to wear on Saturday?"

After folding the dress in half, she laid it across the sofa. "It doesn't matter what I wear. This party is for you."

"Of course, it matters, Julia. If you want the women in town to have you make their clothes, you need to look nice. Besides, you're my sister. What you do and how you look reflects on me."

Well, there she went again acting all high and mighty. "Don't worry. I won't embarrass you." Before she said something she'd regret, Julia went into her bedroom and closed the door.

"How I look and act will reflect on her?" she sing-songed, removing her blouse and hanging it on a hook. Was she going to have to watch her every step for fear that she'd make her sister look bad?

Julia shook her head while slipping a lightweight, frayed, nightgown over her head. Not that she planned on doing anything bad, but having to watch her every move, every step, every word coming out of her mouth, was going to be irritating.

She climbed into bed. Sighing, she pulled the sheet and blanket to her shoulders. She ran a hand over the sheet. Soft. Quiet. No crunch of dried grass in the mattress. No stems poking through worn sheets. No sagging in the middle, at least not until the ropes began to loosen.

What was the mattress made of? Cotton? Wool? Down? Whatever it was, she loved it. After turning on her side, she tucked her hands beneath her cheek and snuggled down for what she hoped was a good night's rest. The next two days were going to be busy.

Chapter Eight

Suzanna grabbed Julia's arm as she left the grassy dance floor and pulled her over to a chair. "Heavens, my feet hurt. I'd love to take off these awful shoes."

"I think it's about time to eat, anyway." Julia rolled her toes as best she could in her confining boots. "At least in Iowa we eat before dancing."

Julia needed the respite from dancing with nearly every man at the gathering at the schoolhouse. Didn't the musicians ever take a break? Hadn't any of the men learned to dance? The ones that seemed to be adept at moving across the lawn were married.

"All these people here can't have children in school, can they?" Suzanna asked, wiping perspiration from her brow. "I've met quite of few of the families, but I know I danced with some men who don't seem to be attached to a woman or children."

"I don't know for sure, but I'd have to agree with you. I've never been swung in so many directions or had my feet stepped on so much on in my life." Julia giggled. "Even big old Johann Swenson back home was lighter on his feet."

People had begun arriving at the schoolhouse nearly two hours earlier. The spread of food grew as more came. The boards stretched across empty beer barrels groaned beneath the weight. The aroma of roast beef, pork, and other delectable foods nearly made her swoon. If she'd known how long it would be before eating, she'd have snacked on something before leaving the house.

Suzanna bumped her shoulder against Julia. "By the way, my dress turned out lovely. I've received many compliments on it."

Julia had to agree. Because of the warm June weather, they'd agreed to make the dress short sleeved. The neckline, edged in cream lace matching the trim on the hem of the skirt, dipped to Suzanna's collarbone, showing off her sister's graceful neck. The way the men lined up to dance with her, it didn't go unnoticed. With her blonde hair in a low chignon and tendrils curling down her rosy cheeks, Suzanna was a sight to behold.

"Well, you look lovely."

"Thanks, but if I am, it's your dress that made me so." Suzanna's stomach gave an un-ladylike growl. "Heavens, are we ever going to eat? I'm so hungry I may make a fool of myself in front of my students by shoveling food into my mouth like a ravenous pig, then licking my plate clean."

Julia turned her attention from her sister to the two men who'd recently shown up and headed their way.

"And I have to say, you look lovely yourself, sister. I know you weren't able to make something new, but the skirt and blouse you sewed before we left Iowa is rather attractive."

"I have to agree with you, Miss Suzanna," Daniel said, standing before them with King at his side.

King bowed as if they were royalty. "Both of you ladies look fetching."

Daniel's grin set her heart jumping. "I was wondering if you were going to come tonight."

"We were here earlier helping set up chairs," Daniel tipped his head to the diming sky, "and worrying about the weather. Then I had to clean up and a meeting to attend."

"And I had to help Leona get pies ready." King smiled. "I'm not very adept in the kitchen, so after changing clothes from helping here, I had to change again."

"Why?" Suzanna asked, her eyes twinkling. "I'm assuming it wasn't from mud?"

King slapped a hand over his heart. "You wound me. It was flour this time."

The music stopped. Colin stood in front of the musicians. "Can I have your attention, please," he called out in a booming voice, halting conversations. "My wife has informed me the food is ready."

A cheer rose from the gathering.

"She also tells me that our guest of honor and her sister will start the line."

Suzanna clasped Julia's hand. Her face turned red. "I can't walk in front of all these people."

"You'll be fine," King assured her.

"But . . . but . . . It's different when it's a bunch of kids, but there's at least forty adults here."

King took her hand and pulled her to her feet. "Will it help if I go with you?"

"Just don't get too close or people will get the wrong idea about us."

Julia didn't miss the raised eyebrow King threw at Daniel.

"Nothing could be further from my mind." He swept a hand forward allowing Suzanna to precede him. "Heck, are we allowed to have a dance?"

Daniel bowed to Julia. "May I accompany you?"

Right now, she was so hungry, she'd allow the smelliest polecat to join her. She glanced at some of the men who'd arrived, looking as if they'd left the mines minutes ago. She shuddered. Maybe not.

The array of food was so vast she didn't know where to begin.

"Take a bit of everything so you don't offend anyone," Daniel whispered in her ear.

"Even with taking small portions, it'll never all fit on my plate. Besides, how can I offend anyone when I don't know who any of these people are, nor what they brought to the table."

Daniel pointed to a dish with corn and some type of meat. "That's Sadie Haywood's. She always brings the same thing to our church meals."

Julia looked over her shoulder at him. "Good?"

"Delicious."

She plopped a spoonful on her plate. As they went down the tables, he pointed out who made the various dishes. By the time they got to the end of the second table, her plate was close to overflowing. Good thing she'd lost a few pounds on the trip, or her seams would burst after eating all the food.

"I'll point out the women who made the food on your plate so you can thank them later."

He tipped his head, indicating she should follow King and Suzanna to a colorful patchwork quilt spread beneath a large elm tree.

"You say that like I'd remember."

"Here, let me." Daniel took her plate, allowing her to sit down and spread her skirt over her legs.

"I'll get us some lemonade," King said, setting his plate on the quilt.

Daniel lowered himself beside her, his knee brushing her leg, sending heat melting through her body. Did he have to sit so close? But with four people sharing a quilt meant for two, there was no place to move. If Daniel had noticed the contact with her leg, he didn't react, merely dug into his food.

"What do you think of the party so far?" King asked, sitting next to Suzanna then taking his plate from her.

"I didn't realize so many people would show up," Suzanna answered. "They don't all have children, so they?"

Daniel laughed. "Not hardly, but when men from the mines hear there's going to be a shindig, they'll come from all over for free food and dancing, especially when word gets out there are a couple of fresh females in town."

Julia rubbed the toe of her boot. "I can attest that most don't know how to dance."

"Or get so excited about kicking up their heels, they forget how," King added.

"Will you dance with me later?" Daniel asked Julia, stabbing a piece of pork.

The idea of Daniel's arms around her sent a shiver down her spine. He'd held her elbow the other day as they'd maneuvered through town and put his hand over hers when she tried to crank the telephone, but this would be different. Depending on the music, their bodies could be in close contact with each other. Good thing she had a plate in one hand and a fork in the other, or she'd fan the heat from her face.

"Of course, but please don't tromp on my feet. I don't think my poor toes could take any more."

"I promise I've never tromped on any woman's feet."

His wink made her think differently.

AN HOUR LATER NEARLY all the food was gone. Empty dishes and dirty plates were packed into baskets then placed onto wagons parked haphazardly around the property. While Suzanna gathered the children for games of blind-man's bluff and follow the leader, Julia helped the women clean up. Along with more lemonade, a wooden keg of beer replaced the food on one of the tables. Loud burps, followed by hurried, embarrassed apologies filled the air. Children giggled. Women scolded.

Julia jumped when someone touched her shoulder.

"I get the first dance," a deep voice whispered in her ear.

Thinking it was Daniel, she nearly said of course, but before she could turn around, a hand touched her rear-end. What on Earth? Did Daniel think he could touch her in such a forward manner because the evening sky was beginning to darken?

"What do ya, say, babe?" he said, this time squeezing her backside.

His body odor rolled over her shoulder, striking her nose, making her full stomach shift and roll. That wasn't Daniel's voice or his clean scent. She spun around and slapped his hand away. "How dare you? Get your grubby hands off me."

"C'mon, baby. Big old Daniel and King aren't here to stop me this time." Despite his words of bravado, he took a step back. "If you're lucky, I may give you a kiss or two."

Oh, no. It was the man she'd kicked between the legs the other day. What had Daniel called him? Mingus. Where *was* Daniel? Would any of the other men come to her rescue if she screamed? "I'd suggest, Mr. Mingus, that you step aside. I've already promised the first dance to someone else."

Mingus narrowed his eyes, tipped his grungy, tattered cowboy hat back on his head, and leaned toward her. "Well, ain't that too bad. Ya tell me who it is. I'll explain to him right nicely that I'll be takin' his place."

If he weren't keeping his lower body away from her, she'd kick him as she had the other day. Kick him so hard he wouldn't walk for a week. But there were other ways to stop a man's unwanted attention. Mingus' hold on her left arm would certainly leave a bruise. She jerked her arm free and smacked his ears with cupped palms. Having had this done by her father when she'd sassed her mother, she knew how much the pressure of air pushing into her ears hurt. She'd never talked back again.

Crouching to the ground, Mingus covered his ears. "Sonofabitch." Except for his cussing, the partiers were silent.

Daniel pushed his way through the crowd to her side, King, Suzanna, and the sheriff following. "What happened?"

"He wouldn't take no for an answer, so I . . ."

"Gave him the ear whack?" Suzanna finished for her.

"Ear whack?" King asked, helping the sheriff pull Mingus to his feet. "What's that?"

Suzanna stood next to her. "To stop someone, you slap them on both ears with open palms. Hurts like crazy."

"Stupid bitch," Mingus swore still holding his head. "I'll get you for that. You'll be sorry you turned me down."

Sheriff Josiah Winkman yanked Mingus' arms behind his back and snapped on handcuffs. "How many times do I have to tell you to leave a lady alone when she says no? If you want a woman, you know where to go." He pushed him forward. "And I have no idea why you thought it would be a good idea to show up here. These are decent folk, not for the likes of you."

Julia took a deep breath and wiped damp, shaking hands down her skirt. "I didn't see him until it was too late."

Daniel placed his hands on her shoulders. "Did he hurt you?"

She blinked away tears. "Other than touching me on my backside and nearly knocking me out with his horrid smell, no."

King raised his arms to the gathering. "Everything's all right, folks. Let's get back to the party." He nodded to the men holding their instruments. "Gentlemen."

After a brief tune-up, the group struck up 'Ol' Dan Tucker.' Even though still shaking from her encounter with Mingus, she tapped her toe to the upbeat song. With the next song, couples partnered up in-to groups of four for a square dance.

"C'mon, let's join in." Daniel took her hand then faced King and Suzanna. "Want to form a square with us?"

True to his word, not once did Daniel tread on her toes. Too bad she couldn't say the same about herself, having given both his and King's toes a what-for. When had she become such a clumsy dancer? Perhaps because every time Daniel's hand touched hers, her heart raced and she became lightheaded. Thankfully she didn't pass out.

DANIEL TOOK OFF HIS jacket, tossed it on a nearby chair, rolled his sleeves to his elbows, and loosened his string tie. Foregoing the beer, he filled two glasses with lemonade and gave one to Julia.

"I haven't kicked up my heels like this in ages," he said, trying to slow his rapid breath. "You're a good dancer." It didn't help that every time he'd touched Julia, his heart nearly burst from his chest. Could a man in his late twenties have a heart attack?

Julia laughed. "Thanks for lying. I imagine your toes are swollen by now."

Her laugh sent shivers straight down to his groin. Damn, why had he taken off his coat? It would have done well to hide the erection he was trying to wish away. Other than the fact that he'd be too close to her, he couldn't wait until a waltz was struck.

A man, one he'd seen about town a few times, stood before her then bowed at the waist.

"May I have the next dance, Miss Julia?"

"She's with . . ."

"Certainly, Mr. Hotchkiss," she answered before Daniel had a chance to finish his sentence.

Daniel held in a groan when the band struck up a waltz. Figures. How did she know the man's name? When would they have met in the short time she was in Deadwood? He ground his teeth together as couples waltzed past. While he didn't have the right to keep Julia to himself, he sure didn't want anyone else dancing with her.

"Quit scowling." King stood beside him. "You look as if you're going to bite someone's head off."

"Hmph." He crossed his arms over his chest. "Why aren't you dancing with Suzanna?"

"If you'd take your eyes off Julia and her partner long enough, you'll see that she's dancing with someone else."

Daniel curled his fingers into fists. "Doesn't it bother you?"

"Sort of, but as much as I enjoy her company, as a teacher who hasn't spent one day with her students in the classroom, she certainly can't favor one man over another. Don't forget the damn contract."

"Julia doesn't have that problem." He drained his glass of lemonade. "I was wondering how Suzanna went from hating you for getting her all muddy, then dumping water on her, to being so chummy."

"She's smart enough to know an intelligent, handsome, charming man when she sees him in his cleaned-up form."

Daniel snorted, keeping his eyes on the couple moving as if they'd been born to dance together. "Oh, brother. You do have quite an ego, don't you?"

"Someone has to." King pointed to Julia and Mr. Hotchkiss. "I couldn't help overhearing her say his name. How do you think she knows him?"

"I have no idea, unless she danced with him before we got here." If Hotchkiss held her any closer, he was going to have to knock the guy out right in front of God and everyone else. He closed his eyes and took a deep breath. He had no right to harm anyone who showed an interest in her. He opened his eyes. Well, wishing Hotchkiss away hadn't worked.

"You look as if you're ready to pick a fight with someone," King said, nudging Daniel in the side. "I don't think doing so would endear you to Julia."

"I know. I know." The music thankfully stopped, but before Julia left the dance floor giving him a chance to step in for his turn, another man took her hand, leading her into a polka. "I'm not sure what the hell is going on with me. Ever since I set eyes on the woman, I can't concentrate on anything else. Hell, I nearly ran Mrs. Woods over yesterday while walking down the sidewalk."

"You falling in love?"

Daniel sniffed as if that one word smelled like a dead skunk. "Not hardly. How can a person fall in love with someone he's only spent a few hours with?"

Rocking back on his heels, King shoved his hands into his pockets. "Damned if I know, but I've heard it happen before."

"Well, not to me, it hasn't. Besides, I have no intention of letting a woman latch on to me simply to have someone to take care of her." As much as his heart sped up and hands sweated whenever he was near Julia, there was no way he was falling in love.

King chuckled. "We'll see, my friend, we'll see."

Chapter Nine

July 1879

"Darn woman," Julia muttered, head bent over a seam she was ripping out from a third dress given to her by Mrs. Woods. "Why some people think they can sew is beyond me." While Suzanna thought it was great Julia was doing work for the banker's wife, Julia grew more frustrated with each passing day. Since the woman was not small, pulling out the zigzagged, uneven stitches on the ugly, bright yellow dress with large green and blue flowers, took longer than usual.

The color alone made her eyes hurt. How she wished she could suggest to the banker's wife that fabric in a paler color with smaller prints would be better suited to her body size, make her appear smaller and her skin less gray. But, of course, she couldn't do that without offending Mrs. Woods and losing her business.

What she wanted to do was create new clothes, not tear out stitches for women who couldn't tell the difference between a thimble and a needle, or a pair of scissors and a paring knife.

In the month since arriving in Deadwood, Suzanna and her students had settled into a routine. Except for a few of the older boys who'd given her some grief in the first week and had to be threatened with expulsion, things were going well.

At least one of them was happy. Excluding the smocks she'd made from the ugly brown material and a few repair jobs only bringing in pennies to their coffers, sewing jobs were non-existent. By re-working Mrs. Woods' dresses, maybe other women would realize the value in hiring her, and she'd could quit feeling guilty for not contributing to the household pocketbook.

While Suzanna was teaching, Julia cooked, cleaned, did the laundry, and took care of their small garden. Since walking into town on her own was a recipe for disaster, she rarely left the property. The men who wanted clothing repaired took their items to Haywood's store. Either Colin or Daniel brought them out to her. When done, either Daniel picked them up, or he escorted her into town.

Grinning to herself, she pulled out the last stitch holding the bodice and skirt together then separated the two pieces. When Daniel came and suggested he walk with her to deliver the repaired clothing, it was always around the noon meal, which meant they spent additional time together at King's restaurant. Time she didn't mind at all. Time spent getting to know each other. Time making her realize how much she was coming to care about the man.

Besides being intelligent, he was funny, caring, and, to her, so very handsome. Lately he seemed to find more reasons to take her elbow or touch her hand. Even through gloves, his warmth seeped into her being. There were times it was difficult keeping her attention on what she was doing so she wouldn't trip on a loose board on the way to town, or nearly cut off the tip of her finger while cutting out fabric.

At least King hadn't come around to pester Suzanna, easing Julia's mind. Had he lost interest in her sister, or did he want Suzanna to fulfill her contract so the school board wouldn't have to look for yet another teacher?

The children's laughter pulled her thoughts from Daniel. It must be lunchtime. She set Mrs. Woods' disaster aside and went into the kitchen to make herself a lard sandwich. Suzanna took a bucket lunch with her every morning. Even though their cozy home was a few steps from the school, her sister didn't dare leave the children alone for the few minutes it would take to grab lunch from home.

These kids weren't any different from their younger siblings and could get into trouble faster than a fish eluded a hook.

She stood by the kitchen window, eating her sandwich, watching the young boys chase each other, the girls jump rope, and the older boys play catch. Like at her old school, the older girls sat together giggling and probably talking about the boys.

A small girl, no older than six or seven, swung a hand bell nearly half her size. Recess was over. Gradually the noise subsided as the children reentered the school. Peace would reign again until the afternoon recess, allowing her to undo the havoc created by Mrs. Woods without interruption.

WITH A SNIP OF HER scissors, the last thread in the skirt's side seam came out. Julia stood, stretched her arms over her head, twisted side to side to ease tight muscles from leaning over the dress, then touched her fingers to her toes. With that done, she went outside to check on their fenced-in garden.

"Miss Lindstrom," a voice called out to her before she'd rounded the corner of the house. A young man, too old for school, waved an arm at her.

At the man's approach, her stomach dropped. Who was he? What did he want? She surveyed the area around her. There was nothing available as a weapon if he had the idea of attacking her.

"Miss Lindstrom?" he repeated.

"Yes?"

"I have a message for you." He held out a piece of paper.

She hesitated before taking it from him. "Who is it from?"

He shrugged until his shoulders almost hit his large ears. "I don't know. A man paid me to run it out here."

If he'd already been paid for his coming out here, did she need to pay him, too? When he didn't move, she knew the answer.

"Stay right here, I'll be right back." She set the note on the kitchen table and removed two pennies. Hopefully it would be enough. It didn't matter, it was all she was willing to part with. It was undoubtedly more than he came with.

Julia waited until the man was out of sight before going back into the kitchen. Who on Earth from Deadwood would be writing her? Had Daniel sent her an invitation to dinner? Maybe Sadie had some work for her. She swallowed around the lump in her throat. What if Mingus was suing her for slapping his ears? He'd be out of luck if he thought he could squeeze any money from her. You can't extract a nickel from a penny.

With shaking hands, she picked up the piece of paper and peeled back the wax seal. The first few words made her drop onto a wooden chair.

Dear Miss Lindstrom, It has come to my attention from my sisters, Dorrie, Ivy, and Franny, that you are a seamstress. We are in dire need of someone to repair, create, and sew garments for us. I'm willing to pay top dollar for your services. If you are interested, please meet me at ten o'clock tonight behind the schoolhouse shed. I don't expect you to come downtown by yourself after dark. It isn't safe. If you don't show up, I'll understand. Yours, Hattie McDougal

She put the note on the table and pressed it down with her palm. Hattie McDougal? Dorrie, Ivy, and Franny? Where had she heard those names before? Tapping a finger on the table, she let the names roll through her brain until it came to her.

"Heavens." She pressed her fingers to her lips. "They're the prostitutes who came into King's. Hattie is the owner a brothel."

The clock ticked the time away as she contemplated what to do. She needed the money. Except for mending, no one was rushing to her door begging her to make clothes for them. What did Hattie mean by top dollar? What did she expect Julia to make? Would she have to go to their place of business, or would they come here? Either way, being seen with the women would harm both her and Suzanna's reputations.

Instead of sitting and mulling over the note, she could think it over while working on Mrs. Woods' horrid dresses. She had only three more days to finish before the banker's wife came for a fitting. The promised bonus for having it done by then would go a long way to refilling their cookie jar.

"YOU'RE QUIET TONIGHT," Suzanna said, handing Julia a clean plate to dry. "Is something wrong?"

So deep in an inner war of whether or not to meet Miss McDougal that night, she nearly let go of the plate when Suzanna spoke. "No. Simply thinking about how to get more work. These repair jobs don't pay enough. I need to get some orders for dresses."

"Maybe you should open up a shop."

Julia set the plate on top of others. "And how do you propose I pay for it?"

"Can't you go to the bank for a loan?"

"Don't you remember when Ma tried to get a bank loan when Pa was laid up with his broken leg? Banks don't give credit to women, especially women who have no way of paying it back." Julia took another plate and wiped it dry. "From what I understand, you have to make monthly payments including interest with only so long to pay the entire amount back."

Suzanna frowned. "Why is that a problem?"

Julia shook her head. "I'd have to make sure I had the money for the payment. What if I don't get enough work one month? I'd lose my business along with all the money I'd already paid the bank."

"Doesn't sound fair."

"I agree. Women never make as much money as men. Since single women don't have a man to help with money, I sort of understand their reasoning."

Suzanna handed her the last dish. "What are you going to do? My pay doesn't go far. Since the school board sets up wood only for the schoolhouse, we'll need to have money to buy winter wood for the house and make sure we have enough food stocked up."

"I agree." Julia hung up the damp towel on one of the three wooden dowels nailed to the wall. "Not everyone goes to Haywood's store, so they may not know what I do. I've thought about making some signs to put up around town."

"Do you think that's safe?" Suzanna asked, blowing out the kitchen lamp then following Julia into the parlor.

"I'm going to ask Daniel what he thinks."

Suzanna lit a lamp by her favorite chair, sat down, and raised an eyebrow. "Speaking of Daniel, how is it going between you two?"

Julia picked up the bright red scarf she was knitting and added a few rows before answering. "I like him."

"Like?"

"Okay, I like him a lot, but right now we're only friends."

"Do you want it to be more?" Suzanna asked, working on a blue and red striped scarf. "Has he kissed you yet?"

Between the two of them, they hoped to have enough scarves and mittens made to sell at Sadie and Colin's store or any other store agreeing to sell them. According to Daniel, miners went through mittens faster than a fox after a jackrabbit. As requested, their mother had shipped their winter clothes, along with skeins of yarn. Now they had enough yarn to make several dozen without spending any of their own money.

A blush crept up her neck to her face. "The answer to the first question is I don't know. The answer to the second is none of your business."

Suzanna set her handiwork in her lap and leaned forward. "So, he has kissed you. What was it like?"

Julia's face burned deeper. If she didn't answer, Suzanna would pester until she wanted to smack her. "No, he hasn't kissed me. We've only known each other a month. Other than the party here, we've only been together a few times during the day. The last thing I want is to have him kiss me in broad daylight where anyone can see."

"Soooo . . ." Suzanna's eyes glittered. A smile played at the corners of her mouth. "If it was dark, you'd let him kiss you?"

Time to change the subject before her skin melted from her face. "So, what about you and King? I haven't seen him in a while."

"He has a ranch a half-day's ride from here. He had to check on his animals, then hunt for meat to supply the restaurant. He won't be back for a week or so."

"When did he tell you that? I don't recall you being with him."

Suzanna face reddened as she picked the scarf back up and turned her attention to her knitting.

"Suzanna? When did you see him? You know you can't get serious about anyone."

"I know. Don't remind me. He sent a note to me at the school the other day. Don't worry about us. He is fully aware we have to wait a year."

"Just as long as you don't forget."

Crickets chirping their evening songs came through the open window, reminding her of the farm when, after chores and supper were done, they'd all sit outside. The younger kids would chase lightning bugs while the older ones put the bugs in jars and their parents talked as the sun went down. Julia glanced at the wall clock and suppressed a sigh. Three hours to make up her mind whether to meet Hattie. She also needed to make sure Suzanna was asleep before venturing out.

Julia's chest tightened. Did worrying about Suzanna being asleep before meeting the madam mean she *had* made up her mind? Her damp palms made her knitting needles slippery. She dropped two stitches. Even though it was still early, maybe she should go to her room. But it would only serve to give her too much time alone to worry about meeting the madam. Staying out here at least gave her opportunities to talk with Suzanna while they knitted.

She picked up the missed stitches. "How are the students doing?" If anything, getting her sister to talk about her classes would help pass the time.

At eight forty-five, a yawn cracked her jaw.

"Tired?" Suzanna said through her own yawn. "Me, too. I'm going to the necessary before I go to bed."

Julia put the scarf on a box next to her chair. "I'll be right behind you." Only an hour left.

Suzanna came back to the house and disappeared into her room, shutting the door behind her.

Forty-five minutes. It wouldn't take her long to use the outhouse. Maybe she should wait in her room before going outside. She knocked on Suzanna's door then poked her head in. "I'm going to read in my room a bit before I head to the necessary. Then I'll lock up. If you hear the front door open, it'll be me."

"Okay," came a mumbled reply.

That should take care of trying to sneak out of the house. Since she didn't know how long the meeting with Hattie would last, she hoped Suzanna would be asleep and wouldn't realize when she came back in.

With the bedside lantern lit, she picked up her worn copy of "The Last of the Mohicans." Instead of stretching out, she sat on the edge of the bed. She yawned.

At fifteen minutes to ten, she slipped from her room and tiptoed across the parlor, flinching at the squeaky front door. Since she had to use the necessary badly, going out early would give her time to take care of her needs.

The full moon lighting the path to the outhouse meant a lantern wasn't needed, but also created eerie shadows, making her skin crawl. Coyotes and wolves were known to come into town looking for scraps or a stray cat or dog.

Her business complete, she opened the outhouse door and scanned the area. With no visible wild animals lurking, she left the whitewashed building then took two steps to the rear. A ghostlike shadow came from a row of bushes at the back of the property. Julia jumped, swallowing a scream. Slapping a hand to her chest, she retreated three steps. Running from a wild animal was never a good thing as most were known to run faster than humans.

She backed up one more step. The bear moved one step closer. If the animal hadn't attacked yet, maybe it wouldn't. With another step, it was in the moonlight.

"Miss Lindstrom?"

Julia let out a breath and sagged her shoulders. "Miss McDougal?"

"Yes. Why were you moving away from me?"

"I'm sorry. Until you came into the moonlight, I thought you were a bear."

Hattie laughed. "That would be scary. You were smart not to run." She held out her hand. "Nice to meet you, Miss Lindstrom. I appreciate it."

Was it wise to touch a prostitute? What did she expect would happen, she'd turn into a soiled dove by simply touching one? Stupid. Julia shook her hand. "Please call me Julia."

"And you must call me Hattie. Let's stand behind the necessary in case someone is watching."

Why would someone be watching? But the madam more than likely knew best, so she followed her into the shadows.

"You got my note?"

"That's why I'm out here."

Hattie tipped her head. She was dressed all in black, with a black bonnet nearly hiding her face. Except for strands of hair peeking from the sides of the bonnet, it was difficult to see what she looked like. As a madam, Julia imagined she was gorgeous.

"What do you think?"

What should she say? The idea was crazy. If caught, it could ruin both her and Suzanna? That she had no idea what kind of clothing prostitutes wore? Curiosity won out. "What type of clothing are you looking to have made?"

"Gowns. Slips. Undergarments. If you can, hats. They need to be fancy enough to draw men's attentions."

"That's quite an array. Why me?"

"Except for the Chinamen, I can't find anyone in this town who can sew, and I won't deal with them. The other women in town are too hoity-toity, have young children and no time to sew anything but their own clothing, or are like myself and too tired during the day from working all night. When I heard you were a seamstress, I thought I'd take the chance to meet you."

"How do you know I'm good at what I do?"

"I know you make dresses. I've seen you in town a few times with Daniel Iverson and admired your work. You have an eye for color. So far I like what I've seen."

"But . . ."

Hattie held up her right hand, a ring on a finger glittering in the moonlight. "I know what you're going to say. What if people find out you're sewing for whores?"

"Well . . ."

"I don't want your reputation ruined. What I suggest is we meet after dark."

"But don't you work at night?"

"I always have a girl who can take my place for a bit."

Julia shook her head. "But how do I meet with the girls? I'll need to measure them, pick out material, do fittings."

Hattie tapped a manicured nail against her lips. "I hadn't thought of the mechanics."

"What if I disguise myself and come to you after dark?" Julia couldn't believe she was suggesting such a crazy thing.

"That would work, but it all depends on what you disguise yourself as."

The quiet crickets started in again as Julia ran various ideas through her head. "What about a Chinaman?"

"You're too tall, and the Chinese aren't safe at night. When men get drunk, the Chinese aren't safe from those who hate them."

"What about a cowboy?"

Hattie eyed her from head to toe. "That would work. It wouldn't matter how tall you are."

"Can you find something for me?" Was she seriously thinking about dressing up as a man and sneaking into a brothel after dark? "It would look rather strange for me to be buying men's clothes when everyone knows I'm single."

"They couldn't be new, or you'd stand out like a sore thumb." Hattie paused. "So, are you considering working with us?"

Julia took a deep breath. "What would the pay be?"

Hattie tapped a finger against her lips again. "I think it would depend on what you're making. I'd certainly pay you more for a fancy dress than for something simple like a camisole or under slip." She opened her coat to check a watch pinned to the bodice of her top. "Let me think on it, and we'll get together again."

"When?"

"Do you have a telephone?"

It was the first time anyone had asked that question of her. "Yes, we do."

"Good. I'll ring you when I have an idea of what I am willing to pay for your work."

"Wait." A jolt of fear rushed through her. "How can you call without the operator wondering why you're calling the schoolteacher's house?"

Hattie stared at her boots. "Good point."

"Also, what if Suzanna answers? She knows who you, Dorrie, Ivy, and Franny are."

The madam jerked up her head. "How the hell does she know that?"

"She was at the restaurant when your girls came in to talk with me. After King told the ladies to leave, they explained who they were and where they work. She's never met you, but she'd certainly recall your name."

"Damn."

Even though Julia had never heard a woman swear, it seemed natural for the woman to cuss. Was it because she was a prostitute, or because she said the words so easily, it wasn't shocking?

"For now," Hattie said, "I'll send a message to you on when we'll meet. I won't sign it, but you'll know it's me by a rose I'll print in the lower right-hand corner."

Things were beginning to sound clandestine. Cloak-and-dagger. Sneaky. If she had to admit, scary. If they didn't need the money so badly, she'd turn down the job. But if she did, she could end up working for Hattie in a different, more sordid way.

"All right. I'll wait for your message."

"I'd best get back. Someone will start wondering where I am." Hattie put her hand on Julia's arm. "Don't worry. We'll figure this out." Without another word, she walked into the bushes, then turned back before disappearing. "I do have one stipulation."

Whatever more could the woman want or need? She was putting her reputation and that of her sister on the line. "What's that?"

Hattie's skirt swished across the grass as she approached. "You only sew for me."

"Who else is there to sew for?"

"There are more than a few brothels in this town. Besides Swearingen, Mollie Johnson is my biggest competitor. She and I don't get along at all. If she were to find out you were making dresses for me, there'd be hell to pay." Hattie tipped her head to the side, then reached out her hand. "Deal?"

Since it sounded as if sewing for Hattie would be a big job, she wouldn't have time to work for anyone else anyway. Julia clasped Hattie's hand. "Deal."

After their agreement, Hattie disappeared. Julia's legs shook as she went back to the house and locked the front door. They didn't stop until she was in bed, curled up on her side, blankets pulled to her chin. What had she gotten herself into?

Chapter Ten

Julia ran her palms down the skirt of her new, pale yellow dress with lavender flowers and matching trim. She drew in a deep breath. Daniel was officially courting her. She nearly dropped the receiver when he called two days ago to ask if he could take her to dinner at King's, then to a traveling theater group performing Shakespeare.

Instead of walking to town, he was picking her up in a buggy. After a month of mud, the streets were finally dry. Only now they were filled with spine-breaking ruts. Someone had dragged boards over the streets at an attempt to level them. In theory it worked; in reality—well, if one had any loose teeth, they were in danger of losing one or two driving through town.

Julia ran her tongue over her teeth. Solid. But seeing Shakespeare performed by actual actors was worth losing a tooth or two.

"Nervous?" Suzanna straightened the collar on Julia's dress and patted a stray hair into place.

"What do you think? I've never been on a date before."

Not only that, but tonight was the night she would start pretending to be a cowboy seeking the warmth of a prostitute's arms. The note she'd received yesterday had said a package of clothing would be hidden in the bushes behind the house. But, besides telling her how to get to the alley and to watch for a lit lantern, there were no other instructions. How would she get into the building? What would she see there? What if someone recognized her? What if she saw a man she knew? What if she saw something she shouldn't?

Every night questions ran through her mind, making sleeping impossible. Now she had dark circles beneath bloodshot eyes. To Suzanna, Julia chalked it up to something in the air bothering her.

"What time is he coming?"

Julia glanced at the wall clock. Her stomach did a somersault. "In ten minutes."

"Do you think he'll kiss you tonight? After all, didn't he say he wanted to court you?"

With one last look in the mirror, she faced Suzanna. "You sure are fixated with Daniel kissing me."

Suzanna slapped her hands at her waist. "Well, don't you want him to kiss you?"

Of course, she did. When trying to keep her mind off working for Hattie, she imagined Daniel's kiss—her first kiss. Would his lips be warm or cool? Would they be soft? Would he be gentle or demanding? What did people do with their noses? Eyes open or closed? Would he stop after one kiss or would he want more?

Julia bit her bottom lip "Maybe."

"Huh." Suzanna plopped onto her chair. "I'll bet." She leaned forward, her eyes sparkling. "If he does, you better tell me all about it. I'll stay up until you get home."

A lump in her throat made it difficult to swallow. The last thing she needed was to have her sister awake wanting to talk all night when she needed to get to Hattie's. "That's all right. I'm not sure how late we'll be, so don't wait up. Nothing will change between tonight and tomorrow, so the story can wait until then." She inched back the sheer curtain on the front window.

Suzanna sighed. "All right. If you say so."

Dropping back the curtain, she pressed a hand against her stomach. Why was she so darn nervous? It wasn't as if they hadn't had a meal together. But so far Daniel had only acted as a friend before. Now it was more.

"He's here." Her voice barely came out as a whisper. "Heavens, Suz. What if I don't know what to talk about? What if I spill something on my new dress? What if . . ."

Suzanna jumped from her chair. "My goodness, Julia. Have you ever spilled on your clothes when you've eaten with him? When have you ever had problems coming up with something to talk about?"

"This is different." She fiddled with the yellow ribbon on her bonnet until it was a mass of knots. "I thought we were simply friends."

"Well, now you know he wants more." Suzanna kept her hand on the doorknob. "He's a nice, attractive man. Certainly much better than ninety percent of the men in this town or back home put together."

As soon as Daniel's knock came, Suzanna threw open the door and let him in. Julia's breath caught in her throat. My word, he was handsome and, as always, impeccably dressed. Even when wearing denim pants and a flannel shirt, he was neat.

"Good evening, Julia," he said, standing before her, holding a small bouquet of daisies. "You look lovely." Holding the flowers in a shaking hand, he tugged on his collar with the other. "Here, these are for you."

Why was his hand shaking? Could he be as nervous as she? She'd always had the impression that men were never nervous with women. They always knew what to say. What to do. The revelation that he may be as anxious about their date as she, calmed her.

"Thank you." She sniffed the flowers. "How did you know they're my favorite?"

Daniel shrugged. "My mother loved daisies, so I guessed maybe you would, too."

"I'll put them in water for you." Suzanna took the flowers to the kitchen.

"Are you ready? We need to get going so we make it to King's in time for our reservations." He winged out his bent elbow.

This was it. A date with Daniel Iverson. Swallowing a fresh batch of nerves, she tucked her hand in the crook of his elbow. "Goodnight, Suzanna," she called. "Don't wait up."

ONCE JULIA WAS SAFELY in the buggy, Daniel rounded the front and climbed in. Thankfully he'd managed to walk into the house, walk back out, and help her into the buggy without tripping, fainting, or saying something stupid.

At least he'd remembered to tell her she looked lovely. Hell, she always looked lovely no matter if working in the garden, leaning over some piece of clothing, or shopping at Haywood's. Julia Lindstrom was the most beautiful woman he'd ever set his eyes on. Not only beautiful on the outside, but inside, too. She'd been cutting to him when they'd first met, but over the past month he'd seen her kindness to children, and the old men and women who'd come into King's while they were eating.

He'd never been this anxious with her, though. Probably because before now, he hadn't spoken his intentions. From the moment he'd seen her that first day, she'd done something to him. Thankfully, she'd listened to their advice about not heading into town alone, giving him ample opportunities to escort her. But those were casual times. This was different. This was serious. This was . . .

From the corner of his eye he caught her adjusting her bonnet. He wasn't sure what these jittery feelings racing through him were, but it was something he'd never encountered before. This racing pulse whenever he was near her or thought about her was both irritating and exciting. He could do without the weak knees, sweaty palms, and jittery nerves. Having King catch him smiling to himself had been embarrassing.

Now his tongue was tied in knots. He'd never had trouble talking with Julia before. Now it was as if his brain had quit working, and he wouldn't be able to get words out of his dry mouth. *Say something, you idiot.* Hell, they were halfway to King's already.

He grabbed her arm when the buggy dipped through a particularly deep rut. "Sorry about the bumpy street."

"At least you don't have to worry about getting stuck in the mud."

He eased the horse to a more level area. "I'm glad it's still light out, so I can see." What a moron. Talking about bad streets and the sun being out. *Idiot.* "It will be a beautiful evening for the show. Not too hot or cold." Now he was discussing the weather. *Moron.*

"I'm glad. It would so disappointing if they had to cancel the show because of rain."

To keep from taking her hand, he leaned his elbows on his knees and snapped the reins against the horse's rump. "I believe it's in a tent, so rain wouldn't be a problem."

Julia gripped his leg as they dipped into another rut then jerked it back. "I'm sorry. I didn't mean to . . ."

"That's fine." Hell, it was more than fine. The quick warmth of her hand sent signals to his crotch. Signals he'd better snuff out—and fast. "Wouldn't want you to get tossed off the wagon."

"At least I wouldn't be all muddy as poor Suz was."

He joined her laughter. "Poor King. He wanted so bad to make a good impression on Mrs. Woods."

"He was supposed to meet her?"

"Since King and Mr. Woods don't get along, I'm not sure why he asked King to meet the stagecoach and escort Mrs. Woods to the bank. By the time the coach arrived, King had already fallen into the mud as he crossed the street. He took a quick dip in the horse trough, but it didn't do much to rinse off the mud. That's why I helped the banker's wife."

Julia snorted. "Too bad those dogs had to come along and knock him back into the street as he was helping Suzanna down. I've never seen her so angry."

"And now . . ."

"Yeah. Now they're attracted to one another." Julia shook her head. "I've talked with her about not getting serious with King."

"Me, too. King gets it and is willing to wait, but you know how nature can be." Fancy black buggies and worn wagons lined both sides of the street as far as he could see. He eased the horse to the boardwalk a block from the restaurant. "We're going to have to get out here."

"Everyone in town must be dining out before heading to the show."

Daniel looped the reins over a hitching post, then stepped into the street to help Julia. His heart raced. He took a deep breath. Helping her into the buggy had been easy as he only held her hand. Now he would have to place his hands around her waist to help her down. Around her tiny waist.

He reached up. Julia's eyes widened. Her face turned a becoming pink.

"Um. Don't drop me. I'd hate to end up like Suz."

He laughed, easing the knot in his stomach. "I won't drop you." She put her hands on his shoulders. "Even if I did, the ground is dry enough that you'd be more likely to break something than get dirty."

"That makes me feel better."

He grasped her waist. His fingers tingled and shoulders burned at her touch. *Down boy.* The last thing he needed to do was get a bulge in his pants. Her body trembled. She hissed in a breath then let go of his shoulders as soon as her feet hit the ground. "Did I hurt you?"

"Um, no."

Did her red cheeks say she was lying? "Are you sure? If I did, I apologize."

"You didn't hurt me. I've never had anyone help me from a buggy before. It was a bit scary being held in the air."

Daniel's heart faltered. Damn. Evidently, she wasn't as affected as he was. That put a different light on things. Maybe tonight wouldn't be the night he'd kiss her for the first time. At least she tucked her hand in the crook of his elbow when he offered it, so that was good.

Chapter Eleven

In his twenty-eight years, Daniel had been to the theatre five times: twice in Boston, twice in New York City, and once in New Orleans. Each had been thrilling, but tonight, sitting on wooden benches beneath a patchwork tent, the stage lit by lanterns, people dressed in whatever they could afford, air filled not with flowery perfume, but the stench of unwashed bodies, was the best.

Julia practically bounced in her seat, turning this way and that, as if she were trying to see everything at once. "It's all so exciting, isn't it?"

He didn't have the heart to crush her enthusiasm by telling her the tent was old, musty, and best used to start a fire, the music out of tune, the stage scratched and worn, and the costumes patched to within an inch of their lives. He leaned into her. "Is this your first play?"

Her smile could have lit the inside of the ragtag, patched pavilion. She clapped her hands like a child on Christmas Eve.

"Yes. Our pastor had an entire collection of Shakespeare, which he let us borrow. Sometimes it was hard to understand, but I loved the stories. But to see it live . . ." She grasped his forearm. "I'll never forget this. Thank you so much for inviting me."

It didn't happen that often, but he'd invite her to every traveling show performing in Deadwood, if only to see her eyes light up, her cheeks turn rosy, and a continuous smile on her face. On impulse, he leaned over and kissed her cheek.

With wide eyes, she stared at him. "What was that for?"

"Because I couldn't help myself."

She touched her cheek. "Why?"

"Because you're so beautiful. Smart. Happy." His heart dropped. "Should I apologize?"

"Apologize?" She bit her bottom lip. "Whatever for?"

Didn't she know he should have asked her first? "Because I didn't ask for permission."

JULIA'S HEART JITTERED. Why hadn't her mother told her men were supposed to ask for a kiss? Or how her skin would burn where his lips touched her? Or how a kiss would start a fever going from her head clear down to her toes, taking a detour between her legs. What was wrong with her? How should she respond? Admit she liked it? Give him permission to kiss her anytime he wanted? Wouldn't that make her a loose woman?

Without looking at her, he faced the front, his hands clutched in his lap as if he were angry. "I'm sorry, Julia. It won't happen again."

She took a deep breath. If she said what she wanted and he didn't approve, this would be the shortest courtship on record. "You needn't apologize, Daniel. I . . . I . . ." She fiddled with the button on her glove. "I liked it."

Daniel's neck cracked when he turned to her. "You liked it?"

Keeping her head lowered, she nodded. "I know that makes me like one of Hattie's girls, but I did."

He raised an eyebrow then grinned. "Admitting you liked my kiss doesn't make you like one of her girls."

That was a relief to know. "Then I give you permission to kiss me whenever you wish, unless I say no." His reply was low as if he didn't want her to hear it. Had he really said *hot damn*? Before she could ask him what he'd said, he angled toward her. His scowl didn't bode well.

He folded his arms over his chest. "Just how do you know about Hattie?"

Julia's chest tightened. His concern was appropriate. Any proper, well-bred young lady shouldn't know about prostitutes. But wait. Had he forgotten he'd told Suzanna and her about them?

"Don't you remember the first time we had lunch at King's when those three women came in?"

He sucked in a breath. "I'd forgotten, but yes, now I remember."

"You and King were the ones to explain about Hattie's establishment."

Daniel nodded and took her hand. "I was afraid you somehow had been spending time with them, which would be completely inappropriate."

Even though he was correct, what right did he have telling her who she could and could not associate with? Her pulse raced. Beads of sweat formed on her upper lip. She blinked her burning eyes. She was playing a dangerous game.

The music increased in volume drawing Daniel's attention back to the stage.

"That means the play is about to start."

Good. Any more talk about Hattie, and she would be telling him what she was about to do later that night.

The play went by in a blur. Having nothing to compare to, she was rather disappointed in the acting. Hamlet slurred his words and staggered about the stage. Even dim lights couldn't make Ophelia appear young. The plump woman had to be sixty if she was a day. But maybe that's the way all plays were.

Mix in worry about the coming night's adventure and excitement about maybe getting a real kiss from Daniel, and her stomach was tied in knots. At the end, she joined the crowd in a standing ovation, then with their laughter when Hamlet's wig fell off during his bow, revealing a pate shining in the tent's lights.

"What did you think?" Daniel asked as they strolled to the buggy.

Julia inhaled air devoid of body sweat and smelly clothes. She tipped her head back to view the sky, which had grown dark during the play. "Well . . ."

"Go ahead, you can be honest." He patted her hand as if he would accept her words no matter however wrong they may be.

"First of all, thank you for taking me to my first play." She swept her skirt aside to avoid a pile of horse droppings. "As much as I love Hamlet, I thought the acting was rather poor. For heaven's sake, was Hamlet drunk?"

Daniel threw back his head and laughed. "Oh my, he was so drunk I'm surprised he was able to maneuver around the stage without falling flat on his face."

"And wasn't the woman a bit long in the tooth to be playing her part?"

"You've hit the nail on the head." He helped her into the buggy. "I'm not much of a musician, but I believe the band at the Gem plays better."

Julia arranged her skirts as Daniel hopped into the buggy with the grace of a gazelle. "I'm glad to hear you say that because I wanted to help tune their instruments so my ears would stop ringing. Do people enjoy these traveling plays?"

"Unless you're willing to go into the Gem, there isn't much. Traveling troupes are big excitement. When they come to town, usually in the summer, they bring in a lot of people, no matter how bad they are. Sometimes the groups are good, sometimes, like tonight, not so much."

Would she see any entertainment when she went to Hattie's tonight? Probably not, as she was to enter by the back door, not step foot in the main part of the establishment. "Are the entertainments always plays?"

Daniel guided the horse around a couple of arguing drunks. Her stomach turned. Would she encounter anything similar when she came into town later?

"No. The Gem pulls in a big crowd with the entertainment Swearingen brings in, but the crowd can be quite rowdy. No place an unescorted woman would want to go. I don't care to go because of the people, even if he does manage to get a wide variety of entertainers."

Without the full moon and clear sky, the stars shone bright enough to cast shadows as they passed trees and buildings. There had to be millions up there. "I do hope more come before winter sets in."

Daniel chuckled. "Yeah. Once winter hits it's more difficult to get acts here, though somehow Swearingen manages it and brings in comedians, singers of all kinds. Believe it or not, as rough as the men are out here, they love to hear opera singers. He's also had the Vaidis sisters, who are exceptional acrobats. And there was the McDonald family."

"Who are they?"

"They have a daughter they call Baby McDonald, who is quite a talented singer and dancer. They say she's seven, but some say she's much older. Her father, James, is an incredible skater and clog dancer."

"Ice skating?" How did one ice skate inside a building? At home they'd skated on the pond.

Daniel chuckled. "No. He has skates with wheels on them. I'd heard so much about the family, I fought the crowds and took in the show." He pulled back on the reins to let in another driver who wanted to cut them off. "He had this little platform said to be ten inches square. It was up on a pedestal about three feet high."

"What did he do?"

"Not only did he roller skate on that small platform, but he clog danced in his roller skates. It was quite the sight."

"I can imagine." Would Daniel take her to see the show if it came back to Deadwood? She wasn't bold enough to ask. Would she and Suzanna still be here this winter? If she had to hogtie her sister to keep her away from King, she would. "You said before that Deadwood gets a lot of snow. How much is a lot?"

"Depends on the winter, but I've seen it pile waist high. So, you'd better make sure you have enough wood," Daniel said, clicking to the horse to move again. "Food, too. It doesn't seem possible, but people can be homebound for days after a storm. The school board puts up wood for the school, but King and I can help you with the firewood for the house. King has a large tract of woods at his ranch. In early fall, we spend a week or so hauling it into town."

Relief washed over her. Being new to the area, they had no idea where to start. "We get a lot of snow in Iowa, too, but with the pigs, steers, and chickens my father butchers and cures we've never lacked for meat. We always had a large garden and fruit trees, so in the fall we' can a lot of food to last over the winter. It's wood for heating and cooking that could be an issue."

"What do you do if you run out of fuel?"

"We never ran out, but it's been close. In the evening, my father banked the fire in the fireplace so there were sparks to start a fire in the morning."

The schoolhouse came into view. It wouldn't be long before she was home. Her stomach flipped. Would he kiss her?

"One year, Pa figured out how much warmer it was in the loft than downstairs. After that, he shoveled additional snow on the roof for insulation and moved his and Ma's bed up there. Us older ones had to make room for a smaller child. With our combined body heat and piles of blankets, we were snug as a bug in a rug."

"Sounds a bit too cozy for my tastes."

"It was. Suz wiggled and kicked all night. We got stuck with Maria, who liked to sleep with her feet at the head of the bed and head at the foot."

Daniel laughed. "Are you kidding me?"

"No, I'm not. It was only for a short time, but there was a lot of arguing until my father told us that anyone fighting would sleep in the barn."

"Did anyone have to?"

"I was tempted to fight just to get out of the house. Pa snored loud enough to wake the dead, so even though we were warm, his noise kept us awake. There were a lot of grumpy people for a few weeks. The day it was warm enough for everyone to sleep where they belonged, Ma cooked a special meal in celebration. I think Pa and Ma drank a bit, too."

Daniel shook his head. "I had only two brothers, so I can't imagine."

"The worst part was with so many warm bodies up there, frost built on the ceiling from our breaths. Pa would go down early to get the fire going. By the time he roused the rest of us, the frost began melting and dripping on us."

"How many siblings do you have?"

"Before we left there were ten kids, but the way Ma was acting, I'm sure she had another one growing."

Daniel urged the horse to the school property. He pulled back on the reins, guiding the horse came to a stop. "I know families who have sixteen or seventeen children."

A distant coyote howl brought her back to how late it was. As much as she'd love to stay longer with Daniel tonight, she needed to prepare herself for her meeting with Hattie. But how did one end an evening with a man?

Daniel sighed. "I suppose I should let you get some sleep."

The buggy dipped as he stepped down. Once at her side, he reached up to help. Julia's breath caught as she put her hands on his shoulders. Her feet touched the ground, but he didn't take his hands from her waist.

"May I kiss you?" His breath whispered across her cheek.

She tipped her head to the side. "Didn't I say earlier you didn't need to ask?"

"I'm a gentleman. Gentlemen always ask. Anyway, that's what my father drummed into us boys."

"Then, you certainly may kiss me." Now what? The questions that had kept her awake night after night ran through her mind, but before she ran into the house as if she were unhinged, Daniel cupped her cheeks. She jerked her head back at the first tentative touch of his lips to hers and the tickle of his mustache.

"Sorry. Did I hurt you?"

"Heavens, no." She bit her bottom lip. "I've never been kissed before." Should she mention his mustache?

"Really?"

Julia nodded.

"Are the men in your hometown daft?"

"A couple tried." She recalled their farm-smelly bodies leaning toward her and shuddered. "There simply wasn't anyone I wanted to kiss."

Daniel grinned. "But you want to kiss me?"

Her heart skipped a beat. "Oh, most definitely."

When his warm lips met hers, her eyes automatically closed. Something skittered down her body, settling to the most private part of her body. *Oh my.* All thoughts of meeting Hattie and worries about if she would kiss properly flew away in the evening breeze. Only his hands gently holding her face and his soft, tender lips registered.

All too soon, he broke away, his rapid breath meeting hers gasp for gasp. Then he stepped back, leaving her lips cold, cheeks burning, and heart empty.

"I'd better go before I do something we'd both regret."

She frowned. "You regret kissing me?"

Daniel leaned forward and gave her a quick peck. "Not in a million years."

"Then what do you mean?"

He sighed sliding his fingers through his hair. "I think it's too soon to explain. Let's leave it at I want to kiss you again." He nudged her toward the house. "But you need to get some sleep." Without another word, he leapt into the buggy and turned the horse toward town.

With trembling fingers against her lips, she strolled back to the house barely noticing her surroundings. Thankfully, no lights shone from windows, but it didn't mean Suzanna wasn't sitting in the dark waiting for a detailed description of her night.

Chapter Twelve

The parlor was dark. No light came from beneath Suzanna's door. Julia removed her bonnet and hung it on a peg inside the door. She sat on the bench beneath the pegs and peeled off her gloves. With the boot hook, she undid her boots, eased them beneath the bench then crept across the floor.

In her room, she removed her dress and stockings then replaced them with her gardening skirt and blouse. After retracing her steps, cringing when a board squeaked beneath her feet, she left.

The damp grass made her remember how it felt going without shoes. Happy. She hadn't gone barefoot since leaving home. She vowed to do more of it in the future. Even gardening at home had been done shoeless.

As the note she'd received yesterday had stated, a brown package was hidden in the bushes. Precious minutes were wasted as she tried to decide where to change. The necessary wouldn't work. If she left her clothes there and Suzanna needed to use it while she was at Hattie's, her sister would ask all sorts of questions. Questions she didn't want to answer.

The bushes wouldn't work, either, as it would be too difficult to maneuver. Snagging her hair or clothes on the branches would slow her down. Behind the necessary would be the best. She'd stash her clothes beneath a metal washtub leaning against the back wall. Even though there were no houses nearby and the chances were slim that anyone would be watching, Julia peered around the area before tearing open the wrapping. On the top was a long, black heavy coat followed by a pair of washed-out jeans; a faded, green plaid flannel shirt with a hole in the elbow; a vest with what she hoped were coffee stains; and a red bandana with frayed edges. Beneath those items were socks, cowboy boots, and a floppy, worn, brown hat with a cut out in the brim as if an animal had taken a bite from it.

Julia sniffed at the clothing. No unwashed body odor. The warm summer air had cooled, raising goosebumps when she removed her clothes. Bloomers and camisole on or off? On. Wearing men's clothing was one thing but wearing them against her bare skin was another.

The flannel shirt fit as if it were made for her. It was a good thing she was small on top, or it would be obvious she was a woman. The jeans were a bit loose, but the rope from the wrapping would suffice to keep them up. It didn't matter if the socks were too long since they'd be inside the boots. Earlier concerns over the boots being overly large were dismissed after she'd tugged them on. Accustomed to tighter women's boots, the wider fit was strange, but comfortable. At least she wouldn't be clomping around like a fool.

She tied the bandana around her neck and tucked her hair beneath the wide-brimmed hat. Hattie had suggested smudging some dirt on her face to conceal her fair skin. Even though it was too warm for one, the coat would further hide her identity. Too bad she didn't have a mirror to see herself as Jeb, the name Hattie had given her for identification.

Taking a deep breath, she recalled Hattie's directions, pushed through the bushes, climbed the hill behind their house, and walked a hundred yards. The hike back down the hill was slippery. The back alleys of Deadwood, dark. In order to appear manly, she used long strides.

Every scrape of boots, whoop of laughter, gunshot, cat screech, or dog bark set her nerves on edge. Two drunks, arms wrapped around each other's shoulders, singing an off-key song, the words turning her ears red, staggered past her, nearly knocking her hat off.

"Hey, cowboy," one of them said, waving a bottle at her, "wanna swig?"

"Um . . ." Her voice cracked like a young rooster learning to crow. She slipped her hand into a coat pocket fingering the thimble she'd brought for luck. She sent a quick prayer to the heavens for luck.

"Ah, hell, Jocko," the other man said, slurring his words, "he's only a young pup learn'n to use his big man's voice. Don' wanna ruin it with this rotgut 'fore it's workin' right." He waved a bottle of dark liquid at her.

Julia tucked her head into her shoulders. "Thanks," she mumbled, keeping her voice as low as possible. When the men disappeared into the darkness of the alley, she released her breath and trudged on, watching for a lantern by a back door. The note had said it would be the only light in the alley.

"Pssst," a voice whispered close to a lantern sitting on the ground. "Jeb?"

Even though the person used her fake name, she wasn't going to take any chances and immediately admit she was Jeb, especially since the person hadn't identified himself. Although, why anyone except Hattie would know her fake name was beyond her.

"Who wants to know?" Would the squeak in her voice give her away?

"It's Dorrie." A woman stepped from the shadows. "Are you Jeb?"

Julia nodded then realized the girl more than likely couldn't see her. "Yes," she answered, inching toward the woman. "What do we do now?"

"I'm going to take you up the back way." Dorrie held out her hand. "Hurry. Ivy is keeping watch to make sure no one is in the hallway."

The rickety, narrow wooden stairs led to a dim, equally narrow hallway. How could anyone find their way up the stairs without falling? The light grew brighter as they passed the top of the stairway where Ivy was leaning, calling down to the men below, taunting them with images of what would happen if they visited the upstairs girls. Lively, tinny music from an out-of-tune piano competed with loud, male voices streaming up a set of stairs from the saloon. The temptation to peek was strong, but Dorrie held her hand and tugged her down to the end of the hallway.

Dorrie knocked on a wooden door painted a pale lavender, then opened it when a female voice called out permission to enter. The room wasn't what Julia expected. In her mind, she pictured dingy walls, shabby furniture, dim lighting, a sagging mattress, and stale air.

Instead, Hattie sat at a bench-like chair before an ornate dressing table, applying rouge to her cheeks. Bottles and jars of what Julia assumed were perfume and face paint littered the top. The largest, four-poster, oak bed Julia had ever seen was covered with a pale pink, flowered quilt. Matching ruffles trimmed the canopy and edged the bottom of the bed. Lamps scattered throughout the room were covered with pink-colored glass with strings of beads giving the room a rosy glow.

And the scent. Instead of the sweat of men, the air was filled with the fragrance of . . . lilacs? Roses? Lilies? Maybe a mix of all three?

"Have a seat," Hattie said, first eyeing herself in the mirror then turning to face Julia. Tipping her head to the side and giving Julia a once-over, the madam tightened the belt of a bright green, silk robe around her waist. "You do look the part of a cowboy. Did you have any trouble on the way here?"

Julia sat on the edge of a padded chair made with the same fabric as the bedding. "Just a couple of drunks wanting me to share a drink with them."

Hattie raised an arched eyebrow. "What happened? Did they accost you?"

"No. When I tried to sound like a man, my voice cracked. They decided I was too young to drink and moved on down the alley."

"What a relief," the madam said, slapping a hand on her ample bosom. "I'm going to bring the girls up here one at a time, so no one gets suspicious. I'm afraid we won't have time for everyone, so we'll have to do more tomorrow night."

"Tomorrow night? So soon?" Her voice squeaked, but this time she couldn't put the blame on trying to change her voice.

"Of course. I know it's only July, but in less than four months, we could be hit with so much snow you won't be able to get down the alley on your own. The sooner we start, the better."

She hadn't thought of that. "How many girls are we talking about?"

Hattie tapped a red fingernail to her painted lips. "I have seven girls. Each will need at least three different dresses, plus corsets, etc. Not to mention the mending piling up."

Julia's stomach rolled over. She should say no. Twenty-one dresses in four months? Was Hattie crazy? "Who did the work before?"

The madam's chin wobbled. "Unfortunately, the girl was shot and killed by a jealous boyfriend who came to Deadwood to ask her to marry him. He was under the impression she was a shopkeeper. When he found her . . ." Hattie shook her head. "Well . . . he flew into a rage. Before anyone could stop him, he killed her."

Julia cringed. In the month since she and Suzanna had been here, they'd heard stories of murders, but until now, hadn't associated them with women. This made what she was doing even more dangerous.

"Should we get started? I can't stay out too late. Suzanna may get up during the night to find me gone. I put pillows under my blankets to make it look as if I was in bed, but she may wake me up to ask about my evening with Daniel."

Hattie snapped her fingers at Dorrie. It must have been from practice, but in less than a minute Dorrie was stripped down to a corset that made her waist seem tiny and her breasts overlarge. Red garters held up black stockings. Not being used to measuring anyone larger than her siblings and Suzanna, who was slim and small on top like her, she wasn't sure where to start or how to do it without touching bare skin.

Before removing her outer garments, Julia took the measuring tape from a pocket, stood in front of Dorrie, then hesitated.

"She won't bite, Julia." There was a hint of humor in Hattie's voice. "I can write down the measurements for you." She poised a pen over a piece of paper. "When you're done, we'll pick out fabric, then she'll trade places with one of the other girls."

Taking a deep breath, she wrapped the tape around Dorrie's neck and called out the inches to Hattie.

"So, Daniel Iverson is courting you?" Hattie said fifteen minutes later, while they waited for the next girl.

Heat filled her face as she sat on the edge of the bed, trying to keep from blushing. "We've spent some time together."

Hattie's grin and raised eyebrow suggested she didn't believe a word of it. "Some time?"

Julia tapped the toes of her boots together. "He's escorted me to town. We've had lunch."

"But what was this about spending the evening with him?"

Their time together seemed likes eons ago, not a few hours. "He asked me to dinner, then we went to the play put on by a traveling troupe. That's all."

"Humph." Hattie leaned her elbows on her knees and tipped Julia's chin up. "Did he kiss you?"

Her cheeks grew warmer recalling Daniel's lips on hers. She kept her eyes downcast.

"Humph. That answers my question." Hattie released Julia's chin. "Let me tell you something about Daniel Iverson, missy."

Julia's heart cracked. *Oh, no. She was going to say something awful about him. Something that could change her feelings. Had he killed someone? Stolen gold? Robbed a bank? Beaten one of Hattie's girls?* She hated to ask but wanted to know what she was getting herself into. "What?"

A small smile played across Hattie's face. "There are few decent men in this town. King Winson, Colin Haywood, Oliver Ogden, and . . ."

Julia held her breath. *Please make her say Daniel Iverson.*

". . . Daniel Iverson. He's never cheated anyone. As far as I know, he's never visited a brothel. He's been the only one willing to help some of the girls in this town when they were beaten or cheated out of what they'd earned."

Bubbles of happiness built inside her, threatening to spill over as giggles. "Really?"

Hattie nodded. "You couldn't have chosen a better man." She patted Julia's hand. "And he's not too bad on the eyes, either. Don't let him get away."

Someone knocked and came into the room before they could continue the conversation. Taking measurements didn't take as long as she had thought, but by the time a clock chimed midnight, there were still three girls to go.

"We can stop here," Hattie said, taking off her robe, revealing a corset that had seen better days. "As you can see, I'll need help, too, but if we wait too long for you to leave, there'll be too many drunken men roaming the alleys." She pulled a low-cut burgundy dress over her head, had Dorrie button up the back, slipped on a pair of high-heeled slippers, and swung a pink boa around her neck, flinging the strands over her shoulders. With her hand on the doorknob, she angled back to Julia. "Of course, I'll pay you for the time you spend here. Keep track of the hours." She opened the door.

Panic streamed through her body. "Wait."

Hattie raised an eyebrow. "Yes?"

"How do I get the material home? Wouldn't it look rather odd for a man to be carrying a package of material, old corsets and chemises at this time of night?"

"Good point. I'll have them delivered to you tomorrow after dark."

Julia tugged on her coat and plopped on the hat, tucking her hair beneath it. "Where will I find it?"

"The usual place." With that, she swept from the room, looking as regal as a queen, a gaudily dressed queen, but a queen, nonetheless.

Dorrie, who had returned, stuck her head out the door. "It's safe right now. Let's go."

The walk home was as dark as the trip to town. *Whatever would Ma and Pa think about my being in a brothel? Suz would be scandalized. Daniel would never want to spend any more time with me if he knew.* She was a fallen woman by association. No one would believe how much she liked Hattie and the girls she'd met tonight. Why, if she didn't know what they did for work, she'd never guess they were prostitutes.

A black cat ran in front of her, nearly tripping her. She'd always been told black cats were a sign of bad luck. To counter it, she put her granny's thimble on her pinky. She was going to need all the good luck she could get to keep this job a secret.

Chapter Thirteen

The sun sliced through Julia's bedroom window far too early. Her mattress dipped, then bounced back up again.

"C'mon, sleepy head," Suzanna said, her voice way too cheerful. "It's time to get ready for church. Besides, you have to tell me what happened last night."

Julia pulled a pillow over her head. "Go away. I'm still tired." By the time she'd gotten home last night, or rather this morning, it was well past one. After removing her cowboy clothes and putting on her regular ones, it had taken several minutes to find a hiding place. She finally settled on wrapping them back in the paper and stuffing it beneath some logs in the bushes. She'd have to make sure to shake them out to get rid of any critters, snakes, frogs, or bugs that might take up residence during the day. She'd find a better place tomorrow when Suzanna was safely ensconced in the school. Then, back in her room, she'd had to undress again then put on her nightgown. She was exhausted.

Suzanna threw back the covers. "Did you have fun? How was the play? What did you have to eat? More importantly—did he kiss you?"

Julia lifted a corner of the pillow. If she glared at her sister hard enough, maybe she'd leave. "I had fun. The play was interesting, but not well acted. I had roast chicken, mashed potatoes, and corn. Now go away."

"You didn't answer all my questions."

"If I tell you he kissed me, will you go away?"

"Yes."

"Yes, he kissed me."

Suzanna's shriek nearly broke her eardrums, even with a pillow over her head.

"I knew it. I knew he was going to kiss you." Suzanna patted Julia's hip through the blankets. "C'mon. C'mon. C'mon. Tell me what it was like."

"Would you please, please, please go away? I didn't sleep well last night."

"Oh, I get it. You were up all night reliving the kiss, weren't you?" Suzanna sighed. "How romantic. Oh, to be kissed by a handsome man."

Julia kicked at her sister. "I answered your question, now let me sleep in peace."

"Oh, all right, I'll go, but church is in two hours, so don't sleep too long."

With the click of her bedroom door, Julia flopped onto her back. Oh, she'd relived Daniel's kiss, his touch, every word they'd said. Then recalled her fear of the trek to Hattie's, meeting the girls, and her discussion with Hattie about Daniel. The anxiety over being caught in the alley and how it would affect not only her sister, but her relationship with Daniel, added to her sleeplessness.

After the first initial impression of him, she'd known in her heart Daniel was a good man. It was nice to have someone confirm her assessment.

At the end of a sleepless night, she was exhausted. Good thing today was the Lord's Day with not much happening. With a sigh, she pushed back the rest of the covers and swung her legs over the side of the bed. She might as well get up to start the day. Since working on a Sunday was wrong, maybe she'd be able to get a nap at some point.

IT WAS ONLY SUZANNA'S elbow jabbing into her side keeping her eyes open, or from resting her head on the pew in front of them, during the minister's endless sermon. Keeping an eye on Daniel, who sat across the aisle and one row up, didn't help.

Daniel's smile as he passed them on the way to his seat, had set her heart racing and delicious tingles spreading through her body. Surely God, or at least the minister, wouldn't approve of her thoughts or reactions to Daniel's kiss, his smile, his arms around her.

"Pay attention," Suzanna whispered.

Huh. The way Suzanna and King had looked at each other with adoring eyes, she'd bet her bottom dollar her sister hadn't any more idea of what was being said from the pulpit than she did. As soon as the last hymn was over, she could get out of the building to fresh air. The day was growing warmer, but there was no breeze, so even with the church windows open, the air became hot, stuffy, and odiferous.

Julia cleared her throat to keep from laughing when the organist hit a long chord signifying the last song before the minister wrapped up his sermon. If the organist wasn't the minister's wife, there'd probably be hell to pay after church. If she could, Julia would give the woman a hug and thank her for putting a halt to a sermon that had been going in never-ending circles.

Outside, they stood with a group of women, many of whom were mothers of Suzanna's students. Using a fan as cover, she eyed Daniel talking with several men. Her heart skipped a beat when he broke away and sauntered in their direction.

"Misses Lindstrom. Ladies." He tipped his dark brown cowboy hat. "Hot one, isn't it?"

Several of the women tittered at his words. What was wrong with them? They were all married with children, so why should his appearance make them act like ninnies? Maybe it didn't matter how old one was, they all liked a handsome, respectful man.

"Miss Julia?" Daniel said, taking her elbow. "May I have a word with you?"

The women's giggles, as he guided her away from the group had her wishing a hole would appear and she'd fall in so far, they'd never find her. When they were a distance away, he released her arm, but didn't say anything, keeping his gaze over her right shoulder.

"Did you want something, Daniel?"

He shuffled his feet. "I wanted to thank you again for the wonderful evening."

"I enjoyed it, too."

"Um . . ." He finally looked down at her. "I was wondering if you would care to join me on a picnic this afternoon. The Colin and Sadie invited me and said I could bring a guest."

Julia raised an eyebrow. Spending time with him last night and in town during the day when there were other people about was one thing. Tongues would wag if they went off on their own.

"They said they would act as chaperones."

A mixture of relief and disappointment swept through her. Relief that people wouldn't think badly of her, disappointment of having chaperones meant no more kisses. She also needed a nap if she was going to make it back to Hattie's tonight.

"What time would we leave?"

"In case you agreed, Sadie already made a lunch for us. How long would it take you to change out of your Sunday finery?"

With the church within walking distance of her house, it wouldn't take her long to get home. "About an hour. I can bring some sugar cookies along with lemonade."

"You don't have to do that, Julia," Sadie said from behind her. "I have plenty."

"Oh, but I want to." She couldn't help grinning at Daniel. "If I do say so myself, I make a mean sugar cookie. Suzanna's lemonade is delicious."

Sadie clapped her gloved hands together. "It's settled then. We'll pick you up in about an hour. Does that work for you?"

Colin put an arm around his wife's waist. "We'll have to take the buckboard instead of the wagon."

"Oh, honey," Sadie said, a frown marring her brow. "Why can't we take the buggy?"

"Because I invited King and Suzanna to join us. There's not enough room in the buggy." He tugged one of Sadie's dark curls. "It doesn't make sense to rent another buggy. We can toss in some quilts and pillows for the ladies. I believe King and Daniel are tough enough to withstand a few bumps. Right, Daniel?"

Daniel hesitated. Was it because he didn't care for the idea of riding in the back of a buckboard, or upset King and Suzanna were joining them? She wasn't particularly fond of either idea herself. The chances of stealing a few kisses lessened with the addition of two people, one her sister, who she would have to keep an eye on so there was no hanky-panky between her and King.

"Uh, sure, Colin."

"Well, let's get going then," Sadie said. "I'll have to throw in more food."

"We'll bring some, too," Julia said, running their stock of food through her mind. "We have some left-over baked beans. Will we be able to start a fire to heat them up?"

Daniel nodded. "Not a problem." He squeezed her elbow. "We'd better get on home to change. Colin will pick up King and me first." With a smile, he headed down the lane.

Suzanna left the group of women and clutched Julia's arm, her eyes sparkling. "Isn't this exciting? Our first picnic in Deadwood."

"By any chance did King tell you where we're going?" Julia asked, hurrying toward their house.

"No. He did mention there was a creek to wade in to cool off since it's so hot."

Julia grinned then widened her stride. "Then we'd better get a move on so we're ready when they pick us up."

Chapter Fourteen

Julia reclined on her back, a rolled-up jacket beneath her head, covered legs crossed at the ankles. Her bonnet rested beside her. A full stomach, the whispering of hundreds of pines, and the buzzing of bees made it difficult to keep her eyes open. Did she dare fall asleep? Wouldn't that be unladylike and rude?

Still within sight, the Haywoods sat on another blanket. Sadie leaned against a tree, her legs outstretched, Colin's head on her lap as she played with his hair.

King and Suzanna were on opposite ends of a patchwork quilt. Suzanna toyed with a yellow flower while King tossed small pieces of twigs at her. Their voices were low, making their conversation difficult to hear. King's deep voice was followed by Suzanna's giggle. What were they talking about?

Daniel, dressed in a plaid shirt, sleeves rolled to his elbows, and denim pants, lay on the other side of her patchwork quilt, arms folded beneath his head, his hat over his face. Was he sleeping? If he was, then she would, too. Her eyes drifted shut, her body feeling as if it was still on the bumping, sometimes tilting wagon.

With a pile of blankets beneath her and pillows behind her back, she'd sat against the sides of the wagon. The trip was longer than she'd hoped. Bouncing along as if they had springs on their rear ends, there were times she thought for sure they'd be flung from the wagon to roll down the steep hills they traveled past. Without the padding she and Suzanna were lucky enough to have, Daniel and King, with only a few cusswords, followed by quick apologies, swore they were bruised for life.

They'd followed a trail leading up into the trees, then a flat area, then back down. With her poor sense of direction and the winding trail, she'd been lost within five minutes outside of Deadwood.

A Bluejay squawked in a distant tree. The water bubbled and gurgled as it flowed down the mountain. Worried they might be trespassing she was surprised to learn this was part of King's ranch. How much land did he own?

Unlike the previous night, nature's quiet sounds soothed her mind. Dappled sunrays through the leaves of the trees flickered against her closed eyelids. Who cared if falling asleep in the presence of men was wrong? She was too tired to care. She opened one eye.

King was stretched out with his hat over his face. It wasn't as if she had any say in the matter. If the men could fall asleep, then so could she.

DRAGGING HERSELF FROM a dreamless sleep, Julia swatted at her face. Something was pestering her. Bees? Flies? Dragonflies?

"Wake up, sleepyhead," a deep voice said.

Whatever it was, hit her on the nose again. She reached up to bat it away, when someone held her hand. Something warm and wet swiped across her skin. What type of animal did that? Swinging out her arm, her elbow connected with something solid.

"What the heck? Why did you hit me?"

She threw open her eyes. Daniel held a hand over an eye. "Oh, my gosh. I'm sorry. Did I hurt you?"

"For a woman, you sure pack a wallop. Do you always wake up swinging?"

"I'm sorry. I was dreaming an animal was licking my hand."

Keeping a hand on his eye, he lay back down. "I was kissing the back of your hand."

Julia tugged at his arm. "Let me see." She gasped.

"What?"

She hesitated. Already swelling, it was bound to look worse later. "Um. You may have a black eye."

Daniel's eyebrows drew together. "Great. Just great. How do I explain that a woman gave me a black eye?"

Why did men always think a woman couldn't best them? "We could make up a story." She knelt beside him. "You could say you walked into a branch. Or . . . or maybe you saved me from a bear." When he didn't respond, she pulled a handkerchief from her pocket and stood.

"Where're you going?"

"Is the water cold?"

Daniel leaned up on his elbows. "Should be. It's melted snow from the mountain."

"Good. I'm going to get this wet so you can put it on your eye." She took a few steps then took in the empty quilts. "Where is everyone?"

"They went for a hike."

And left them alone? The temptation to kiss his injury was stronger now that she knew they were by themselves. Too bad she didn't have the courage to follow through. "I'll be right back."

Thankfully the bank wasn't steep. To keep her footing, she side-stepped down to the creek. Water this clear certainly had to taste good. She raised her skirts above her knees, knelt at the water's edge, cupped her hand into the cool liquid, and sipped. A deep growl came from the other side of the stream. Without moving her head, she glanced across the burbling water.

Dear heavens. A bear, its black coat shining in the sun, looked her way, then rose to its hind legs. *Please don't let it be a mama bear.*

Please don't let it be a mama bear. Her prayers were dashed when first one small cub then another bounded around their mother, splashing in the water as if they didn't have a care in the world. Of course, they didn't. They weren't about to get mauled.

As a child there were four things she'd learned to do when meeting a bear. Don't scream. Don't look it in the eye. Don't approach. Don't run. Ice-cold water dripped through her cupped hands, dripping onto her boots.

The mother bear dropped to all fours and moved toward her. *Don't blink. Don't sneeze. Don't move a muscle,* her father's words came to her. *She'll lose interest.* The only problem with the scenario was that the cubs were splashing through the water toward her. The temptation to scream and run was strong. Doing so would only make her appear to be prey.

"Don't move, Julia." A whisper came from behind her.

Did he think she was a fool? She was tempted to say that, but any movement would send the mother into action.

"I'm going to crawl to your left, then shoot my gun into the air."

Julia held her breath. Nothing moved. The mama bear growled. The little ones scampered back to shore then up a tree. Silence. Where was Daniel? Behind her, the gun went off. She jumped. Her boots slipped in the mud. Waving her arms in the air like a windmill, she hit the water face first. Hair dripping, skirt weighing her down, she knelt on all fours in time to watch the bear take two steps toward her, then turn into the woods, growling to her cubs.

Splashing came from her left side. Keeping sight on the bear's rump and the cubs scuttling down the tree, she blew at strands of wet hair obscuring her view.

Daniel bent beside her. "Are you all right? Let me help you."

"How are you going to do that?"

He moved behind her. "If I lift you under your ... um ... armpits, I should be able to help you stand."

Heat rose to her face. But what choice did she have? The cold water was making her numb. Not to mention with the weight of her skirts holding her down, she'd never be able to stand on her own. "All right."

Sloshing through the water and standing behind her, he put his hands beneath her arms.

"On the count of three," he said in her ear. "One. Two. Three."

His warm breath sent shivers down her spine. Of course, she shivered. The creek water was cold. He lifted her. She pushed against the creek bottom. His hands brushed the sides of her breasts. This time there was no denying the shivers weren't entirely from the cold water.

"Sorry," he mumbled.

Gaining purchase on the slippery rocks wasn't easy. She was nearly upright when her foot slipped. Daniel wrapped his arms beneath her breasts. One leg tangled with his as the other went out from under her. With trees and sky flashing before her, she was back in the water. On her back. On her back on top of Daniel. With his arm still beneath her breasts. His breath whooshed from him, blowing against her cheek.

The water wasn't deep, yet her face submerged when she rolled off him. Luckily, she'd been taught as a child how to exhale under water. She let out a short breath, stopped, let out another, then repeated until she pushed herself to her hands and knees.

"Are you all right?" Daniel said, kneeling beside her. He stood shaking his head like a dog. "Let me help you."

She pushed his hand away. "I think it might be safer if I crawled to shore. It's not far." By the time she reached the bottom of the bank, her knees hurt from the rocks she'd scrambled over. Her palms were scratched. Her skirt was torn. Her hair hung in wet strands over her face. She probably looked like a wild woman.

Her boots squished as she walked up the bank, shaking out her heavy, wet skirt. Daniel scrambled up the bank beside her. "How did you know to come down here?" she asked.

"I heard the bear's growl. Besides, it doesn't take that long to wet a handkerchief."

His grip on her elbow was strong. "Thank goodness you came." She sank to her knees at the top of the bank. "I knew I couldn't scream or run, so I was stuck like a statue waiting for the mama bear to charge."

Daniel pushed a strand of hair from her cheek. "I nearly had a heart attack when I heard the bear growl."

"*You* nearly had a heart attack?" With shaking hands, she tried to unhook her boots. The day was warm, yet goosebumps speckled her skin. "I almost fainted."

Daniel knelt at her feet and pushed her hands away. "Let me."

Voices came from their picnic area, then closer. "Are you guys all right?"

"We heard a gunshot."

"Why is Julia all wet?"

Suzanna shoved Daniel until he landed on his rear. "What did you do to my sister, you brute?"

"Ouch." Daniel leapt to his feet. "You Lindstrom girls are dangerous."

"Take it easy, Suzanna. He didn't do anything except save me from a mama bear protecting her cubs."

"Then why are you both wet?" Sadie asked, tugging on Julia's other boot, then helping Suzanna pull Julia to her feet. "C'mon, we need to get you dry."

As they trudged back to their picnic, Julia explained what happened.

Suzanna's face paled. "Oh, my gosh, Julia. You could have been killed." Before Julia could respond, she narrowed her eyes at Daniel. "What happened to your eye?"

"I accidentally punched him."

"What? Why?" She stomped to Daniel until they were nose-to-nose and poked him in the chest. "What did you do to my sister that she punched you?"

Julia grabbed her sister's finger and jerked her away from Daniel. "Thank you for protecting me, but what part of 'accidentally' didn't you understand?"

Suzanna scraped the tip of her boot in the dirt. "I guess I didn't hear that part."

"Obviously not. All he did was startle me from a dream and I elbowed him in the eye."

Suzanna slapped her hands on her hips. "And *how* were you trying to wake her?"

Evidently Suzanna wasn't about to cut Daniel any slack. "Suzanna, it's none of your business. He came to my rescue with the mama bear. He didn't hurt me. Now drop it."

Colin handed a quilt to Daniel. "My question is why are you both wet?"

"Don't worry, Julia," Daniel said. Instead of using the quilt on himself, he swung it around Julia's shoulders. "Suzanna, I was tossing bits of twigs at her. I was only trying to wake her."

Suzanna laughed. "Waking her up is like trying to wake a hibernating bear."

"Could we please forget about bears for now?" Julia clutched the edges of the quilt together. "Thank you, Daniel." She blew a wisp of hair from her eyes. "The reason we're both wet is . . ."

"Why don't you sit down. I'll tell the story."

With chattering teeth, she eased onto Suzanna's blanket and tucked the quilt around her shaking legs. She closed her eyes, listening to Daniel recount their adventure. When the only sounds were the birds singing, she opened them. Five pair of eyes were focused on her.

"What?"

Colin snickered.

Sadie covered her mouth.

Shoulders shaking, King turned away from them.

Suzanna snickered.

"Are you guys laughing at me?"

"No." Sadie giggled.

"Yes, you are."

Daniel plopped down beside her and touched his red eye. "And the worst part was, I never did get that cool, wet hanky."

Julia pulled out the hanky in question. "Here." She dumped the sodden item in his lap.

Daniel sniggered, then threw his head back and roared.

King bent at the waist and slapped his knees on his hands. "Oh my gosh, I wish I had seen that."

Julia clenched her fists on the sides of the blankets. "You wouldn't think it so funny if it had been you face to face with an angry mama bear."

"That part wasn't so funny," King said. "It's the idea of you two splashing about in the water like a couple of fish."

"Well, at least we didn't land in the mud like two people I know," Daniel said, rubbing his red eye.

Julia swallowed past a laugh. "True. At least *we* were clean when our disaster happened." Then she lost it. Every time she thought she was done laughing, one of the others would let out a snort or snicker or giggle making her start all over again.

Finally, after a few minutes of levity, Julia, followed by the others, took a deep breath. "Can we go home now? I need to change."

While the others gathered food and the rest of the blankets, Julia stood, legs still shaking from her encounter. With her soaked boots in hand, she stumbled to the wagon, her stockinged feet cutting on the rocks and twigs with each step. Why had Colin parked so far away? She shook her head. Dumb question. There was no way he'd have gotten the horses and wagon through the woods.

She'd gone only a few steps when she was swept from the ground. "What do you think you're doing?"

Daniel held her in his arms. "You can't walk barefoot to the wagon. You'll cut up your feet."

"But . . ."

"But, nothing." The muscles in his jaw clenched. "I'm only doing what any gentleman would."

She highly doubted it but arguing wouldn't do any good. Too bad her arms were encased in the blanket or she would wrap them around his neck and settle in for the ride. All too soon he was setting her on the edge of the wagon.

"There, all safe and sound."

"Thanks to you. You're my shining knight."

Daniel grinned. "I doubt that. However, if you think so, I'll take it." Before stepping back, he glanced over each shoulder.

What was he looking for? Voices from the others were still a distance away. Was he making sure the bear hadn't crossed the creek and ambled in their direction? He planted each hand on either side of her legs and leaned in. Her heart fluttered.

"Quick, before they get here."

Daniel's smile slipped as he gazed into her eyes, then her lips. His kiss, although quick, hit her as if she'd been bowled over by the mama bear plus both her cubs at the same time.

"Wow," he whispered against her lips before stepping back.

Wow was too simple a word to describe his kiss, but right now she couldn't come up with anything else. Her brain was mush. She licked her lips and nodded.

"You guys ready to go?" King asked, appearing from the woods, Colin, Sadie, and Suzanna behind him.

While the men hitched the horses and, keeping the blanket wrapped around her shoulders, Julia slid back the best she could to make room for her sister. Colin helped his wife to the seat beside him. King climbed in and, thankfully, sat across from Suzanna. Daniel sat next to her, an arm resting on his bent knee. Even with the bumpy path jostling them, her eyes grew heavy. Something warm and comforting pressed against her shoulder. Before she had a chance to figure it out, she was asleep.

JULIA'S HEAD RESTED on Daniel's shoulder. Ignoring King's raised eyebrows, he tucked her deeper into his side. Not only was he keeping her warm, her body heat was helping him, too. He'd like to think the scent coming from her hair was roses, or lilacs, or something else equally feminine. He sniffed again. No doubt she'd be upset when she realized she smelled like fish. Or was it a wet dog? He couldn't put his finger on it, but she would want a bath.

He sniffed his shirt. Hell. Maybe he was the one smelling rank.

"Cozy?" King whispered across the wagon.

Daniel nodded.

"Don't get too cozy, there, man."

"Shut up, King," he said, ignoring the nasty look Suzanna sent his way. Had she seen their kiss or was she letting her imagination run wild? Hell, between the quilt Julia was wrapped in, their wet clothes, and four chaperones, there was no way he could do anything to Julia. Not that he didn't want to. He raised both hands in the air. "Not touching her."

"You'd better not." She pointed a finger at him. "I don't want my sister hurt."

"Who said I'm going to hurt her?"

Suzanna shrugged and squinted her eyes at him. "You just be careful."

Daniel had seen the way Suzanna and King looked at each other but refrained from reminding her of the teacher's contract. Julia wasn't under any obligations, so why should it make any difference if he was courting her?

He closed his eyes, shutting out their glares, letting the afternoon' events pass through his mind. The bumpy ride to the picnic area. Sharing a blanket with Julia—even if they barely touched fingers. Fear when he realized it was taking too long to wet the hanky then hearing the bear growl. Terror when he'd reached the creek where Julia was standing in the water, an angry, large sow threatening to attack. Shooting his gun in the air. Her breasts brushing his arm when he attempted to help her up. Her body on top of his—even if it was in freezing water. Carrying her to the wagon.

His blood warmed clear down to his crotch. He squirmed and he turned his thoughts from Julia's delectable body, and the kiss that had nearly sent him to his knees, to a case he was working on.

Men were getting sick. A few had met their maker. The doctors in town all agreed it wasn't typhoid fever, or any other known disease, but couldn't decide what it was. It wasn't something in the water, or everyone would be getting sick. With the docs taking care of the sick, the businessmen decided someone else should figure out how or why men were falling ill. For some reason, they'd chosen him to solve the mystery. The sooner, the better.

Julia's heat seeped through the quilt. When he closed his eyes, he hadn't planned on falling asleep since he'd taken a nap earlier. He faded into slumber, dreaming of having Julia by his side at night. In his bed. In his life. A passel of kids . . .

"Ouch." Daniel jerked awake. Blood pooled in his mouth. "What the heck?"

Julia drew away from his arms and rubbed the top of her head. "What happened?"

King laughed. "Ol' Daniel here was snoring with his mouth open."

Suzanna giggled. "The wagon hit a rut bouncing you in the air."

"And the top of your head connected with Dan's jaw," King continued, shaking his head.

"Muth ha' 'it my ton." Daniel mumbled, wincing over each word.

"It's been quite a day, hasn't it?" Julia said, sounding as if she was trying not to giggle.

That was a simple way of putting it. Too bad he couldn't say what he wanted to. Like, sonofabitch his tongue hurt. How the hell did a person stop the bleeding? He couldn't put the hanky in his mouth. He wouldn't anyway because it was more than likely covered in germs. How was he going to eat? Would it hurt to kiss Julia? It shouldn't be, as he used his lips to kiss, not his tongue—at least not so far.

He slid into Julia's side as the wagon descended into Deadwood. "'Orry."

"That's all right." She tucked her hair behind her ears. "I'm the one who should apologize. You poor man. Between your eye and tongue, you look and sound as if you've been in a fight."

King chuckled. "Better not tell anyone how you got a black eye and damaged tongue, or you'll never hear the end of it."

Colin glanced over his shoulder. "Looks as if we have something to hold over his head in the future."

He clenched his hands into fists. These guys were supposed to be his friends? Maybe he would do well to stay out of sight for a week or so. King and Colin's laughter needled. Hell, maybe a month.

Chapter Fifteen

Late July 1879

Julia sat back on her haunches on the parlor floor. The clock struck twelve times. Noon. Only three and a half more hours before school let out and then another half hour until Suzanna waltzed through the door. The fabric she was working with today was particularly wicked to handle. The silky, shiny, red fabric with gold flowers that was to be made into a robe simply wouldn't stay in place. The bottom of the fold slid one way and the top another as she tried to pin the pattern pieces down. Putting weights on the material didn't help.

Then there was the breeze coming in through the open windows flapping up the edges of the pattern pieces. Along with high humidity, a summer heat wave had descended on the valley. Even though the breeze was hardly refreshing, she didn't dare close the windows or she'd die of heatstroke.

Cussing didn't help, either, but saying dammit instead of 'gosh darn' was more satisfying. If her mother ever found out the cuss words she'd learned while in Deadwood, she'd drag Julia back to Iowa by her ears faster than she could utter 'dammit.' Sometimes saying 'heavens' or 'golly gee' simply didn't help frustration. A good old dammit, or shit, or hell worked much better. She made sure not to swear in front of Suzanna, although she thought she'd heard her sister mutter a cuss word or two under her breath while correcting papers.

In the ten days since the picnic, she'd made several evening trips to the brothel to measure the girls, pick out fabric, return the scrap material to them for burning, and visit with the women. She'd learned the hard way the first time she'd cut out a dress to get rid of all the scraps and not put them in the stove to burn later. First, she'd missed a scrap that had slipped under the couch. Then Suzanna had asked why there was a fire in the stove in the middle of summer.

Each time she was at the brothel, she came to know the women. Other than their type of work, they weren't much different than Suzanna or herself. Maybe Hattie was a bit brass at times and the girls jaded, but they had same the womanly dreams of marrying, having children, or simply getting out of the life they hadn't planned for themselves. They hated being called names by the men in town and shunned by their wives.

Julia sighed and put more weights on the fabric. If she didn't get it right this time, she'd toss the entire thing in the wood stove and suffer the consequences with Hattie. But with having to purchase new boots to replace the ones destroyed in the creek, she couldn't afford to ruin it. How was she to know the boots would shrink? Guess that's what happened when you couldn't afford more expensive goods.

One of the problems with her evening forays was becoming too complacent. One night, a few days before, she very nearly ran into the sheriff. She'd been daydreaming about Daniel, wondering when she'd see him again, when the sheriff came from a shadowed nook behind the bank. At least she'd remembered to use her deep voice when questioned about why she was in the alley so late at night. Her heart didn't quit racing until she entered Hattie's room. Lesson learned—pay attention to her surroundings.

So far, by starting her sewing as soon as Suzanna left for the day, and working all day, she'd managed to finish three outfits. The girls were so happy at their fittings, they'd hugged her. But she'd need to up her production. The agreement between her and Hattie was that she'd get paid at the completion of five garments.

Another problem, besides the damn fabric mocking her, was hiding her work from Suzanna. Ruffles, lace, and other gewgaws the women wanted on their clothing were hard to hide. They had agreed at the beginning of living together that their rooms were private. Neither could enter the other's without permission. Right now, she had so much fabric under her bed, if the ropes holding up her mattress were to break, she'd have a soft cushion to land on.

Julia stifled a yawn. How she'd love to stretch out on her bed for a nap. It had been a few days since her last night trip, so she'd been able to get a couple of nights' decent sleep. Suzanna's questions about why she looked so tired made her realize she needed to spread her trips out. Except for working in the garden to keep up with the weeds, she spent all day inside. After supper, she took whatever mending she had to get done outside to enjoy the summer evening. Suzanna either graded papers, read, or messed around in the yard. A father of one of Suzanna's students gifted them with hand-made rocking chairs as thanks to Suzanna for getting his son interested in learning.

Occasionally, Daniel would walk over to join them, sitting on the ground between the chairs, entertaining them with stories of the town's happenings. Too bad her sister didn't take the obvious hints to leave. What part of "Suz, go into the house," or "Suz, leave us alone" didn't she understand?

With the pattern pieces *finally* pinned in place, she picked up the scissors, hesitated, and then took a deep breath. "Here goes nothing."

It was bad enough that she daydreamed about Daniel while hiking into town in disguise, but as she sewed her thoughts went back to him time and time again. Why couldn't she keep her mind off the man? Forcing her mind to thoughts of her family, old neighbors, the trip to Deadwood, whether their garden would produce enough food to get through the winter, plus anything else she could think of didn't work. Even counting the number of times a long-legged spider crossed her foot as she leaned over the mending hadn't done any good.

What was it about the man that set her heart pounding, her palms sweating, and her dreams settling on him? Was she falling in love? If only she could talk to her mother about her feelings. There had to be a woman in town to talk with. Hattie and her girls? Was she wrong in thinking they wouldn't know what it was like to fall in love?

Sadie? Every time Julia went into town she was escorted by either King or Daniel. She certainly couldn't talk about her feelings with either man in their presence. King more than likely would tell Daniel what he'd heard. And if Daniel were to overhear her, well, that didn't bear thinking about. Heat rose to her face. How embarrassing would that be? She'd never be able to look at Daniel again.

Much to Suzanna's chagrin, an invitation from the society ladies had yet to arrive, so they hadn't made any new friends that way. The mothers of Suzanna's students were too busy with their children, housework, gardening, cooking, and shopping to take notice, let alone spend time gossiping. Except for weekends when Suzanna was home all day, she was so busy sewing, her fingertips were sore. Too bad she couldn't work with thimbles on each one. She set aside the first cut out piece.

The Fourth of July was over. Daniel and King had escorted them to the downtown festivities. Miners had erected a tall liberty pole using rags the ladies of the city had donated to decorate it. A twenty-one-gun salute followed the reading of the Declaration of Independence. As the day wore on and the alcohol flowed, the revelers became so rowdy, Daniel and King had decided it wasn't safe to stay for dancing.

Julia set the cutout sleeves to the side, then started on the back piece. If they were in Iowa . . . Julia blinked away tears she didn't want to fall on the precious material. She had to quit comparing life in Deadwood to back home. Home was now here. In Deadwood.

What would winter in Deadwood be like? Would there be more social activities in the colder months like in Iowa? With no gardens, no canning, no work in the fields, well . . . no mining, what did the people do to get through the winter? Did they hold card parties? Quilting bees? Dances? Would she spend time with Daniel or be stuck in the house with Suzanna when snow closed the town?

She finished cutting out the back. Only two front pieces and the ties to go, and then she could start stitching. What she wouldn't give for one of those fancy machines that did most of the work for you. Maybe she should save some of her money for one. It would certainly save her time. She'd have to talk to Sadie about it the next time she went shopping there.

Julia sighed. Thinking about home hurt. Thinking about Daniel confused her. Maybe she should create a story in her head. When she had any spare time, she could write it down.

She snapped her fingers. What a great idea. Suzanna was always asking her how she spent her days when she didn't have mending to do. If she were to write a bit each day, she could use it as an excuse. It didn't have to be good, simply fill sheets of paper. Of course, it didn't matter if she insisted, Suzanna would never see the words.

When the pieces were stacked and the scraps wrapped in paper, she hid them next to two dresses ready for delivery. Then she took a sheet of paper and pen from the desk. Sitting at the kitchen, she let her imagination run wild.

HOURS LATER, LOST IN the world of dragons, princesses, and heroes, she jumped when Suzanna entered the kitchen.

"What in heaven's name are you doing?"

"Nothing."

Suzanna picked up the first page and turned her back before Julia could yank it away. "Hey, this is pretty good," she said a minute later, taking the next page from the table. "What made you decide to write a story?"

"I needed something to fill my time between mending jobs." Julia closed the inkwell. With Suzanna home, her concentration had broken. She'd get no more words written today. "There's only so much dusting to do, and so many dishes to wash and weeds to pull. I was getting bored."

"Can I read the rest of it?"

Why would she want to do that? Even though she'd had fun creating the characters and plot, it was merely something to do so she wouldn't have to lie to Suzanna about her day. "It's not done. The last page isn't dry."

"I don't care. I want to find out what happens." Suzanna held up a hand, palm out when Julia tried to scoop up the pages. "Shh. Let me finish."

Julia left the room, her stomach jumping as if she had completed one hundred rope jumps. It never occurred to her that having someone other than herself read what she'd written would be quite so nerve-wracking. Suzanna giggled. What part was she reading? Julia had tried to add humor to the story. Was her sister laughing at the part where a frog rode on the back of a dragon, telling him where to fly? Or was it when the princess refused to kiss the frog?

To keep from going back into the kitchen and throwing the entire mess in the garbage, she searched the parlor for any scraps of material she may have missed.

"Oh, my goodness, Julia," Suzanna said, entering the room with the story in her hand. "I didn't know you could write."

Julia swallowed around the lump in her throat. Was it that bad? "What do you mean?"

"This is fantastic. When you're finished, I want to read it to my students. I think they'd love it."

"Are you serious?"

Suzanna nodded. "Dead serious. I think you should try to have it made into a book."

"Well, I never . . ."

"Never, what?" Suzanna frowned as she set the papers on the desk.

Stepping on a small piece of red material peeking from under the corner of the couch, Julia shrugged. "I don't know. I never thought about writing anything until today. Didn't have a clue I had an idea for a story. Didn't give any thought to having it published. Plus, I wouldn't know how to do that."

"Why don't you finish the story before you start worrying? Right now, I need to change. Then we can think about supper." Suzanna went into her bedroom, closing the door behind her.

Julia moved her foot and picked up the stray piece of fabric, searched beneath the couch and chairs, and shook her head. Sewing for prostitutes, writing a book, and having feelings for a man. Life was sure taking surprising twists and turns.

Chapter Sixteen

Daniel snapped the reins on the horse's rump. Today he was picking up both the sisters for a weekend trip to King's ranch. He rubbed the itchy eye that had turned from black to a shade resembling the clay from back home. It had been two weeks since the 'creek incident' as King called it, never letting him forget one woman had punched him in the eye and made him bite his tongue, and another knocked him on his ass.

Since then, he'd seen Julia only a few times. Whenever she'd call to be escorted into town, he was busy with his current case. Since it was easier for King to leave the hotel and restaurant, he usually took over the duty of collecting her. If he didn't know King's feelings about Suzanna, he'd be jealous of the time he spent with her older sister.

Now that they'd have two days together, they would possibly have some time—alone. He crossed his fingers on one hand. With the other rubbed the rabbit's foot in his pocket. Childish gestures for sure, but he didn't want to take any chances. Thinking of King's she-bear of a housekeeper, Hilda Kearney, he'd need it.

The woman had to have eyes in back of her head, as he'd never seen anyone else who knew what was going on all the time on the entire ranch. If she couldn't keep an eye on them, she'd sic her husband, Paddy, on them. Since Paddy resembled an ox, large and muscular, Daniel didn't know who would be worse. He palmed the rabbit's foot and crossed the rest of his fingers. If it were possible, he'd cross his toes, too.

He grinned. Was he crazy over Julia or just going crazy? If it weren't for his current case, she would be all he thought about. He couldn't pinpoint what it was about her that sent his senses reeling. All he knew was he'd been struck by something the first time he'd seen her. Was it love? He shrugged and leaned his elbows on his knees. How the hell should he know? He'd never been in love before.

Dammit. While mooning over Julia he must have pulled back on the reins. Instead of clomping along in his old, plodding gait, Sizzle had stopped in the middle of the street. He whistled to the horse. "Get going, Sizzle." He snapped the reins. "Who the hell gave you that name, anyway? You don't have any more Sizzle in you than those rocks over there." Great, now he was talking to the back end of a horse. He certainly was going crazy.

"Get your mind on the case, Daniel James Iverson." In his mind, he ran over the reports in his satchel. He hoped to run his ideas past King this weekend. Maybe the girls, too, since both were intelligent women.

Somehow, somewhere, in the past few weeks, the men in Deadwood were getting sick. There was no rhyme or reason as to how or where they were getting ill. Some while at their camps, some after being in town, and some who couldn't recall where they'd been before their bodies gave up anything they'd eaten or drunk. He would blame it on the living conditions of the miners, but the illness wasn't confined to them. Many of the men who lived and worked in town were also affected. It took nearly a week for them to feel well enough to get back to work.

Was it the food they'd eaten? The water they drank? It was well known how polluted some of the water was from mining runoff. Since none of the women had been affected, they'd considered the possibility the men had contracted something from the brothels. Usually the pox didn't arrive one day then leave in a few more. Getting some of the men to admit where they'd been was like trying to blow up the side of a mountain with a match.

Was someone purposely poisoning the men? While it seemed unlikely, he couldn't ignore the possibility. He ran a hand over his daily stubble. Why, and more importantly, who? Shutting down the saloons and brothels until they found the culprit would set the men to rioting.

Al Swearingen would more than likely shoot anyone who tried to close his doors. Same with wild Mollie Johnson. Not that she'd shoot anyone. There were other ways to injure a man. He ran other establishments through his mind. Any one of them could be suspect. Why would the owners want men to get sick? If men couldn't drink or whore because they were ill, gold coming through the business doors would drop significantly.

Something niggled at the back of him mind. He snapped his fingers. Sizzle stopped and glanced over his shoulder. "C'mon girl, that wasn't a signal for you to rest." He flicked the reins. Sizzle let out a low whinny before continuing her plodding steps.

Maybe one or more of the saloon owners had banded together to put the other places out of business. There weren't any he'd trust more than Sizzle could jump a fence. Nah, that didn't make sense. How would they be making the patrons of other places sick? Besides, he was being paid by some of the businesses to solve the problem before no one wanted to come to town for fear they'd get ill. The owners were up in arms demanding a resolution to the situation.

The schoolhouse came in sight. His mind returned to a more pleasant subject, one Julia Lindstrom.

AS USUAL, DANIEL WAS greeted at King's ranch with a wide grin and a hug nearly squeezing the breath from him, along with a kiss on the cheek. For all her gruff and bluster, Hilda was an incredibly kind woman. For some reason, she didn't want anyone to know it. He didn't understand why, but then he never was good at figuring out women.

King received a nod, which made sense since he owned the ranch and rode out here at least once a week. He'd seen Hilda smile many times before, but when she spotted Julia and Suzanna it was if she'd found long lost friends, or the children she'd never had. Her eyes sparkled. Dimples deepened in her plump cheeks.

With open arms, she approached the sisters. "My dears." Her German accent deepened. "So nice to have women on the ranch. Ya. Such pretty ladies, too." She gave the men speculative looks, then slapped her hands on her ample waist. "Who are dese lovely ladies?"

Daniel grinned. "Hilda, this is Julia Lindstrom and her sister, Suzanna, who is Deadwood's new schoolteacher. Ladies, this is Hilda Kearney, King's housekeeper."

Hilda took the women by the elbows and led them to the front porch. "Come join me for coffee and some of my special apple strudel." Before they entered the house, she yelled over her shoulder, "King, bring da bags in for dese ladies."

King grinned, shook his head, and handed a bag to Daniel. "You know what she's thinking, don't you?"

"'Fraid so." Daniel carried two of the bags. "How are we going to convince her we're not out to marry them?"

"Maybe you aren't, but I am," King said, coming to a halt at the porch stairs.

"Really?"

King frowned. "Is it that hard to tell Suzanna and I are interested in each other?"

"Well, no." Daniel followed his friend up the porch steps where King set his bag on the floor. Evidently this conversation wasn't over. "What about her teaching?"

"We've discussed it and agreed to wait out her year. We'll need to be careful to always be seen with other people. I don't want her to lose her reputation or her job." King raised an eyebrow. "And what about you and Julia? I've seen how you look at each other, so you can't tell me you don't have feelings for her."

Daniel's face heated, which surely meant he was blushing like some schoolgirl. "That obvious?"

King snorted. "A blind man could see it. So, what are you going to do about it? She doesn't have the strictures of a teaching contract."

"I don't know." He removed his hat then raked his fingers through his hair. "I know you're going to think I'm stupid, but I'm . . ." Could he even say the word?

"Falling in love with her?"

Daniel peered through the screen door. "Shh. Keep your voice down. How does one know if they're in love or not?"

"Beats the hell out of me." King ran a hand down his face. "If thinking about someone all the time, wanting to be with her all the time, and worrying about what the rest of your life would be like if they weren't with you is love, then I'm head over heels with Suzanna."

"We're a lost cause, aren't we?"

"At least we're in good company."

"You gents coming in or not?" Hilda's strong voice came down the hallway. "Dese ladies would like to freshen up."

Daniel chuckled. "Better do was we're told, or we may not be fed while we're here."

AFTER A LUNCH OF COLD ham sandwiches, hot chicken soup, and warm lemonade, they accepted King's invitation to tour the ranch. She'd always wondered what the difference was between a farm and ranch. The first thing to strike her was the size. Their farm in Iowa was twenty acres, which was enough to have milk cows, chickens, sheep, and rabbits, and to raise crops to feed their animals and family.

Here it seemed King's land went on for miles. "How many acres do you have, King?" Suzanna asked.

"Just shy of a thousand." King propped his foot on the bottom board of the fenced-in paddock. "With the woods, rocks, cliffs, rivers, and creeks on the property, I don't have nearly that much to work, just enough to raise most of what we need at the restaurant and feed the hands here at the ranch."

Sandwiched between the men, she and Suzanna stood side-by-side, leaning their arms on the top board of the fence. "Is this where the wood for the school will come from?"

King nodded. "Even though I don't have any children in school, it's my contribution to the education of our youth. We still have more to put up before winter sets in."

"How will we get the wood for our house?"

Daniel bumped his shoulder against hers. "There are a couple of axes in the shed. You and Suzanna can come out any time you want, cut down a few trees, split the logs, and haul it back to town."

He was kidding, right? There was no way they could handle hauling wood. Again, Suzanna spoke before she could.

"He's not serious, is he, King?"

King chuckled. "No, he isn't." he tucked an errant strand of hair into Suzanna's bonnet. "Don't worry, we plan on making sure you have enough wood for the winter."

"Thank you," Julia said, relieved she wouldn't have to help. They'd done enough putting up wood back home. It would be nice to have someone else do the job for once. "Let us know how much you'll charge us."

With her hand tucked in his elbow, Suzanna and King strolled away, her sister asking farming questions Suzanna could have answered herself. Why was she being such a nitwit?

"A kiss."

Had she heard Daniel right? "What?"

"I said a kiss. You can pay for the wood with a kiss."

"A kiss?" Was he kidding again?

Daniel nodded and smiled down at her.

"Just one kiss?"

"Well. . ." Daniel's eyes sparkled. "It's going to take a lot of wood to get you through the winter, I suspect one kiss wouldn't be enough."

Interesting thought. "How many kisses are you talking about?"

"A lifetime." His face turned red before turning away from her. "I apologize, I shouldn't have said that."

Her mother had always told her children to think before they spoke because the first words out of someone's mouth were usually the truth. Sometimes the truth hurt. Was Daniel telling the truth? Did he want to spend the rest of his life kissing her? With his broad shoulders turned away from her, he wouldn't be able to see her lick her lips, blush, or hold back an excited giggle. Nor could he see her mouth 'yes' behind his back.

"Do you ride?"

What a switch in topics. "Sort of."

He finally turned, his face no longer red, or eyes sparkling. He draped his forearms over the top board and stared at the horses in the corral. "What do you mean 'sort of?' You either do or don't."

"While we were growing up, Pa had a couple of work horses. We couldn't afford anything fancy like King has. They were used for plowing, pulling stumps, hauling us to town in the wagon." She fiddled with the strings on her bonnet. She had no idea what Daniel's background was. Based on his dress and that he had attended college to become a lawyer, he more than likely came from money. Would he think she was a hick?

Daniel turned his attention from King's thoroughbred horses and nodded toward King and Suzanna's retreating backs. "We'd best catch up with those two."

An excellent idea, as they seemed a bit too cozy. Time to take her thoughts from Daniel and focus on her sister.

"Go on," Daniel said when they'd caught up to the other couple.

"Anyway, Dell and Dale were plow horses. Maybe seventeen hands. Big heads. Big back ends. Wide middles. If Pa wasn't using them, whenever we had a spare moment Suz, our brother, George, and I hauled blocks of wood to whichever horse was free and climbed on, one behind the other."

"No saddle?"

"Are you kidding? I don't think there is a saddle big enough for either of the horses. We didn't use a bridle or reins, either. The person in front held on to the mane while the other two held on to the one in front of them."

Suzanna turned and grinned. "Oh, my gosh. Are you telling him about Dell and Dale?"

"Yes. Since I was maybe eight, Suzanna, seven, and George, six, we must have looked ridiculous on top of the horse, plodding around the yard, our dresses hiked up to our knees."

"The horse was so wide," Suzanna added, "and our legs so short, they stuck straight out from their sides, our dirty bare feet flapping in the breeze like Ma's sheets on the clothesline. We thought we were something else riding miles from the ground."

Julia smiled at the memory. "For their sizes, I've never seen two more gentle horses." They stopped at a fence facing toward the woods. "Their offspring were just as gentle."

"Did you have pigtails?" Daniel asked. She frowned. "Of course. Why do you ask?"

His eyes returned to sparkling. His smile deepened his dimples. "I'm trying to get a full picture." He tapped the tip of her nose. "I'll bet you were adorable in pigtails."

"I doubt it, but we had fun."

"Since you have ridden before, do you ladies want to go for a ride now?"

Julia shook her head to clear it. Had she heard right? "Um. What part of *we rode a pokey plow horse with no saddle or bridle* did you miss?"

With his hand at her back sending shivers down her spine, Daniel guided her toward the barn where Suzanna and King had disappeared. "Being brave enough to get on a horse, especially without a saddle, is the first step. How old were you when you quit riding them?"

He'd think it ridiculous if she mentioned her age. "Just before we left for Deadwood. We took turns giving the younger kids rides."

"Then this will be easy for you."

The silhouette of the other couple was all she could make out in the dim interior. As her eyes adjusted, she took in the length of the barn with stalls lining each side.

"I breed some horses for racing," King said, running his hand down the forehead of a pure-black horse poking his head out the stall. "I also raise sturdier ones for miners and any farmers we have in the area, which aren't many."

Suzanna rubbed her nose against the horse's muzzle. "Are there races around here?"

Daniel stood in front of the next stall scratching the ears of a brown horse with a white star on its forehead. "Hi there, Penny. How's my girl today?" He waved Julia over. "King raises the racers for a couple of men who own a racetrack in California. They come out here in the fall and spring to see what he has for sale. King has quite a knack for raising fast horses."

The last thing she wanted was to be on the back of a fast horse. "Um, if we're going to ride, do you have anything in the slower range? Something old, lazy, doesn't care if the rider has never used a saddle before?"

King laughed. "You, too, Suzanna?" When she nodded, he went on. "I'm sure I can find something like that for you. I'm afraid I don't have a side-saddle for you ladies."

"We don't know how to use a regular saddle, let alone a side-saddle. Do we, Julia?"

Suzanna smiled at King. "Plodding sounds good to me."

Chapter Seventeen

Julia lay on top of her blankets, replaying the weekend while waiting for Suzanna to fall asleep. Throughout the weekend, as they rode horses, played cards, took hikes, and sat on the front porch drinking lemonade, the thought she had to deliver two dresses and finish several others played in her mind. There were times her fingers itched for her needle and thread. Plus, tonight was the night she got paid—finally.

Her time with Daniel was more than she'd hoped for. Talking about their families, their dreams for the future, which, he'd hinted more than a few times, included her. What life had been like in the early days of Deadwood, which was all of three years earlier. How he'd first panned for gold and quickly realized standing in ice-cold water or digging into hills wasn't for him.

Then there were the kisses. His delicious, heart-stopping, kisses. Her dreams of being kissed by a man hadn't come anywhere close to reality. His earlier ones had been amazing, but the more they'd kissed, the longer, more passionate, they'd become. The first time he'd urged her mouth open and she tasted his tongue, her skin burned, and lady parts clenched. She had to squeeze her thighs together to stop something overwhelming from taking over her body. Something she'd never experienced before, as if she'd been spun into the sky. When he'd broken the kiss, she wanted to pull him back and sink her body against his. To devour, consume, lay down on the grass with him, and let him ease the ache coiling between her thighs.

She opened her eyes and stared at the ceiling, willing her breath to slow down. How could simply thinking about him and his kisses re-create those same sensations? She released her clenched fists and took a deep, cleansing breath. *Think about something else, Julia May Lindstrom.*

Several times she and Suzanna had been left alone while the guys holed up in King's office. Once or twice they helped Hilda with her baking. Other times, they talked about the letters they'd received from home, comparing what was said in the other's letters. How in between helping Pa with chores, George had taken over teaching the little ones their letters—when he could tie them down long enough, anyway.

The clock's chiming the tenth hour came through her door. She scooted to the edge of the bed and leaned her elbows on her knees. Better get the night over with. Since the miners were done with their shopping and headed back to their camps, Sunday evenings at Hattie's were quiet, making it a good night to trek into town.

She eased open the bedroom door, wincing at the door hinge she'd forgotten to oil, tiptoed across the parlor, then slipped out the front door. By now, getting dressed as a down-and-out cowboy was routine. Noting the package with the dresses was gone she stepped through the bushes and headed to town.

"THESE DRESSES ARE BEAUTIFUL," Hattie said, handing a thick, white envelope to Julia. "I couldn't ask for anything better. The girls love them, too."

Without looking inside, she tucked the envelope in the inside pocket of her vest. "Thank you. It's been a challenge both sewing and keeping this a secret from Suz."

Hattie picked up the low-cut teal dress and, with one hand, held it to her waist. With the other, she held the bodice to her front. The silver beads, meticulously stitched into the bodice and skirt edges, sparkled in the lamplight.

"Once we've caught up on the dresses for downstairs, I'd like you to start on some day dresses for the girls. You know, ones they can wear outside this house. Or if they want to leave, they'd have decent clothes for the outside world."

Julia raised an eyebrow. "You don't mind if your girls leave?"

"No. As much as I hate to admit it, there's always some poor girl out there to take her place." She swayed from side-to-side letting the satin skirt sway and shimmer. "It's a sad world when a woman can't find a man to support her. Her options to take care of herself are so limited, she must resort to taking care of men's needs in a brothel."

Hattie was right. About the only thing a woman could do, other than be a wife and mother, was to become a teacher or nanny, and she couldn't think of anything else a woman could do that wasn't allowed by a man. "Is that what happened to you?"

Hattie shrugged. "Sort of. I fell in love with a man working as a hand at a neighboring farm. I thought he returned my affections and followed him to Chicago." She spread the dress across the bed and smoothed the fabric. "When he tired of me, he stole what money I had from my parents then left without a word. I couldn't pay the rent on the rat hole we lived in, couldn't get a job, so when the owner of our building gave me the name of a woman who could help me, I jumped at the chance to earn some money."

"Did she?"

"Did she ever." A tear ran down her cheek. "Once inside her *business* they took my things, and I was given fancy clothes to wear and a room to sleep in. Until the first man showed up at my door, I had no idea I was in a brothel."

"Couldn't you leave?"

"We were guarded twenty-four hours a day."

Julia couldn't imagine what it must have been like. "How did you get away from the brothel?"

"Ever hear of the Chicago fire?"

"Of course. Who hasn't?" Even in her small hometown, the horrible news had spread.

Hattie closed her eyes. As if reliving the event, she answered in a monotone. "The brothel wasn't far from where the fire started. We hadn't had any rain for months, so everything was brown and dry. With all the wooden buildings, when the fire started, it had plenty of fuel to keep it going. It roared to us so fast, we didn't have a chance to put on shoes. The madam screamed at us to get out of the building. With the flames licking at our feet, we ran and ran until we hit the river. It was the only safe place.

"The fire went on for several days until it finally burned itself out. I knew for sure our building plus all our belongings were gone."

Julia couldn't imagine how anyone survived the disaster. "What did you do?"

"With everything in piles of smoking rubble you couldn't tell the streets apart, let alone buildings. Even if I'd been able to find it, I didn't want to go back to the brothel and take a chance of being seen." Hattie shrugged as if what she'd gone through was no big deal. "I wasn't the only one who had only the charred clothes on their backs and no place to live. I followed a large group of people heading out of the destroyed area. Some not affected by the fire came with supplies. Others brought wagons to transport us out.

"I caught a ride to a shelter. After a few days, we were given clothes and a bit of money to help us get started again. Many went back to Chicago to rebuild their lives."

Julia fingered the pile of new fabric sitting on the table next to her chair. "You didn't?"

Hattie shook her head. "No. I didn't have anything, nor anyone left, so this was my chance to leave. At home, my folks weren't too interested in having me back. I'd left with a man I wasn't married to. Left them with one less body to help with the work. To them, I'd turned my back on family to be a whore, as my father put it. I sure as hell didn't say it was exactly what I'd turned out to be."

"Did they make you leave right away?"

"No. They did show some compassion when I said all my belongings were lost, including the jackass I'd left with, in the fire. They let me stay as long as I went back to helping with chores and my younger siblings."

Julia could relate to having to help with younger siblings. However, it sounded as if her parents were more caring than Hattie's. "How long did they let you stay?"

"After a year, I was tired of being treated as a slave, so I thought I'd head west. Eventually, I ended up in Deadwood."

Julia's mind raced. There had to be more to Hattie's story, but unless she was willing to share, Julia wouldn't ask. "If you wanted to start a new life, why did you end up owning this place?"

"Working in a brothel was all I knew. Other than working on a farm, I had no other skills. With a lot of time to think as I traveled out here, one of the things I realized was I didn't want to be under the thumb of any man. Working and slaving for what? A man? Children?"

"Didn't you ever want children?"

"At one time I thought I did. Now I don't want to be tied down."

Hattie pulled a lacy curtain aside and stared out the window. Julia didn't know what to say. Didn't every woman want at least one child? Daniel's handsome face came to mind. She did, but not for a couple of years. After a few minutes of silence, Hattie sighed before dropping the curtain.

"When I finally arrived in 1877, there were a few bawdy houses, including Al Swearingen's Gem Theater. It soon became clear to me how he and other men treated the women. Beatings. Rapes. Their cruelty knew no bounds. There had also been some deaths. Then there were madams such as Mollie Johnson."

There was a name she'd heard before. "You told me a bit about her."

Hattie shrugged. "While she didn't allow her girls to be beaten, she made them dye their hair a brassy yellow, so everyone knew they belonged to her. To make sure none of her girls left, they had to stay in town unless chaperoned by her or one of her men. It wasn't much different than where I lived in Chicago." Hattie opened a bottle of perfume and sniffed before placing a drop behind each ear. "She also picks on the girls from other brothels. Calls them names. Tells men they all have the pox or some other disease.

"When I arrived and saw the condition at Swearingen's, I took as many girls as I could then opened my own place. You'd better believe old Al wasn't happy about that."

A shiver went down Julia's back. That was the man Daniel and King had warned them about. She'd always thought they'd been exaggerating. Now she knew they were right to caution them. "Is that why you'd allow a girl to leave, because you weren't able to in Chicago?"

Hattie nodded. "A woman's life should be her own, regardless of what they do. The only requirement I have of my girls is that they keep their rooms and bodies clean, and don't swear or drink." She lifted a curl draped over her shoulder and let it drop.

What a world they lived in, where a woman was the property of a man, or a madam, no matter what they did. Maybe someday things would change—probably not in her lifetime, though. Julia glanced at the gold filigreed clock on Hattie's nightstand. "I better get going, or I'll be too tired to work tomorrow."

Hattie wrapped Julia in a hug. "Thank you for listening to me rattle on. I can't tell you how much I appreciate your helping us. What I paid you isn't nearly enough."

If Hattie only knew how any amount of money would help her and Suzanna. "I should thank you. I've never worked with such beautiful fabric before or made such gorgeous gowns." She tucked her hair under her hat.

"I'll send the material for the next dresses the usual way. I have notes on what we want made from it," Hattie said, ushering her to the door.

At the bottom of the stairs, Julia poked out her head and perused the alley before leaving the building. She couldn't afford to slip up now. Tonight, on the way into town, she'd sensed someone watching her. While she hadn't seen anyone, it still gave her the jitters.

Reminding herself to keep her steps long, she added a hitch to her giddyap. Hattie's story was amazing. Outrunning the fire had to be terrifying. Leaving the city, wise. Going back to her parents, brave. Heading west on her own with no job or prospects of one, daring. Each time she met with the madam, she was more and more impressed.

Halfway down the alley, her skin prickled. Something clattered behind her. Was someone following her, waiting to rob her? Was it the sheriff again? A drunk? She patted the envelope holding her earnings to make sure it was still there. Another crunch sounded back down the alley.

Get hold of yourself. It's probably a cat or dog looking for something to eat. The sound came again. Definitely footsteps, not loud, more like someone trying to be sneaky.

Julia slipped into the dark opening of a building and flattened her back against the wooden door, praying the rickety wall wouldn't collapse. She held her breath, closed her eyes, then popped them back open. Wouldn't it be better if she knew who was out there?

"I tell ya, I saw someone walkin' down the alley in front of us." An unfamiliar, deep voice came from her right. "And I swear I smell perfume."

The next voice was more familiar. Where had she heard it before?

"And I say ya had too much to drink. With all the whorehouses around, of course ya smell perfume, ya idiot."

"I din't have mor'n two drinks." The first man said. "If'n I did, the boss would have my neck."

"Did ya get it?"

Something, like a chain, clanked in the darkness. "Ya. But the boss better be careful. That lawyer guy has been sniffin' around askin' questions."

Julia suppressed a gasp. They had to be talking about Daniel. Why hadn't he mentioned it to her? This sounded dangerous. Was that why he and King were held up so often in King's office over the weekend? The urge to peek around the doorway was strong. If they saw her who knew what they'd do? Beat her up? If they found out she was a woman in the process? She shuddered. Too scary to consider.

Should she tell Daniel what she'd heard? No. If she did, wouldn't he ask what she was doing in the alley at midnight? By herself? She certainly couldn't explain her disguise. She had to come up with something about where she was when she heard the men talking.

"C'mon. Let's get this to the boss before we're fired."

There was the clanking sound again. "Yeah. We were supposed to be back by midnight. It's nearly that now."

The men's boots scraped along the ground as they passed. A waft of cigarette smoke ticked her nose and burned her eyes. A sneeze threatened. Thinking of something other than an imminent sneeze always worked, so she concentrated on Daniel's kisses until the men's footsteps faded in the night.

Glancing right, then left, Julia left her hiding place. Being careful not to kick any loose rocks, she headed straight home, praying all the way she wouldn't encounter anyone else.

SET TO FOLLOW THE TWO men, Daniel rose from behind a pile of whiskey barrels. Why were they so concerned about him trying to figure out why the men were getting sick? Who was the boss they were talking about? What did they get for him? Why couldn't the men have said more?

The men hadn't been gone long when someone stepped from a doorway. He wore a cowboy hat and, even in the warm evening, a long coat. The man's cautious steps didn't make a sound. Twice he glanced over his shoulders. Since Daniel was dressed all in black, the cowboy couldn't see him.

Unfortunately, because of shadows, he couldn't see the cowboy's face or been able to identify the two men, even if one of the voices was familiar. A voice he couldn't quite place. Such had been his luck throughout his investigations. So close, yet so far away.

Daniel stopped and stared at the skulking cowboy. There was something off about his walk. Was his stride too short? Were his shoulders too narrow? The hitch in his walk a bit forced? The cowboy turned again. Only his chin was visible from the shadow of the hat. A chin too feminine for a man. Was that a strand of light hair curling around his chin? A skitter went down his back. Daniel shook his head.

Hell. He was imagining things at this late hour. What would a woman be doing in the alley at night dressed as a cowboy? Even the ladies of the evening knew better than to venture out after the sun went down. Besides, it was too dark to get a good look at the person to tell if it was a man or woman. The cowboy hadn't been with the other two and was probably a young pup sowing his wild oats, so it wasn't worth his time following.

Since the first two men were long gone, it was no use going any further. He cut down past the Grand Central Hotel then crossed the street. Ignoring the boisterous shouts, swearing, and a drunk thrown from a saloon, he took the steps two at a time to his second-floor rooms.

Daniel unlocked the door, struck a match to a lantern on his desk, and tossed his jacket on the back of his desk chair. Carrying the lamp to light the way, he pulled aside the curtain separating his bedroom from his office. After removing all but his pants, he toed off his boots, then draped his socks over the rusted, metal footboard. He flopped back onto the mattress and threw an arm over his eyes.

Someday he'd have a better place to live. The makeshift room was only big enough to hold a bed too short for his frame, making it necessary to curl on his side to sleep. A bedside table held the lamp plus the current book he read before sleeping. That left only enough room for a small dresser. Hooks on the wall were used to hang his clothing. A tiny window barely let in enough light during the day to find his clothes and enough air to keep the room from becoming hot and stale. A potbellied stove in his office sufficed to keep both areas relatively warm in the winter.

With the exorbitant rooming prices in town, creating a separate area in his office space was the only way he could afford a place to sleep. Julia's sweet face came to his mind. If he wanted to consider marrying her, something he did way too often, he needed to find better living quarters. Getting paid to solve the issue of the sick men would go a long way to helping fill his bank account and, with a bit of luck, bring in new clients.

Daniel folded his arms beneath his head. The lamplight wavered on the ceiling. Like it did whenever he had a spare moment, his thoughts turned to Julia. As the weekend at King's had progressed, he'd been drawn more and more to her humor, sweetness, intelligence, and, it went without saying, her femininity. As their kisses evolved from pleasant to exciting, it took everything in his power not to go further. He itched to unbutton her dress and caress as much of her bare skin as he could. His palms hurt from digging his fingernails into them. He'd been raised a gentleman, and gentlemen didn't take advantage of ladies.

Had Julia known he'd wanted more from her? His erect member pressed against her stomach certainly should have been a clue. She was an innocent. Expecting an innocent to understand a man's needs was wrong. And it was his duty as a gentleman to keep her virtuous until they married.

Daniel unbuttoned his pants releasing the pressure on his penis. He'd spent nearly the entire weekend with a hard-on. When he wasn't with Julia, all it took was thinking about her to grow hard. He rolled to his side. He needed his sleep to keep his mind sharp to solve the mystery. It was going to be a long night again. Turning his mind from her, he focused on the issue at hand. Before long, he was asleep.

Chapter Eighteen

Julia rubbed her burning, itching eyes. By the time she'd returned home last night, it was past one o'clock. As usual, sleep was hard to come by. Now she was suffering the consequences today.

The package of material had been in a different place this morning which had taken her longer than usual to locate. A note was attached saying the path was getting too worn down, so another hiding place had to be found. Julia understood, but it might have been nice if Hattie had warned her last night. Now she was a good hour behind in cutting out the next dress. At least Suzanna didn't expect her to produce something on her book every day, giving her time to sew.

Concentrating on making the correct cuts to the emerald fabric, she jumped when a knock came on her door. With a grunt her mother would chastise her as being unladylike, she rose and hobbled to the door, shaking out her legs. Sometimes, when she sat too long on the floor, they fell asleep.

After tipping the young man who'd delivered the note, she sat on the couch and removed the dab of wax keeping the folded paper closed.

Im knowin what your doin. Im kepin an eye on you. Money will help to kep my mouth shut. Ill rite soon so we can talk. Member, your bein wached.

Julia's breath caught. Good thing she was sitting down. She dropped the paper to her lap then re-read it. Who would write such a thing to her? Was it possible the message was meant for someone else? Whoever wrote it had sloppy penmanship, making it hard to tell if a man or woman wrote it. No curlicues, no bold script to identify the gender of the writer. Not to mention the horrific spelling, which meant the person didn't have much of an education. Not that knowing this helped any. From what she'd seen of the men in town, it described a good share of the population of Deadwood.

Was the person referring to her sneaking into Hattie's place at night or sewing for the madam? Who had seen her well enough to recognize her through the disguise? Had one of Hattie's girls, without thinking about the ramifications, talked to one of the men who visited her, who in turn had blabbed it to someone else?

Julia balled the paper and stuffed it in her apron pocket. There wasn't one girl she'd suspect who'd reveal her secret on purpose. Was there? Her skin prickled. Had Mingus Thoreson recognized her? Dorrie had been careful not to let any men see Julia as she went up and down the stairs, but that didn't mean someone wasn't listening outside Hattie's door, recognizing Julia's voice.

What did this person mean by discussing the situation? Blackmail? With her arms hugging her waist, she paced the room. If anyone thought they could get money from her, they were in for a big surprise. While their situation had improved with the money from Hattie, there wasn't enough to pay someone to keep silent. She stopped at the telephone, fingered the cord, then stopped. Other than Hattie, there wasn't one soul she could talk to about this.

Daniel would never want to see her again. King was Daniel's friend who might turn his back on both of them. Suzanna would either faint or yell at her so loudly, their parents would hear her all the way to Iowa, then insist Julia leave and never come back.

There was Sadie. As much as she liked the woman, she didn't know her well enough to know how she'd react. Stop selling goods to them? Spread the news to all the church members? What if she understood and could help? Julia fell back to the couch and covered her face with her hands. What was she going to do?

The only one she trusted was Hattie. She wanted to believe she trusted Hattie's girls, too, but someone blabbed the secret. Wait. She snapped her fingers as she went to the desk. What if no one had recognized her? What if someone followed Hattie or one of the girls delivering fabric to this house and put two and two together?

Julia needed to warn Hattie right away. She tapped the tip of the pen to her lips. But how? Showing up at Hattie's back door without giving her advance warning wouldn't be a good idea. She placed the pen back in its holder. If she sent a note directly to the madam, the messenger could easily spread news the new school marm's sister was communicating with one of the madams in town.

Fear trickled down her back. What should she do? She stared out the window until an idea popped into her head. An idea so preposterous, it could possibly work. An idea that, if caught, would ruin their lives forever. It was the only way she could think of to get in touch with Hattie. Every nerve in her body spiked with fear. A bead of sweat trickled down the sides of her face. It was a risky chance, but a chance she had to take.

"YOU SURE ARE QUIET tonight," Suzanna said, placing slices of the apple pie she'd baked the night before on their plates. "Something wrong?"

She should have known Suzanna would pick up on her distress and paid more attention to her sister's recounting of her school day. "No. I've been struggling with a scene in the book. I had no idea how hard writing a story could be." Would the excuse satisfy her sister?

"Well, here's something you can put in a book."

Julia swallowed a chunk of cinnamon-flavored apple along with the flaky crust. Other than Leona's, Suzanna's pie crust was the best Julia had eaten, surprisingly better than their mother's. "What's that?"

"You know who Josiah is, don't you? He's the ten-year-old who has made it his mission to antagonize me."

"What did he do this time?" Julia asked, trying to keep the laughter from her voice. So far, the brat had greased Suzanna's chair, hidden her chalk, brought in bugs to try to scare everyone, dipped one of the girl's pigtails in the ink well, and hid a harmless grass snake in his sister's lunch pail.

"Well, today, while we were out for recess, he managed to get into the school and put a frog in my desk drawer."

Julia snickered. Since they'd caught frogs all the time back home, she couldn't imagine Suzanna doing this, nonetheless, she had to ask. "Did you scream?"

"Are you kidding? I closed the drawer before it could escape. When the children were reading their stories for the day, I put the frog in my apron pocket."

"Did you do what we did to that bully, Sam, when he wouldn't leave us alone?"

Suzanna nodded. "Yep. Josiah always wears a shirt with these large pockets where he hides all sorts of things like rocks, sticks, bugs. As I walked around the room checking their work, I slipped the frog into one of his pockets. When I got back to my desk, I told the children they needed to wipe off their slates. I knew Josiah kept his rag in his pocket."

"Did he yell?"

"Oh, my goodness." Suzanna rocked back in her chair, her eyes twinkling with glee. "Did he ever. He squealed like a stuck pig. I'm surprised you didn't hear him in the house. Knocked over his chair and ran from the building."

Julia wiped away her tears from laughing so hard. "That's just what big old Sam did."

"When the children finally quit laughing, I set them to a new task to work on while I went in search of him."

"What did he do?"

Suzanna propped her elbows on the table and rested her chin in her hands. "I was surprised he didn't realize it was me who'd hidden the frog in his pocket. He swore he'd get back at whoever did. Once I made him realize the shock he felt when he'd touched the frog was how he made others feel when he pulled jokes on them, he apologized and swore he'd never pull another trick on anyone again, ever."

"Do you think he'll keep his promise?"

"Probably for at least a week."

Julia wiped her mouth with a napkin. "What happened to the frog?"

"You know what?" Suzanna tipped her head to the side. "I have no idea, but I'm sure it'll show up in someone's desk."

"You're a good teacher, Suz. Not only did you teach him you're not scared of frogs, you taught him a valuable lesson."

"One can only hope." Suzanna took Julia's plate. "Now, are you going to tell me why you're so quiet tonight?"

Darn, her sister never could forget a question when someone ignored her. She shrugged. "You know. Just one of those moods. I miss everyone back home, and I'm worried about expenses."

The hand pump squeaked as Suzanna filled the dishpan. "Me, too. It seems your mending is picking up. You also have the dress order for Mrs. Jenkins."

Thankfully, Suzanna hadn't paid any attention to how little mending she'd actually been doing. And she'd forgotten about Mrs. Jenkins' dress. "It's only an alteration, so it shouldn't take me long. She doesn't need it until next week, anyway."

"At least it's a start. Once word gets out, you'll have so much work, you won't know which way to turn."

Hopefully, it wouldn't be the wrong word getting out. "I'm going to work on my book a bit, then read before going to bed." Then toss and turn and wait until Suzanna fell asleep. Another attack of nerves nearly sent her supper into her throat. It was going to be a long night.

Chapter Nineteen

Dressed in her cowboy disguise, coughing and sneezing into a handkerchief, Julia made her way down Main Street. Sneaking down the dark alley was different from making her way through the throngs of men, yelling, shouting, and occasionally shooting off a gun. How did they ever get any mining done when they were kicking up their heels in town all the time? Whenever anyone came too close, she sneezed, wheezed, and coughed. Not only did it make the men give her a wide berth, it also protected her nose from the scent of unwashed bodies and animal dung. No one stopped her to ask who she was or realize she was a woman.

Scantily clad prostitutes hung over second-floor railings of the houses of ill repute, calling the men to come visit. She'd had no idea it was part of their job. In between summoning the men, a blonde-haired balcony girl from Mollie Johnson's yelled nasty comments to the girls at Hattie's and others down the street. Their caterwauling only added to the raucous noise of the Badlands.

While she was nervous walking among drunken men during the night, it was spotting Daniel and King leaning against a post outside one of the banks that nearly made her faint. She had two choices—pass them on the way to Hattie's or take her chances crossing the street, walking down a few buildings then crossing back. Since horses ran up and down the street with riders yelling and screaming, it would be better to make her way around the two men. At least she wouldn't get trampled.

With a deep breath, she tugged her coat collar to her ears and held her balled-up hanky over her nose and mouth. With her hat pulled low, someone would have to look closely to see she wasn't a man.

Setting into a fit of coughing, she approached Daniel and King. One step closer. Two steps closer. Almost by them.

"You all right, stranger?"

Daniel's deep voice recalled their kisses. She caught herself before tripping. That was all she would need—fall into his arms.

"Sounds like you're ready to cough up a lung," King added. "You might want to see the Doc about that."

"I'm fine." The hanky served to disguise her voice, which she lowered as much as possible without sounding like a sick frog. "A strong drink will settle the dust."

Daniel tipped his hat then paused. "Do I know you?"

"Don't think so. Just arrived in town. 'Night, gents."

Even though she'd passed by them and the air was filled with noise, their conversation still came to her.

"I swear I've seen that guy before," Daniel told King.

"Hell, Dan, with so many men coming into town, how can you remember who you've seen?"

Taking a chance, Julia glanced over her shoulder. Daniel removed his hat and raked his fingers through his hair. "I know, but there's something about the guy."

"Do you think he has something to do with the men getting sick around here?"

Daniel shrugged. "Don't know. I'm keeping an eye on him."

With the sense of Daniel's eyes boring into her back sending shivers through her, Julia moved on toward Hattie's. Great, now she had more than one person watching her. Maybe it was time to change disguises.

It didn't seem possible, but the noise grew as she approached Hattie's. A body came through the swinging doors landing in the muddy street. Had it not been for yesterday's downpour, the street would have been hard-packed, probably breaking some part of the man's body.

Startled, she pressed herself against the wall, dropping her hanky in the process. Keeping an eye on the saloon man, she bent to retrieve it, nearly unseating her hat. With the hanky safely in one hand, and the other on her hat, she looked toward the bank. Daniel and King hadn't moved. Maybe it was her nerves, but both appeared to be watching her.

"Don't come back in here," a deep voice yelled, startling her. "We don't cotton to cheaters at Hattie's. You want to cheat, go to the Gem. Swearingen will take money from anyone."

The hinges squeaked as the man uttered a few cuss words and reentered the saloon. With a deep breath, she turned her back on the men and stood before the saloon doors that were too tall to see over. Tinny music from an out of tune piano mixed with laughter, cussing, and the occasional slapping of cards on tables.

With the hanky pressed against her mouth, she pushed the doors open. Instantly, her eyes watered. The blue, smoky haze made it difficult to recognize anyone. Not that she expected, nor wanted to.

Now what? Thinking about getting into the saloon was different from actually being here. She scanned the room. After reading dime novels in the newspaper, her expectations of what it would look like were dashed.

Yes, the room was hazy and loud. Instead of a board laid across two wooden barrels, the bar was nearly as long as the room. Made from wood, the front had scrollwork etched across it. A low, metal bar, where men rested their boots, stretched from one end to the other. From what she was able to see between the men leaning against it, the top was scratched, but polished. A large mirror reached from the ceiling to a row of bottles on a counter behind the bar. Two men raced back and forth, filling glasses as fast the men emptied them. On both sides were paintings of scantily clad women reclining on couches. While they made her blush, the men seemed to pay no attention.

Tables were filled with men playing cards. Some of the women wore the dresses she'd made. Seeing the dresses on the girls upstairs was one thing. It was another to see them in the bar where they sat in men's laps, leaned on their shoulders as they played cards, carried trays with drinks, or, much to her embarrassment, led men up the stairs. Where was Hattie, the one person she needed to see the most?

Someone pushed her away from the doorway. "If'n you're not gonna drink, at least get out of the way so's the rest of us can."

"Sorry," she mumbled, keeping the hanky to her lips. Now what? She needed to get upstairs, but so far, she hadn't seen any men heading that way without a woman on their arm. They were all escorted by one of the girls. If only Hattie would appear so she could approach her. Did a man approach the madam or did one wait for her to notice them?

Thankfully, no one took notice of her as she wove her way across the scarred, wooden floor slick with tobacco juice. Despite signs telling them to, obviously the men didn't bother using the spittoons scattered about the room.

"Hey, honey. Lookin' for some fun tonight?" a woman said, her voice rising above the racket in the room. She slipped her arm through Julia's. "Julia, what the hell are you doing here?" she whispered, her voice frantic. "What if someone notices you're a woman?"

Julia faced the prostitute. "Dorrie?" she whispered.

"Yes." In a louder voice she went on. "If you have gold, you pay for what you want." Dorrie shoved a piece of paper into Julia's hands.

Julia glanced at the list. Her stomach flipped. Did people really do these things to each other? Her stomach rolled. "Um, I'll do

Number One." Whatever that was. Under her breath she added, "I need to talk with Hattie. It's urgent."

"Show me your gold, then we'll adjourn to my room."

How did one show gold they didn't have?

"Just open your palm and pretend," Dorrie whispered then, with her arm linked with Julia's, guided her to the stairs.

As they passed the bar, someone came from behind and slapped her on the back, nearly sending her hat to the floor. "Have fun. Dorrie is a handful. Ya won't be walkin' in the morning." The men at the bar laughed at the joke. "Yer first time, boy? Don't worry, Dorrie'll take good care of ya. She'll teach ya real good how to be a man. Then ya can have any woman ya want."

"Like the schoolteacher's sister you want and gave you hell between your legs?" the man next to him said.

"Shut the hell up, McComb. The bitch will get what's comin' to her. No one treats me like that."

"You shut your mouth, Thoreson, or you won't be walking for a week again," Dorrie yelled.

Julia nearly stumbled. *Thoreson? There could be more than one Thoreson in Deadwood, but not more than one she'd kneed. Was he the one who sent her the note?* It was a good thing she always came to town with either Daniel or King. But what if Thoreson decided to accost her at home? Was that what the note was about?

"Ah, hell, Dorrie. I'm jus' funnin' with the kid. I'd come up and join ya, but I'm savin' myself for the Lindstrom bitch."

Panic jerked through her. He planned to get his revenge? Dare she tell Daniel or King? She mentally slapped herself up the side of her head. Like overhearing those men in the alley, there was no way she could mention Thoreson's threats without exposing where she'd heard them.

Dorrie lifted one side of her skirt and tugged on Julia's arm. "Come on, sir."

RESISTING THE URGE to glance over her shoulder to see if Thoreson was watching, she headed up the stairs beside Dorrie.

"What's this about having to see Hattie? She's resting tonight," Dorrie asked when they reached the upper hallway.

"Someone sent me a note saying they knew what I was doing. Someone knows who I am."

"Damn it." Dorrie scurried down the hallway. "I hate to disturb her, but this isn't good." She stood before Hattie's door, lifted her hand to the door, hesitated then knocked three times. "Hattie. It's me, Dorrie. I need to see you. We have a problem."

After a few minutes, a chain clanked against wood. Hattie cracked open the door. "What's so damn important that can't wait until morning? You know I don't feel well."

Dorrie glanced up and down the hallway. "It's Julia. She's here."

"Tonight? She's not supposed to come for two more days." Through the crack, Hattie eyed Julia then swung her attention back to Dorrie. "How did you know to meet her?"

"Can you please let us in before someone hears us? It's important."

With a sigh, Hattie widened the door and stood to the side. Back in the room, she lay back down on the bed. Julia had never seen the women so disheveled. Hair resembling a tumbleweed, dressing gown askew as if she'd put it on without paying attention, and dark circles beneath her eyes. Was she ill like so many of the men in town or did she have something contagious?

"Don't worry, I'm not sick," Hattie said as if she'd read Julia's mind. "The first two days of my monthlies are awful. Can't do a damn thing except curl up in bed."

Julia certainly understood. "My mother was that way, too. At least when she was carrying one of my siblings, she had nine months' reprieve, then at least nine more while she nursed. Maybe that was why she kept having babies."

Hattie chuckled. "No, thank you. I'd rather suffer two days a month than worry about dying in childbirth or go through all the pain of pushing out a kid."

Julia sat on the edge of her favorite chair. She both agreed and disagreed with the madam. Her mother did go through a lot of pain during labor, but holding a newborn was one of the most blessed things in the world. Hopefully, one she'd experience herself someday. A picture of holding Daniel's child flickered in her mind's eye, then disappeared. The way things were going right now, he'd find out what she'd been doing and never speak to her again.

"So, what's this about a problem?" Hattie asked, pulling the blanket to her chin.

Julia pulled the note from her pocket and handed it over. After a few seconds, Hattie got up. A frown marked her surprisingly young-looking, makeup-free face. "Do you have any idea who wrote this?"

"No. It was delivered yesterday by a stranger. I've been racking my brain trying to figure out who and how someone knows what I'm doing." Julia toyed with the thimble in her pocket. "Could one of your girls have said something?"

"No. They were under strict instructions to keep this a secret. They know if any did, they'd be fired, kicked out without pay, and have to leave all those beautiful clothes behind."

"It's possible it's Mingus Thoreson."

Hattie snorted. "Why would he care what you do?"

"Um, I kinda kicked him between the legs when he accosted me. Another time I gave him an ear clap."

"He stopped us before we came upstairs," Dorrie said, twisting a handkerchief in her hands.

"Did he recognize you?" Hattie asked, frowning.

Julia shook her head. "Thank the heavens, no. But he did say he was going to do something to me."

Hattie tapped the note against her lips. "I know the man. A real . . ." She flipped a hand. "I can't say the words to describe him. I think someone wants to blackmail you. Thoreson doesn't have the brains to do more than get dressed in the morning, and he probably needs help with that. No, this sounds like someone with an agenda."

"Who?" Dorrie asked. "Julia isn't doing anything wrong."

"In the eyes of society, I am." She bit her bottom lip. Why had she agreed to help Hattie? "We've been so careful. I've been so careful."

"Besides those two men in the alley a few weeks back, has anyone else seen you?"

"No. Though tonight I ran into Daniel and King. Daniel thinks he knows me."

Hattie held up a hand. "Wait. You saw them in the alley?"

"Um, no." She tugged on her bottom lip with her teeth. She couldn't meet Hattie's eyes. "I had no idea how to get a message to you, so I . . . Um . . ."

"Well, spit it out, girl."

"I came through town and then the saloon."

Hattie slapped a hand to her chest. "Oh, lordy, girl. What if someone realized you were a woman? There's no way you'd have made it here without someone like Thoreson attacking you."

"I know. I know. But I didn't know what else to do. I had to see you right away." Julia held out her hanky. "I kept this over my mouth and coughed and sneezed all the time. Made the men nervous enough to stay clear of me."

"How did you get her up here without anyone suspecting anything?"

Dorrie grinned. "Just treated her like I would any other man who wanted me."

Hattie laughed. "I knew you were something special, Julia. What's this about Daniel thinking he recognized you?"

"I don't know. It sounded as if he'd seen me in this getup before, but I have no idea when he could have. As I walked away, I heard them say that maybe I had something to do with the men getting sick and would need watching."

"Oh, that's just great." Hattie read the note again. "Whoever wrote this didn't have much of an education."

"That's what I thought, too, but I don't know anyone in this town well enough to know if they can read and write or not."

Hattie handed the note to Dorrie. "Have you ever seen Thoreson read or write?"

Dorrie shook her head. "No. We . . ." She glanced at the note, then Julia. "Well, you know."

"I'll figure out a way to find out." Hattie took the note back. "Mind if I keep this?"

Julia shook her head. "That's fine. While you're at it, could you get him to stay away from me?" Julia shuddered. "He kinda scares me."

"He should. Whatever possessed you to kick him in his man parts?"

"One time he accosted me in town, then wouldn't leave me alone at the get-together at the school. It's what my parents taught us to protect ourselves. It worked, but now he wants revenge."

Dorrie tightened her shawl around her bare shoulders. "Couldn't you tell Daniel or King? They'd protect you."

"I thought of that, but how would I explain how I know what Thoreson said?"

Silence filled the room before Dorrie spoke. "No matter what, we need to come up with another disguise."

"Either that, or she doesn't come here anymore," Hattie said, lying back down on the bed.

Not come to see her or the girls? The idea made her heart drop. "But I love seeing all of you."

"That's so sweet of you, Julia, but I can't risk you losing your reputation because you're helping us. Besides, you have all the girls' measurements, don't you?"

"Yes, but I'll miss you."

Dorrie snapped her fingers. "What if we came up with a couple of different disguises?"

She liked the idea. "It would throw off anyone who thinks they know who," she swept a hand down her coat, "this cowboy is."

"Have any ideas, Dorrie? Because I don't." Hattie frowned. "We already agreed dressing her as a Chinaman wouldn't work. She's too tall."

"What about an old miner? There are enough here, no one would notice one more."

Julia gave an inward shudder. "Would I have to be dirty?"

"Probably only your face and hands. We could find you a different, scruffy hat to hide your face, some old pants and boots."

"That would work." Hattie sat up and leaned against her headboard. "What about a fancy man? I think we could find a beard, top hat, long elegant coat."

These ideas were great, but where on Earth was she going to find a place to hide the disguises? "Then I can keep coming?"

Hattie nodded. "I'll make sure to get the clothes to you. We'll have to make damn sure no one follows whoever delivers them. Meanwhile, I'll try to figure out who would have sent this note." She waved it in the air. "If you get any more, let me know. And for heaven's sake, don't talk to anyone on the way home."

"You can bet on that." Julia slapped her hands on her knees and stood. "I'd best be getting back."

Hattie pulled an envelope from her bedside table. "This is for you."

"But I'm not to be paid until I finish another dress."

"This isn't for the clothes."

Julia took the envelope and peeked inside to find several coins. "I can't take this."

"You can, and you will. While thinking only of myself and my business, I've put you in a bad position. It won't make up for the hassles, but I want you to know I appreciate your work and friendship. Women like us don't get many friends from the outside world." Hattie scooted down in the bed, rolled over, and pulled the blankets to her ears. "Now leave. Take the back way. It'll be safer."

JULIA RELEASED A PENT-up breath when she finally crawled into bed. She hadn't seen or heard anyone on the walk home. Not running until she'd reached the safety of their backyard had been a challenge. Before dropping off to sleep, she said a quick prayer. Did God protect people like Hattie and her girls? Did He protect people who helped women in their position? She prayed so, because it seemed things were quickly getting out of hand.

Chapter Twenty

Daniel took a seat near the restaurant kitchen. "Have you seen him lately?"

King placed a cup of coffee in front of Daniel. "Who?"

"That cowboy we saw last week." He took a sip of the black brew and sighed. He might be able to think now. "The one I thought I recognized?"

"No. Have you?"

Daniel shook his head. "He can't simply disappear. Got a minute? We haven't had a chance to talk since that night."

King took a chair across from Daniel. "It's been busy here, plus I had to go to the ranch to get some meat. What have you been up to?"

"Still trying to figure out why the men are getting sick. It's slowed down some, so maybe whatever was making them ill has run its course." He cupped his hands around his coffee mug. "I've narrowed it down to a couple of the saloons."

"Not all of them?"

"No, and that's the strange thing." He held his cup out for a refill. "I've talked to everyone I can who got sick. Doc kept a list of names. I've trekked all over the area this past week. My feet hurt."

King snorted. "Poor baby."

"Ass. Anyway, I can't find any connection with those getting sick except that the men drank at the Gem, Mollie's, and Nuthall's. It has to be the alcohol being served there."

"Not Hattie's?"

"Nope. At first, I thought maybe she was somehow involved since her business has increased, but she's not that type of woman. Besides, why would she sell her liquor to the other saloons? Doesn't make sense."

"I agree. I would think the same would apply to the other places. Since no one makes their own liquor, I guess you need to find out where everyone is getting their booze from."

Daniel shook his head. "You'd think Al, Mollie, and Billy would be willing to give up the information, but they won't."

"Underground?"

"That's what I'm thinking, which makes my job more difficult. They say they want me to solve the problem before they pay me, but they won't help at all."

"So, you think that cowboy may be part of it?"

"Yep." He blew across the coffee before taking a sip. "Damn. How can one cup be lukewarm and the next nearly burns my tongue off?"

"Old post versus fresh."

"You could at least warn a guy." Making sure no one was paying attention Daniel stuck the tip of his tongue in a glass of cold water. The pain was nearly as bad as when he'd bitten his tongue.

"What would be the fun in that?" King clapped his friend on the back. "Have you seen Julia lately?"

He tried to suppress a grin, but just her name made him smile. "I escorted her to town the other day for supplies and ate lunch here. You must have been at the ranch."

"Probably."

"Saturday night I took her to the Colin and Sadie's to play cards."

"Sounds fun."

Daniel kicked King under the table. "You and Suzanna need to join us the next time."

"You know I can't do that. It would look like I'm sparking her."

"Geez, too damn bad, isn't it? We sure had a good time. Got a kiss when I took her home, too."

"Ass. Don't rub it in."

Daniel stood. "I need to get back to the office. Colin and Sadie want me to draw up a will."

"Why would they do that? If something happens to Colin, wouldn't the store go to Sadie?"

"Not necessarily. Besides . . ." He glanced around the restaurant to make sure no one was listening. "Sadie is in a family way."

King's eyes widened. "Really?" He slapped the table. "That's fantastic."

"Found out last night. See what you miss when you have to stay away from Suzanna?"

"Ass."

"So, you said." He chuckled at King's middle-fingered salute. "See ya later."

AFTER MEETING WITH King, Daniel sat at his office desk pouring over the notes he had on the sickness case. When had he become a detective? More importantly, what made people think he was? While more interesting than lawyering work, it was also more frustrating.

He tossed his pen across the desk. He was missing something. Every night for the past week, he'd waited in the alley, positioned himself by the bank, or made the rounds of the saloons hoping to see the elusive cowboy. The guy *had* to be part of what was going on. All he'd seen in the alley were Doc Williams leaving Mollie's, two old coots singing and weaving their way home, and an old miner bent over so far he was surprised the man didn't scrape his forehead on the ground.

Since the doctors in town all agreed whatever had made the men sick wasn't typhoid, diphtheria, or anything else contagious, it had to be poisoning. But who and why? Tonight, he'd wait in the alley for the cowboy. Maybe his next step would be to watch the road into town to see who was delivering booze and then follow them back to wherever they had come from. Relieved he had another plan in mind, he plopped his hat on his head and left for Julia's. He'd never surprised a woman before, but it seemed like a good idea. He paused at his phone. Maybe he should call first. Nah. Women always loved surprises. Anyway, his mother had.

JULIA HUMMED AS SHE sewed the last stitch into Mrs. Jenkins' dress. After seeing the alterations she'd done on the last one, the woman brought over two others for her to remake, and another one to take apart for a dress for her ten-year-old daughter.

Before turning to Mrs. Jenkins' clothes, she'd been adding embellishments to a gown for Hattie and cutting out fabric for a day dress for one of her girls. Hattie's dress, bright red with ruffles at the rear and cut up to the thigh on the right side, was draped across the back of the couch. She hadn't taken the time to clean up scraps and pieces of ribbon before starting on Mrs. Jenkins' dress. Since the birth of her fourth child, the woman had lost considerable weight, so all hers needed to be altered. Julia hoped the woman was worn out rather than sick. Neither sounded pleasant.

A knock at the door made her jump and prick her finger. "Heavens." She stuck her finger in her mouth. Who on Earth could be visiting? Social norms said people should send a note before they arrive. She set Mrs. Jenkins' dress aside, stood at the edge of the window by the door, and peeked around the edge of curtain. Her heart in her throat, she stepped back.

Daniel. What was he doing here? The mess in the room grew in proportion to her nerves. Except for the dress she was working on, she couldn't let him see the other clothing. He knocked again.

"Julia?" he called. "Are you there?"

She turned to the room, then the door. What should she do?

"Julia?" he called again.

"Be right there." She opened the door a crack with enough space to slip through. She pressed her back against the closed door. "Daniel. What a pleasant surprise. What brings you out here?"

"Can't a guy visit his girl?"

Her heart fluttered. "Is that what I am? Your girl?"

Daniel twisted his hat in his hands. "I hope so. I'd like you to be."

A spiral of joy skittered through her. No one had ever asked her to be his girl. "I'd love to."

He rested his forearm on the wall above her head and ran a finger down her cheek before leaning closer. "Good."

His kiss was warm, tender, sweet, and so powerful her knees nearly buckled.

"Can I come in?"

"I don't think that would be a good idea, Daniel."

"Why not?"

Now that she was officially his, would he expect more from her? The idea sent tingles over her skin, but was she ready for more?

"For one thing, it wouldn't be proper. What if Suz and the children saw? They know I'm here alone. They could tell their parents and Suz could get in trouble."

Daniel shook his head. "Sometimes the idea that what one family member does reflects on the others is crazy. Just because I want to spend time with you alone shouldn't affect Suzanna and her job."

Julia toyed with a button on his shirt. "I agree, but that's the way it is." It certainly would make her job with Hattie easier, too. "But the parlor is a mess. I was working. There are fabric and dress pieces all over the place."

"I don't mind."

"But I do." Julia swept a hand toward the chairs. "Why don't you sit in the shade. I'll get us some lemonade and we can visit."

Daniel took a step back and sighed. "If you insist."

"I insist."

"Then at least let us sit away from view of the playground."

Conceding to that, Julia slipped into the house. In case her sister should happen to let school out early, or Daniel found an excuse to enter, she scooped up dresses, patterns, and scraps of material. She shoved it all beneath her bed and closed the door. She left Mrs. Jenkins' clothing laying on the chair. After all, it was a legitimate job.

"WHAT TOOK SO LONG?" Daniel asked when she handed him a glass of lemonade. True to his word, he'd placed the chairs beneath the oak tree back by the garden, out of sight of the playground.

She couldn't miss the fact that the chairs were side-by-side with barely an inch between them. "I straightened up the parlor in case Suz should come home early."

Daniel leaned back, crossed an ankle over his knee, and smacked his lips after draining his glass. "This is the best lemonade."

"I wish I could take credit for it, but it's Suz's recipe."

"She needs to share it with Leona. Her lemonade tends to be a bit on the tart side." He set his empty glass on the lawn, swung his body to face her, and, glancing over his shoulder, took her hand in his. "Now tell me what you've been up to since we last met."

How in heaven's name was she supposed to think when he was rubbing his thumb across the back of her hand, making her rethink the idea of letting him into the house—alone—with her. "I've been working on some dresses for Mrs. Jenkins. With three young children and a new baby, she doesn't have time to sew for her children or herself."

"I imagine. With her husband being the only blacksmith in town, they can afford to hire a seamstress. What else?"

Should she tell him about the book she was working on? The response from the school children had been positive; so much so, they asked for more. She hadn't found the courage to send it off to a publisher yet, but she was working on it.

"What is it? Why are you frowning? Is something wrong?"

She'd been frowning? "I um . . ."

Daniel kissed the back of her hand. "You can tell me anything, sweetheart. Anything at all."

Those words meant a lot, but there was no way she could tell him everything. He'd never want to see her again. But the stories? She took a deep breath. "I've been writing."

He released her hand and raised his eyebrows. It wasn't surprising he was shocked. Not many people knew someone who wrote books, but stories had to come from somewhere, didn't they?

"Writing?"

Julia nodded. "I'm used to being busy. At home there were chores, gardening, helping with the kids. Since moving here, I've had more time on my hands than I'm used to. There's only the two of us, so we don't make much of a mess. One can only do so much cooking and cleaning."

"So you decided to write?"

The lack of censure in his voice helped her to go on. "It wasn't an outright decision. I've always had stories floating around in my head, ones I used to tell my brothers and sisters. So, one day, I decided to write one of them down."

"I'm impressed. Has anyone read them?"

Julia chuckled. "Not because I asked."

Daniel took her hand in his again. "Let me guess. Suzanna."

"Right the first time. One day I was so engrossed with the story, I didn't hear her come in. She grabbed the pages before I could hide them."

"I bet she thought they were wonderful."

His grin made her heart kick up speed. "Why would you say that?"

"Because I think anything you do would be wonderful."

Julia bumped her shoulder against his. "I wouldn't be so sure about that. I can't make lemonade as good as Suzanna's."

Daniel's laughter scared a flock of robins searching for worms. "Geez, I . . ." He glanced off in the distance.

Was he going to say he loved her? Wasn't that a bit premature? She liked him very much. Loved spending time with him. He was always on her mind, especially as she sewed. What should she do now? Ignore him or ask what he was about to say. His next words solved the problem for her.

"So, what did Suzanna think?" he asked, obviously changing the subject.

"She really liked the stories and asked me to share them with her students."

"Did you?"

Julia nodded.

"And?"

"They want me to write more. Suzanna wants me to try to get them published."

Daniel raised an eyebrow. "Will you?"

"I don't have the foggiest idea how to go about it."

He was silent for a moment. Did he think she was crazy for thinking such a thing?

"I don't, either, but I have connections back East. I'll contact one of my brothers for names of publishers."

"You'd do that for me?"

Daniel kissed the backs of her fingers. "I'd do anything for you."

Maybe this made her a loose woman, but she leaned over and kissed him. "Thank you."

"You're most welcome." He tapped her on the nose. "And if that's the thanks I get when I do something for you, please ask me to help you with anything."

"Of course I will." Except for the one thing that could get her in trouble the most. He seemed like an open-minded man, but most men would hate it if their wife worked with prostitutes, no matter if it was done innocently. Time to change the subject. She stood.

"Let me get more lemonade. When I come back, you need to tell me what you've been up to."

IT HAD BEEN A LONG time since he'd played hooky. But sitting beneath a tree on a warm August day with a beautiful woman made ignoring all the work he needed to do worth it. Other than the Sunday they'd gone on the picnic and the weekend at King's, he hadn't taken a day off in a long time.

Did he feel guilty for not working on the case? Yes. But sometimes taking a step back from a problem made the answer clearer. And spending time with Julia was special. As much as he'd wanted to sit on the couch in her parlor and do more than kiss, she'd been right about what people would think. If they'd gone beyond kissing, there would be wedding bells sooner than he was ready for.

A green inchworm crawled over his boot. Would wedding bells be so bad? A robin landed at his feet, tipped its head back, tugged at the worm, and took off. Marrying Julia was a pleasant idea, but not until he had enough money to give her a nice house.

"Here we go," Julia said, handing him a full glass of lemonade. She slipped a hand into her apron pocket. "I brought us a snack, too." Two large sugar cookies rested in her palm.

Lost in his thoughts of marriage, he hadn't noticed her return. "Thank you."

"Now tell me what you've been up to. Have you figured out what's making the men sick?"

"No, but I've narrowed down the places where the ones who fell ill were drinking." He took a bite of the cookie, catching a broken piece before it landed on his clean shirt.

"That's good, then you can figure out what's making them sick."

"I wish it was that easy. Since men from the other saloons didn't get sick, I'm thinking it was the liquor, but finding out where it comes from isn't simple."

Julia tugged on her bottom lip. "Why don't the owners simply tell you where they get their liquor?"

"I've tried, but they won't give up their sources."

"That's stupid."

He chuckled. "Exactly what I think. They're only making my job more difficult."

"What are you going to do?"

Would she think he was crazy? "I'm going to watch the road coming into town and maybe see where the alcohol is coming from. There's Black Hills Brewing Company at the edge of town, but I can't imagine anyone poisoning their own product. Besides, it's only the three places."

"Can I help?"

The question set him back. She wanted to help? "I'm not sure what you could do."

"Couldn't I ride with you when you watch the road?"

"Um . . ."

"What if you're attacked? I can handle a gun. Two guns are better than one, aren't they?"

She had a point, but it would put her too close for temptation. "I don't think that's such a great idea."

"Why not?"

"I don't know how long I'll be gone. What if we have to sleep out in the open?"

"I've done that before." Her eyes shone with excitement. "I can pack some food and blankets."

He was possibly crazy, but the idea of having her alongside him was inviting. King couldn't go, and Julia was a darn sight better looking than King. "What about your concern about us being alone? What would people think if they found out?"

Julia sighed. "Heavens, I hate worrying about what people think. What about the men who visit the brothels? No one thinks ill of them, do they?"

"Well, their wives would if they found out." He rubbed his hand down the back of his neck. "Besides, you're a woman."

She yanked her hand from his. "What does my being a woman have to do with anything?"

"It's rough country we'd be traveling, so we can't take a buggy. Even on horses, it'll be grueling. Sleeping out in the open is not easy."

Julia flapped a hand at him. "Do I look like some simpering wallflower from back East? I was raised on a farm, worked as hard as my father and brother, slept outside when it was too hot in the soddy, cooked over an outdoor fire, trapped rabbits, and shot deer for food. The only thing I haven't done is spent long hours in the saddle." She pointed a finger in his face. "Now tell me why I can't go with you."

Well, hell. She'd done more than he had. Probably better, too. While he'd gone hunting a few times with King, he'd never actually shot an animal. King said he was a lousy shot—and he was. He had to come up with something to make her stay behind. She was too much of a temptation to spend two days alone with.

He snapped his fingers. "You'd have to wear men's britches. A long skirt would get in the way of riding astride and climbing over rocks." Hell, there went the wrist flip again, meaning she had a response for that, too.

"Oh, heavens. Us girls wore britches all the time on the farm. Can't bring in hay and corn in skirts. My mother wore them, too."

"Where would you get a pair?" When Julia didn't immediately answer, he glanced at her. Why was she blushing and biting her bottom lip? "What's wrong? Decide you can't go?"

She shook her head. "Just thinking about where I can get a pair. If you can take me into town, I bet Sadie would sell me some." She grinned. "I have another idea."

He was afraid to ask. Closing his eyes, he took a deep breath. "What would that be?"

"What if we have Suzanna come along? She likes a good adventure every bit as much as I do. Since today is Friday, she has the next two days off. Could we leave early tomorrow morning? I know her size, so if you can take me to town, I can get some britches for each of us."

That *would* solve the problem of a chaperone. "How do you know if she would want to go?"

"I'll go ask her. The kids'll be having recess soon."

He opened his mouth to respond, but Julia took off before he uttered one word. "Women." He fished a bee from his glass of lemonade then downed the rest. It would be nice to have company while sitting around and waiting for something to happen. Could they keep quiet, though? In his experience, women loved to talk. He'd never be able to sneak up on anyone with a jabbering female present.

Children yelled and screamed, jerking him from his thoughts. He pulled out his pocket watch. Ten-thirty. If Suzanna agreed to the trip, there would be time to take Julia to the store and go to lunch.

Julia came into view, running across the yard. Imagining their daughter doing such a thing brought a smile to his lips. If she looked anything like her mother, she'd be quite a cutie. Shit. Thinking about marriage and children all within the span of a few hours. He had it bad.

Even though Julia's wide grin hinted at what her sister's answer was, he had to ask. "What did she say?"

She dropped into her chair. "Yes. She said yes. Oh, this is going to be quite an adventure. Suzanna's as excited as I am. How early do you want to leave? Should we go to town now to get what we need? Should we rent horses tonight and leave them in the school stable for an early start in the morning. What kind of food should we bring? Do you think it'll be cold at night?"

He couldn't help laughing at her exuberance. "Good lord, Julia. Give me a chance to answer one question before you bombard me with a bunch more."

"Sorry. It's been so long since we've done anything this adventurous."

"What about your trip to Deadwood?"

"That was different. Besides being long, dusty, bumpy, and smelly, we had to act as ladies all the time. We were told by one woman that ladies don't get excited over every little thing they see."

She sat back in her chair and folded her hands in her lap as a proper princess would. He liked her excitement better. The way it lit up her eyes. The way her smile warmed his heart. "That's all right." He stood and pulled her up. As much as he wanted to wrap his arms around her and hold her for a bit, the children were still outside. One might come running around the schoolhouse. "If we leave now, we can get what we need at Haywood's then have lunch at King's. We can discuss the rest of your questions on the walk to town."

Chapter Twenty-One

Following Daniel through a narrow passage between boulders the size of mountains, Julia wiggled in her saddle. Was she angry or happy that Suzanna had bailed after a half hour on the trail? Claiming a headache, she'd turned around for home. It was the sly little grin Suzanna had sent over her shoulder making Julia think her sister had planned her early departure all along. As long as no one realized she was now alone with Daniel, there shouldn't be a problem.

It didn't take long for the sun to burn off the cool, early-morning air. A trickle of sweat rolled down her back. She adjusted her feet in the stirrups, rising off the saddle. Two hours in and already her backside was sore. She didn't dare complain since coming along on this adventure was all her idea.

Daniel moved his horse to a trot toward a grove of trees. Without any encouragement, her horse followed suit. Besides letting her rear end slap against the saddle, she had no idea how to handle herself when a horse trotted. Heaven help her if it decided to gallop. As it was, she wouldn't be able to walk for a week.

"We'll stop here for a bit," Daniel said, dismounting in the shade and tying the reins to a branch. "The horses need a rest."

Horses needed a rest? What about her? *Shut up, Julia.* Daniel would head back if she complained. He took her reins.

"Need help?"

Did she ever, but she wasn't about to admit it. Grabbing the pommel, she swung her right leg over the saddle. Before she fully dismounted, large, warm hands encased her waist.

"Since you haven't ridden much, you might be a bit wobbly. I'll hold you until you get your land legs back."

He'd get no argument from her. The second her feet touched the ground her legs crumbled beneath her. If it hadn't been for Daniel holding her, she would have collapsed. Instead, he pulled her against his chest. Too bad she wasn't facing him, or she'd give him a kiss for his thoughtfulness.

"Do you think Suzanna actually had a headache?" he asked against her hair.

Snorting was one of those unladylike things, but she couldn't help it. "No." Something hard pressed against her. Was he . . .? Her heart skipped a beat. Why hadn't she asked more questions of her mother before leaving home? "What she fails to realize is if people find out we're out here alone, it'll ruin her as well as me."

"I don't think she's going to announce it to the town." Keeping his hands at her waist, he moved her away. "Walk around a bit to loosen up your legs."

Goodness, she was going to sore tomorrow. Heck, she was going to be sore tonight. She could walk a mile and not loosen up. Daniel handed her a canteen. After taking several swallows, she bent her knees. The freedom of wearing men's britches was wonderful—especially since now she didn't have to worry about someone recognizing her. Whoever said women needed to wear dresses was nuts. And since she wasn't sneaking Deadwood's back alleys dressed as a cowboy, she could enjoy them. She touched her toes to stretch her legs, stood, and glanced over her shoulder. Daniel's frown made her pause. What was he thinking?

HELL, IF JULIA BENT over one more time, he'd lose it. There were reasons women wore dresses and not pants. Dresses hid the curves of their asses. Pants only accentuated them, not only their backsides, but the front and their legs. Holding her against him when he helped her from the horse had been torture. Had she noticed he was hard? Since she didn't react, he doubted it.

He turned his back on her, walked to Dusty, and removed some jerky for a snack. Maybe chewing the tough food would keep his mind from Julia's delectable body. Why had Suzanna pretended to have a headache? How was he ever going to get through the next two days?

Julia winced as she sat on a tree stump. Was she going to be able to continue? So far, she hadn't uttered one word of complaint, but the day was early. "Here." He handed her a small piece of meat and eased to the ground.

"What is Suz going to do with her horse when she gets back home?" she asked after yanking a piece of meat off with her teeth.

"I told her to leave it in the shed. She said she could take the saddle off herself."

"Huh. I wonder how she plans on doing that since she's never unsaddled a horse before."

"I wonder . . ." He'd better stop talking.

"Wonder what?"

He nearly choked on a sliver of meat before answering. Damn, why hadn't he kept his mouth shut? "Nothing."

Julia tapped him on the shoulder. "Come on. You can tell me."

Would she throw a fit? Demand to go back home? "Maybe King will help her."

"I thought you said he was gone."

Daniel took a drink from the canteen. "Only until this afternoon."

She jumped up. "Do you think we need to go back? What if they do something improper?"

"Relax." He pulled her down to the ground beside him. "King and I have talked about it. He swears he'll make sure she fulfills her contract."

"Thank the heavens."

Now all he had to worry about was not comprising Suzanna's sister, which was getting more difficult to do the more time they spent together. He stood and held out his hand for Julia. They'd removed their gloves. The touch of their fingers sent a spark through his body. Her eyes widened. Had she felt it, too? Resisting was futile when she licked her lips. Drawing her into his arms came as naturally as breathing.

His breath hitched when she raised her face to his then wound her arms around his neck. The explosion inside him when their lips touched was as strong as the dynamite used to mine gold. His body trembled. Sweat dampened his hair. His penis swelled. *Heavens*, as Julia was fond of saying.

Dusty's whinny seeped into his consciousness. With reluctance, he pulled back. Was someone watching them? He swept the area. Was a mountain lion or bear skulking in the woods, making Dusty nervous?

He took a deep, shuddering breath going clear to his toes and touching every spot in between. Julia's chest rose and fell as if she'd run up a hill. "I think we'd better move on."

The trail widened, making room to ride side-by-side. At first relieved Julia didn't talk much, now the silence wore on him. "What do you think of Cinnamon?"

"She's fine. Did anyone ask why you needed three horses?" Julia asked, breaking his growing thoughts of what tonight would be like.

"I told the kid at the stable I was taking the schoolmarm and her sister out to see the countryside. All he did was shrug, so it was no big deal."

He wasn't about to tell her he'd been stopped a few times as he'd walked the trio of horses toward the schoolhouse. Why did he have three horses? Why was there a bedroll on only one horse? Where was he headed? How long would he be gone? Had he found gold? Swearingen confronted him in front of King's and gave him an earful about leaving town and not working on the case.

Not wanting word getting around that he was staking out the road, he told the Gem Theater owner he was spending some time in the wilderness to clear his head and come up with an idea of what was going. With narrowed eyes suggesting he didn't believe Daniel, Swearingen finally stormed off.

What no one knew was he'd been deputized by the sheriff allowing him to arrest anyone. With a shortage of law enforcement officers leaving them unable to investigate anything less important than cattle rustling, shootings, and bank robberies, Daniel was given free rein to investigate and charge anyone breaking the law.

After dropping off the horses at the school, he made sure people saw him returning to his own place for the night so they wouldn't think he was staying with the sisters. It would have been easier if he had since he wouldn't have had to get up so early. Even if he'd slept in the schoolhouse or the stable with the horses, people would get the wrong idea. He was getting mighty sick of worrying about what people thought. When he married Julia, and he had no doubt it would happen, life would be a whole lot easier. Less than a year from now, when King and Suzanna got hitched, things would be even better. Usually when a female teacher married, she wasn't allowed to continue teaching. In his mind, it was ridiculous. With the difficulty in keeping teachers, hopefully it wouldn't be hard to convince the board to let her stay on.

Julia adjusted her seat in the saddle. She must be getting uncomfortable, but he didn't want to stop until they were at the place he'd chosen to watch the road.

"Where are we stopping tonight?"

"There's a place where the road splits. One way goes to Lead, the other to Hill City. There's a hillside with plenty of boulders and thick with pine trees and brush. I know a spot where we can camp."

A pesky fly flew around her cowboy hat. The instant he'd seen the decrepit thing, he thought it seemed familiar, but he couldn't place it. Hell, with so many men in the area, he could have seen it anywhere. Anyway, more than one man could have the same hat. It was the part looking as if it had been chewed by an animal making it distinctive.

"Where did you get your hat? It looks as if it was run over by a team of horses, then chewed for lunch."

JULIA'S STOMACH FLIPPED. Darn. She shouldn't have worn the hat from her cowboy costume. Had Daniel recognized it from the night outside the bank? Quick come up with something. "Um. I'm not sure. Suz gave it to me last night. Maybe she got it from one of her students." Seemed like a plausible story. Didn't it?

"I'd be nervous about lice or fleas if I were you." He pointed at her head. "I'd hate to see you have to cut off all that gorgeous hair."

Lice? Fleas? She shivered. She'd never thought of that. But since she'd been wearing it for several weeks, if there'd been fleas, she'd have known by now. Even so . . . "Thanks. Now I want to scratch my head."

"No problem." He tipped the edge of his hat. "We have about an hour to go before we get to the crossroad. I want to go the rest of the way through the woods. That way no one can see where we are. Are you up for it?"

Of course, she wasn't. Not only was her backside sore, but her inner thighs were screaming. Her toes ached from keeping the tips of her new boots in the stirrups. After drinking so much water at their last break, it wouldn't be long before she'd have to relieve herself. At least if they were riding through trees, they wouldn't be able to go fast. Maybe they'd have to walk their horses. As her granny said, 'Always look for the positive.'

"I'll be fine," she lied. With luck, she'd have to concentrate on following Daniel and wouldn't constantly replay their last kiss. All she'd wanted to do was pull him to the ground and let him do what she hoped he knew how to do. She sure as heck didn't have a clue, but the ache in her woman parts wouldn't go away. And it wasn't from riding Cinnamon.

Daniel turned into a grove of trees. Where was the trail?

"Lean forward when we go uphill and back when we go down."

They were going to go up hill? Wasn't that what they'd been doing?

"Lean forward. Lean forward," she repeated to herself as their horses struggled up a steep, rock-filled slope. "Don't fall off. Please don't fall off."

"Did you say something?" Daniel called over his shoulder.

"No," she yelled back. Sweat ran down the sides of her face, burning her eyes. She was going to die. How much further should she lean before she could look into Cinnamon's ears? Or fall off and hit her head on one of the rocks they were winding their way through? "I'm fine."

Finally, after what seemed like hours, she stopped beside Daniel at the top of the hill.

The view took her breath away. "We must be able to see for miles." When she thought she'd seen the most distant hill, her eyes adjusted to another and another. Pine trees as far as she could see turned the hills as dark as night. "I can see why this is called the Black Hills."

"Spectacular, isn't it?" With a tap of his heels, Daniel nudged his horse forward. "Wait until you see the stars tonight. The place I want to stop has an open view to the sky."

Julia followed. "Living out in the country in Iowa, we have wonderful views of the stars. Sometimes they seemed so close, we thought we could grab one and put it in a jar like we did with lightning bugs."

"I remember catching lightning bugs as a kid." Daniel said over his shoulder. "My mom punched holes in the lids of canning jars. We'd collect so many, we could light up a room, or at least one of our forts."

It was nice to know he'd done the same thing as she had growing up. "Even with holes in the lids, Pa made us release the bugs before we went to sleep so they wouldn't die. He thought anything in the wild should be left free."

"Can't disagree with that."

The land flattened out, giving her relief from leaning over Cinnamon's neck. With fewer rocks, she was still able to enjoy the view as they traveled over what they'd call a prairie back home.

Daniel stopped again. "Let's take a short break before going any further."

Without Daniel's help this time, she dismounted with less grace and more pain than she wished. He walked to the edge of trees. She limped alongside him. "Is that a cliff?"

He removed his hat and wiped his arm across his forehead. "Um. Not exactly a cliff."

"Sure looks like one to me. Tell me we aren't going to go down it?"

"Okay, I won't tell you." He pointed downhill. "Besides, it's more of a slope. We came uphill, now we have to go down."

Julia suppressed a tremble, but, even though it was cooler up in the trees, sweat rolled down her back and the sides of her face. It didn't help any to see Daniel sweating, too. Was he nervous, too? She had to know.

"Are you scared?"

He shook his head. "Not for myself. Dusty and I have done this several times."

"This hill?"

"Well, not this hill, but similar ones. Your horse has, too." Daniel removed a canteen from his saddle and poured water into the horses' water bags.

Julia dug in her saddlebag for the cookies she'd packed. "If you're trying to make me feel better, it's not working."

"You'll be fine. Remember to lean back and let Cinnamon do the work. It'll be faster going down than up."

"That's what I'm afraid of," she muttered, handing him a cookie.

Daniel tipped his hat to the back of his head and cupped a hand over his eyes, surveying the scene. "Wouldn't a house be great up here?"

"I have to agree, but the trip getting here would be horrible." She plunked down on the ground, sat cross-legged, and soaked in the view, eating her cookie while trying to ignore what was coming. Her eyelids grew heavy. While she was accustomed to getting up at the crack of dawn, she didn't normally spend the entire day riding a horse. Maybe she should have done a better job of thinking this adventure through. The chirping of crickets soothed her into a deep sleep.

"Julia." Someone prodded her shoulder. "Time to go."

Where was she? Something dug in her back. The air was filled with the scent of pine. Horses whinnied.

"Come on, Julia. We need to head out. I'm getting some bad feelings up here."

Time to go where? Julia peeled her eyes open. Daniel stood alongside her, the reins of the horses in his hands. That's right. She was on top of a mountain, about to put her life in the hands of a horse. "Give me a minute."

After taking a few minutes to relieve herself behind a boulder large enough to hide her from Daniel's sight, she returned.

"Ready?"

Julia took the reins. "As I'll ever be."

If she'd thought going up the hill was treacherous, going down was darn-right frightening. Leaning back in the saddle as they descended used every muscle in her body, and not being able to see where Cinnamon stepped was terrifying.

The trip down was done single file, so talking was out of the question. When they reached the bottom, Daniel stopped. "We'll take a short break here. There's a creek a bit to the right where we can water our horses. Hopefully it won't be full of prospectors."

Her hands cramped around the reins, making it difficult to let go. Her inner thighs quivered against the saddle. "I'm not sure I can dismount." She hadn't said that as a hint for him to help her but welcomed his outstretched hands.

After swinging her right leg over the saddle, he circled his hands around her waist. Once on shaking legs, it was easy to lean into his chest to steady herself.

"Are you all right?"

Daniel's deep voice vibrated in his chest. She pressed an ear against his shirt and nodded. "I'll be fine in a minute." Maybe more if she had anything to say about it. His arms were comforting, safe.

"Don't take too long. We need to take care of the horses and move on."

Taking a step back, she wrapped Cinnamon's reins around her hand, then led her to the burbling creek. "Earlier you said you were getting some bad feelings. What did you mean?"

He didn't answer until the horses were done quenching their thirst. "It's just a sense I have that we're being followed."

Grateful they didn't immediately mount, she walked her horse alongside Daniel, trying not to look over her shoulder to see if anyone was behind them. "Who would be following us?"

Daniel shrugged. "I don't know. I made sure no one knew the real reason we were leaving town in case someone got the idea to stop us. Maybe someone thinks we know where there's gold and followed us to take over our claim."

"How could they do that?" She swallowed around a lump in her throat. "Kill us?"

She veered one way around the largest tree stump she'd ever seen, while Daniel went the other. When they met on the other side, Daniel answered. "Far too often that's the way it's done."

"But—"

Daniel stopped, put a finger to his lips, and pointed.

A shiver of fear skittered down her spine until she spotted a mule deer and fawn. It was the first time she'd seen one. The mother's large ears flickered in their direction before she snorted and crashed through the woods, the fawn close behind. It didn't take long before the noise of them racing through the woods disappeared.

"They're so much bigger than the deer back home," she said, tugging on Cinnamon's reins.

Daniel raised his hand. She stopped. Something rustled in the brush behind them. A two or four-legged animal? Goosebumps rose on her skin. Daniel was scaring her. It was in all probability another deer or elk or maybe a small rabbit. Cinnamon snorted breaking the silence in the woods.

"Guess it was just an animal," Daniel said, leading his horse on.

Julia walked beside him. "How much further?"

"Tired?"

"I hate to admit it, but yes."

"You're the one who wanted to . . ."

"Stop right there. I know I was the one who wanted to come along, but you asked if I was tired. What was I supposed to do—lie?"

Daniel shook his head. "No. Truth be told you've done a fantastic job." They stepped over an old, half-rotten log. "And, I have to admit, I'm tired, too. It's been a long morning and almost time for lunch. We'll stop in about an hour to give the horses a longer rest, then it's only a few more hours until we get to our final stop. Going through the woods takes longer than if we'd taken the main road."

And a lot more difficult, she thought, but didn't say. If their night's stopping place was near a creek, she'd sit in the icy water for an hour to ease her aching muscles.

Chapter Twenty-Two

Daniel finally halted Dusty at a flat spot at the top of a hill. "This is where we're going to camp. We're far enough off the road so no one can see us, but we still have a good view of traffic from all three directions." He undid the saddle, pulled it and the saddle blanket from his horse, and set them on the ground. "There's a creek for water. The area is flat enough we won't roll down the hill in our sleep." Although he didn't plan on falling asleep. A person couldn't sleep and catch bad guys at the same time.

He still couldn't shake the feeling someone was following them. It was more of a sense he had than seeing anyone. Julia unstrapped her saddle. It would be interesting to see how she handled the heavy piece of equipment. Although with her having been raised on a farm, she probably was strong enough to manage it by herself.

As he expected, with only a few grunts, she had the saddle on the ground, led her horse to the creek, and tied the reins to a bush. Daniel followed suit allowing the horses access to both food and water.

It had been surprising how little Julia had talked on the ride. Although it was possibly due more to handling the rugged terrain than not wanting to talk. Now that they were at their destination, she'd more than likely start gabbing like a magpie.

Julia turned in a circle, surveying the area. "Where should we bed down?"

Daniel pointed to a space near the edge. "I'll be over there so I can keep an eye out for any travelers."

Without another word, she lugged her saddle near where he'd pointed, placed it on the ground, spread out the saddle blanket in front of it, and sat down, stretching out her legs. He didn't miss her flinches or soft, barely discernable groans as she did so, but she never complained. His estimation of her increased by the minute.

Julia reached around and dug in her saddlebag.

"What are you looking for?" he asked, setting his saddle a few feet from her. Being too close to her was dangerous.

"The food I packed. I'm glad I didn't put any food in Suz's bags, or we'd run short." She pulled out a bulky wrap. "Will we be able to have a fire? I want to heat the beans for supper."

"Maybe a small one." He spread his saddle blanket on the ground. "There are plenty of trees to mask any smoke."

"What about the smell?"

"There are enough camps around here that anyone who smelled our fire wouldn't know where it came from. I hope."

Julia frowned. "You hope? You don't know?"

"I have no idea what other people will think, but I believe we'll be safe." If he could only shake the feeling of being watched. But then, maybe it was better if he didn't discard it to keep him on his toes. A small fire would be nice, though as it got cold in higher elevations at night, a bigger one would be better. "Can you collect some rocks and make a fire ring? I'll gather wood."

An hour later, his hunger satisfied with cold fried chicken and hot beans, he lay on his stomach across his saddle, watching the intersection of the roads below. Not only did he have a good line of sight, but hoof beats would let him know someone was passing by. He'd situated Julia a bit further away to observe from a different angle.

So far they'd seen an old-timer leading a donkey loaded with clanging pots; three deer; a man, obviously drunk, weaving and swearing; a turtle; a peddler with a wagon filled with goods; and someone galloping down the road whooping, hollering, and waving his hat in the air.

"Think he struck gold?" Julia had asked.

"Probably, but he's not going to keep it or his claim long if he keeps acting like that. Most prospectors try to keep their finds under their belts so as not to attract attention. Claim jumpers are a dime a dozen." Daniel gave Julia a quick glance, then returned to watching the road. "Except for illnesses, more men have been killed jumping claims or trying to save their claims than any other way."

Julia aimed her binoculars back to the intersection. "These things are amazing. I've only seen a pair in a catalogue. My brothers would love them." She adjusted the focus. "I'm curious, what do you hope to accomplish by watching the roads?"

"I'm beginning to think someone is selling bad liquor to another person, who is then bringing it into town. I'm hoping to see them on the road."

"But isn't there a brewery? Couldn't a person be hauling the booze into town from there?"

"Yes, but they have a large wagon with their name on it. Besides, a brewery would be crazy to sell poisoned liquor. They'd go out of business in a few days if they tried that. Not to mention they mainly make beer, not liquor."

A rustle in the woods took their attention from the road. Daniel placed a finger against his lips, scooted backward then turned to face the direction of the noise. As far as he could tell, there was nothing out there. Probably only a squirrel.

As the sun headed toward bed, the sky glowed swirls of pink, yellow, and purple. It wouldn't be long before it would be too dark to see anyone on the road. Thinking he'd need to stay up all night to watch it was a bit foolish. Might as well get some sleep. Heaven knew he was tired enough to sleep through a tornado.

"Let's get some shut eye. There won't be any more people coming through in the dark."

"I need to wash up these dishes first."

Daniel stood and brushed dirt from his pants. "I'll help."

"You don't need to," Julia said, stacking their plates. "There's not much."

"That's true, but I'd feel better if I went with you. Remember the bear?"

Her shudder made it plain she hadn't forgotten the incident. "All right. If you insist, you can help. Bring the pot and our cups. We'll leave the coffee pot for the morning."

Daniel used his saddle as a pillow. Not as comfy, but better than planting his head on the hard ground. The fired burned low, lending a soft glow to the campsite. Julia lay a few feet away, already breathing slow and steady. It had taken her only a few minutes to drift off. Why couldn't he be so lucky?

It was one thing to be with her while riding horses, in town, or near the school in broad daylight; another having her beside him in the dark, sleeping on her side, hands cupped under her cheek, blanket tucked beneath her chin. It conjured up ideas of stretching out beside her. Taking her in his arms and doing things to her body that would get his face slapped—or worse.

A vision of her wrapping her arms around his neck as he kissed her popped into his head. She'd never once turned away his kisses. Maybe she wouldn't be opposed to doing more. He adjusted the tightness in his pants, then inched closer, then stopped when she muttered something in her sleep. What the hell was he thinking? She was an innocent woman. He didn't take innocent women, unless they were awake and agreeable.

With a sigh he tugged his blanket to his ears and drifted to sleep.

Chapter Twenty-Three

Julia tossed off her blanket and stretched her aching muscles. Was there any part of her body that didn't hurt? Maybe her earlobes. The back of Daniel's dark hair peeked from his blanket. The dawning sun barely filtered through the tree branches. She picked up the binoculars and lay across her saddle, taking in the roads below them. Nothing stirred.

With nature calling, she eased to her feet and tiptoed toward the creek, searching for the boulder she'd used last night before falling asleep. It was far enough away from their camp and creek that she wouldn't disturb Daniel or dirty the clear, clean water they needed for personal use.

When she was done, she knelt beside the creek. The water bubbled and gurgled over rocks, covering up any sounds. She scooped up a handful of water and splashed it on her face, washing away the night's sleep. A squeal escaped at water cold enough to wake a dead person. With a vision of what her hair must look like after sleeping on the ground, she undid her braid, and dampened the tresses to make it easier to re-braid. She was halfway done when a voice, not Daniel's, came from behind her.

"Well, well, well. Who do we have here?"

Without thinking, she turned around and gasped. Mingus Thoreson. She dropped her braid and clenched her shaking hands together. Had he been the one creating the noises in the woods, making Daniel nervous? "What are you doing here?"

"If it ain't uppity Miss Lindstrom herself," he answered, ignoring her question. "Just the bitch I've been waitin' to get alone. Where are all yer admirers to rescue you now, *Miss Lindstrom?*" He took a step toward her.

She glanced over his shoulder. Did she dare scream for Daniel?

"Don't worry about old lover boy. I didn't kill him, only made sure he wouldn't interrupt our fun and games."

Anger, the likes of which she'd never known before, grew in her stomach and expanded into her chest. How dare he do something to Daniel, much less think he could have his way with her?

Mingus crooked a finger. "Now why don't you come over here an' let me show ya how a real man treats a woman. I can do a much better job plantin' myself between yer legs than old Iverson ever could." He eyeballed her from her head to toes. "These men's britches yer wearin' could be a mite harder to get into than a dress, but don' worry, it'll happen one way or another. Why don' you make it easy on yerself and take 'em off for me."

His snake-in-the-grass grin sent bile into her throat. "I'll never let you touch me. You're disgusting and not a tenth the man Daniel is." Mingus' nostrils flared. He curled his hands into fists. Maybe she shouldn't have said that, but there was no way she was going down without a fight. She wasn't her mother's daughter for nothing.

"I know what kind of woman ya are, Miss High and Mighty."

What did that mean? Did he know about her trips to Hattie's? Had he been the one to send the note?

"All women are like you. Good for only one thing." He snatched a handful of hair. "Don't think of kickin' me man parts again, bitch." He yanked her head to the side.

With a hand at his crotch to protect himself, he leaned down, his mouth coming closer to her neck. Her heavy boots had to be more of an advantage than her usual ladies' boots. She swung back her leg and caught him in the shin as hard as she could.

"Son of a bitch!"

As he hopped around on one foot, holding his shin, she raced around him, screaming Daniel's name. She'd made it a few steps before Mingus grabbed the back of her shirt, knocking her to the ground. He flipped her onto her back and slapped her face. The back of her head struck the ground.

"Bitch," Mingus screamed into her ear. He straddled her and yanked at her shirt, tearing the fabric in two.

Dear Lord, he was going to rape her. If she screamed loud enough, maybe someone on the road would hear and come to the rescue. She bucked her hips, trying to dislodge him.

"That's it, bitch, give me a ride. I don' have much time before my meetin'."

Filling her lungs with air, she screamed as loud as she could before his face descended on hers.

DANIEL STRUGGLED AGAINST the ropes tying his hands together. When he'd woken to find Thoreson standing at his feet and Julia gone he'd jumped up, only to have the bastard hit him in the jaw, sending him sprawling onto his blanket.

"You've been following us?"

Thoreson laughed. "Damned right. When I saw ya sneaking out of town, I knew if I took my time, I'd get a chance to get even with the bitch. But why'd ya have ta take such a shitty route? It damn near killed my horse." He waved a large knife, the blade shining in the sunlight, at Daniel. "Ain't so high and mighty are ya now, Iverson. I'll have your little gal before the day is done and there ain't nothin' ya can do about it. And don' go thinkin' about yellin' for her."

Knife or not, there was no way he was going to let this bastard get his hands on Julia. "She's a fighter, you know. She won't let you hurt her, and neither will I."

Thoreson tossed the knife from hand to hand. Did he think that was intimidating? Well it was, but he wasn't about to show his fear. If he could get the bastard to take a step closer, maybe he could get a drop on him.

Taunt him, Daniel. "You couldn't damage a flea."

Thoreson narrowed his eyes and stepped closer.

C'mon, jackass, a bit closer. "All you do is pick on people smaller than you. Bet if you attacked someone bigger and smarter, which wouldn't take much, you'd drop like a ton of gold." *He bit back a smile as Mingus took the bait and walked closer.*

"You won' talk so damn smart when I take yer woman in front of ya."

Outrage filled him, but if he wasn't careful, he'd do something stupid. Instead he met Thoreson's eyes, then kicked out, catching him in the legs, sending the bastard to the ground. Before Thoreson had a chance to recover, Daniel jumped on him, squeezing his hand to dislodge the knife.

Where was Julia? Why didn't she hear the scuffle? Had Thoreson already done something to her? Fury urged him to take a swing at the bastard's face. At the last second, Thoreson turned his head. Daniel's hand struck the hard ground.

"Shit." *Daniel let go of Thoreson and clasped his hand giving the bastard an opportunity to get up.* "Dammit."

Thoreson yanked Daniel up by the neck of his shirt. "Thought ya could take me, huh?" *he threw Daniel on the blanket, kicked him in the ribs, then removed a length of rope from his back pocket.* "This'll keep ya." *He seized Daniel's hands and tied it around them.*

Daniel swore as the rope cut into his wrists. It didn't help any that he might have broken his hand.

"Now where did my damn knife go?" *Thoreson asked, turning in circles, searching the area.*

*So that's what was digging into his ass. Well, the bastard could look
all he wanted, he wasn't going to move an inch and let him know where
it was.*

Thoreson threw his hands up in the air. "Don' matter none. I won'
be need'n it for what I'm gonna do to your gal." *He saluted Daniel.* "I'll
try ta make her scream so's ya know when I'm pokin' her."

Daniel struggled against the ropes, tearing at the skin on his
wrists, then stopped. He needed to calm down and think if he was
going to save Julia. He was sitting on the knife, and since the idiot
tied his hands in the front, all he needed to do was get the knife between his knees and saw the rope in two.

Careful not to slice his pants, he rolled to his side then scooted
back to the knife. Daniel put the handle between his knees, keeping
the blade away from him. Squeezing his knees together to hold the
handle in place, he lifted his hands over the blade and sawed. The
blade wobbled. His knees weren't holding the handle tightly enough.

His boots. They'd be stronger than his knees and the handle
wouldn't dig into his skin. With the knife in place between his boots,
he began moving the rope against the blade. A scream rent the air.
Julia. He increased his frantic motions. He had to get to her before it
was too late. He wouldn't put it past Thoreson to kill her after he was
done.

JULIA TURNED HER HEAD to avoid Mingus' beer and tobacco
breath. He bit her neck. Since struggling seemed to incite his pleasure, she lay still, clearing her mind of his hands at her breasts and
the bulge in his pants pressing against her. What had Mingus done to
Daniel? She'd be a damaged woman when Mingus was done. Would
Daniel still want her after being raped?

A tear rolled down her cheek.

"C'mon, bitch. Don' lay there like a dried-up old hag."

She winced when he squeezed her breast. If he wanted her to move, it would be the last thing she'd do. Even if he slapped, kicked, bit, or tore off her clothes, she wouldn't move. If only she could get her knee between his legs again, but his weight pinned her down. Instead . . .

Mingus howled and wiped a hand over the scratches she raked down his cheek. His hand came away bloody. She held her breath waiting for the slap she knew was coming.

"You bitch," he yelled, raising his hand in the air.

"I wouldn't do that if I were you."

Daniel.

Mingus jumped to his feet. "You! How did ya get loose?" He crouched as if he was ready to charge Daniel.

Like a crab, Julia inched away from the men. The last thing, besides being raped, she wanted to have happen was to get in the way of their fight.

"Don't move, Thoreson, or I'll be forced to use this."

She hadn't noticed the gun Daniel pointed at Mingus.

Mingus's chuckle lacked power. "Ya wouldn't dare. A fancy-pants lawyer don' have the guts to shoot an unarmed man." He lifted a chin at Daniel. "'Sides, it would be murder."

"Are you willing to take the chance, Thoreson?" Daniel cocked back the hammer. "It wouldn't be the first time I've had to shoot a man. And . . ." He grinned. ". . . seeing as how I've been deputized it wouldn't be murder at all. Purely self-defense and protection of a woman being harmed."

Mingus's face paled. "How'd ya get loose?"

Daniel waved the gun at the man. "Face down on the ground now," he said, handing the gun to Julia.

What kind of person was she to hope Mingus would do something stupid so she could shoot him? She aimed the gun at his chest.

Mingus' laughter rang in her ears. "What kind of man are you, Iverson, lettin' a woman protect ya? Besides, I doubt she has the nerve to shoot me."

Enough was enough. Attacking her, trying to rape her, tying up Daniel, threatening to kill them. She cocked the gun. "Care to try me, Thoreson? You're nothing but a piece of trash." She gestured toward the ground with the gun. "Didn't Daniel tell you to get down on the ground? I suggest you do as he says."

Mingus took a step toward her. "Bitch, ya just signed yer death warrant."

Julia sighted on his hat and squeezed the trigger, sending the dilapidated thing into the air. "That's a warning, Mingus. I've shot smaller varmint than you. Now do as Daniel says. Get the hell on the ground."

"Hell, woman. Ya could have killed me."

Daniel patted her on the back as he approached Mingus. "If she had wanted to kill you, you'd be breathing your last breath."

"Oh, I want to kill him all right. Get rid of this piece of horse manure who thinks women are only good to satisfy his disgusting needs." She aimed the gun back at his chest. "Now, before I get truly angry and take a shot at you again, I suggest you get the hell on the ground."

Finally doing what he was told, Daniel stood over him and yanked Thoreson's hands behind his back. "Next time you tie someone up, remember to tie their hands behind their back and don't leave your knife behind. You're under arrest for the attack on Julia Lindstrom and an officer of the law."

"Where the hell did you find my knife?" Thoreson asked over his shoulder, grunting when Daniel pulled the rope tight.

Daniel kept his foot on Thoreson's back. "I landed on top of it when you shoved me to the ground." He wiggled his fingers to Julia.

Relieved Mingus was safely tied up, she uncocked the gun and ran into Daniel's arms, handing over the weapon.

"You all right, honey?"

She nodded into his shoulder. In the comfort of Daniel's arms, tears streamed down her face. Why was she crying? Except for the bite mark on her neck and bruises that would show up tomorrow, she was unharmed and Thoreson in custody. She should be rejoicing, not crying.

Daniel patted her back. "It's all right to cry." After a few minutes, he released her then jerked Mingus to his feet.

"Would ya really have shot me?" Mingus asked, frowning.

"You're darn right I would have." She stood in front of him, no longer afraid. "But since I can't, this will have to do." With a balled-up fist, she punched him right below the ribs. His bellow of pain satisfied her—almost. With open palms she gave him an ear slap, one harder than the day of the school party. His howl echoed across the valley. "Not done, yet, Mingus."

"Julia, stop," Daniel said.

"Not on your life." With Mingus doubled over, she kicked him in the shin. First one and then the other. She slapped her hands together as if she were brushing away a pesky gnat. "Now I'm done."

Daniel shook his head. "I wouldn't do anything more to upset her, Thoreson."

Thoreson glared at Julia. If his hands weren't tied behind his back and Daniel beside her, she might be intimidated. Instead she fisted her hands into Mingus' face. "You ever touch my sister, me, or any other woman again, you'll have me to deal with." The brief flash of fear crossing his face satisfied her. Daniel still had his gun trained on the man. Was that what scared him? Who cared what frightened Mingus as long as he continued to cower?

"Now what do we do?" she asked Daniel, raking her fingers through her hair. Twigs, leaves, and dirt fell to the ground. "Quit watching for someone and take him back to Deadwood?"

"No. I have more rope. I'll tie him to a tree while we watch the road." He took a handkerchief from his pocket, tied it around Thoreson's mouth, and pushed him toward their camp. "It's still early, so maybe we'll see something."

AFTER SECURING THORESON to the tree, Daniel lay across his saddle, and put the binoculars to his eyes.

"I see movement coming from the woods up the road heading to Lead." Julia whispered.

"I see it, too." He focused his binoculars on the woods. A person pulled a cart from the woods then stopped at the side of the road. "Does that look like a woman to you?"

"With the pants, baggy shirt, and hat, it's hard to tell, but I think I can see a long, blonde braid."

Behind them, his prisoner mumbled and kicked at the ground, sending dirt across Daniel's back. "Shut up, Thoreson, or I'll shut you up."

"She seems to be waiting for someone," Julia said. "She keeps looking up and down the road."

"Can you tell what's in the cart?"

Thoreson growled, pushing his boots into the ground again, sending more dirt and leaves flying. "Dammit, Thoreson . . ." Daniel glanced over his shoulder at the man. Eyes narrowed, face red, he looked ready to explode. What the hell was going on?

"Daniel, she's coming closer."

He took a minute to gather his thoughts. He prodded Thoreson's boot. "Did you come here to meet someone?" Thoreson narrowed his eyes and didn't answer. Daniel picked up his gun, aiming it at

Thoreson's chest. "I'm removing the gag so you can answer me. If you yell or make any other noise, I'll put this bullet through your chest. Understand?"

"Daniel, wait," Julia whispered. "Earlier he said he had time to . . ." She shuddered. "You know." When he nodded, she went on. "He had time before his meeting."

Daniel left the gag in place. "So, you're meeting someone?"

Thoreson nodded.

"Maybe a woman?"

While struggling against the ropes, Thoreson nodded again.

Daniel tipped back his hat. "I'll be damned." Was it possible he'd caught one of the people who was bringing in bad liquor? Could he be so lucky as to have a chance to catch the other? "Were you meeting someone to buy booze?" Thoreson's narrowed eyes and mumbling behind the gag gave him his answer.

"Can you keep an eye on him?" he asked Julia.

Julia took her attention from the road. "Of course. Why?"

"I think I know what's going on." Daniel stood and holstered his gun.

"What are you going to do?"

"Catch someone making bad booze."

Thoreson struggled harder, kicking up dust, jerking his arms hard enough to pull bark from the tree.

"Keep your gun on him."

"Don't you want me to keep an eye on you?"

Daniel shook his head and wrapped his arms around Julia. Keeping her safe was important, but catching the bootleggers was, too. "No," he called over his shoulder. "Keep the gun on Thoreson."

AVOIDING STICKS, BRANCHES, and rocks, Daniel managed to maneuver down the hill to the road without landing on his rear or tumbling headfirst. He came in from behind the woman. Before saying anything, he peeked into the small, wooden cart resting on two wheels. Bottles. At least two dozen, filled and corked. To pad them, hay was stuffed between each container. The scent of strong liquor wafted to him. Definitely not beer. Whiskey?

"Are you waiting for someone?" he said, making her jump.

She squealed, twisted around, and slapped a hand against her chest. She wasn't very tall. The men's shirt she wore barely concealed full breasts. A piece of twine around her narrow waist held up her pants. If she was trying to hide that she was a woman, she wasn't doing a very good job of it.

"Heavens, you scared me." She peered into the woods. "Where's Thoreson? I'm delivering booze to him."

Damn. "He got tied up at the last minute, so he sent me. What's your name?"

"Why do you want to know?"

Channeling Thoreson, he answered, "I enjoy learning the names of all the beautiful women I meet."

She tipped back her hat and laughed, making the hat fall to her back, its string keeping it from falling to the ground. "That's a good one. I haven't been called beautiful in ages. Name's Emmaline."

Even though she was slim, with the way the west aged women, it was hard to tell how old she was. She could be twenty or forty. Her bare head revealed dark roots. Not a true blonde? Dyed? His breath caught. Only women who worked for Mollie Johnson dyed their hair blonde. Had she left the house or was she fired?

"Pleased to make your acquaintance, Emmaline."

"I don't need no fancy talk, what I do need is the money. Do you have it?"

Her question brought him up short. Damn. He hadn't thought of having to pay for the liquor. But what if this wasn't what he was looking for? Thoreson must have the money on him. "Can I taste it first?"

"No!" she yelled, glancing frantically around, not meeting his eyes. "I can't open any of the bottles. It'll ruin the whiskey. They'll know there is less than they're paying for. The next time, I won't get any money."

Think. Think. "This is the first time I've done this."

"I don't know why they sent someone different this time."

Daniel shrugged. "Don't know. Just doing what Thoreson asked me to."

How was he going to get her to say who sent her and who was making the liquor? "I was given a note to meet a woman on the road to Lead. It said she'd have a cart filled with liquor bottles. I came last night and camped up on the hill to make sure I found her—you." Instead of pointing directly to the campsite in case she should somehow notice Julia, he pointed back to where he'd come down the hill. He leaned against the cart and folded his arms across his chest as if he had all day to gossip with the woman.

"I'm curious as to how this works." She frowned. Maybe she didn't know. "I mean, who makes the liquor? Thoreson didn't tell me where to deliver it, either. Do you know?"

She shrugged. "I make it."

Well, that was easy—maybe too easy— but was this the liquor making the men sick? "Where do I take it when I get to Deadwood? Do I take it in your cart?" He removed his hat, raked his fingers through his hair, and sighed. "I wish Thoreson had given me more directions."

Emmaline rolled her eyes and twisted the braid in her fingers. "Thoreson's a jackass. I'm not sure how he finds his way anywhere."

He couldn't disagree. "Where should I take this stuff? As far as I know he left town, so I can't ask him."

"As soon as you pay me, I'll tell you. Can't have you taking the booze then disappearing with my money."

Damn. "I left it in my saddlebags at my campsite. Can you stay put while I go back and get it? I didn't want to bring it all with me and chance being robbed on the road. All right?"

"Yeah. I'll go back into the woods to wait for you."

"By the way, how much do you get for the liquor?" At her frown, he went on. "Thoreson handed me some money without telling me how much was to go to you."

"A dollar a bottle. I brought thirty bottles."

Hell, that was cheap. With a dollar per shot, someone was getting rich. He merely needed to find out who. He'd better get going if he wanted to leave for Deadwood at a decent time. "Wait here, I'll be right back."

"WHAT'S GOING ON?" JULIA asked, still pointing the gun at Thoreson. "Why did you come back to camp? I saw you talking with the woman. Isn't she the one?"

Resting his hands on his knees, he tried slowing his heartbeat. "Let . . . me . . . catch . . . my . . . breath." Running all the way uphill to camp may have not been the wisest thing to do. He took a deep breath and straightened. "She's the one making the liquor and meeting Thoreson. Don't know if it's the bad booze or not."

He kicked Thoreson's boot. "Emmaline the one you're supposed to meet?" His prisoner nodded. "You got the money on you?" Another nod. Daniel tugged down the gag. "How much do you pay her?"

Thoreson spit at Daniel's boot. "Buck a bottle. She's supposed to have thirty bottles, so's that's thirty bucks. Not a penny more."

"Where's the money?"

"Ain't tellin'."

Daniel removed his gun from the holster and pushed the barrel against Thoreson's nose. "Want to answer again, because putting a bullet in your face won't make you any uglier than you already are."

Julia snickered, eliciting a swear word from Thoreson.

"Inside me coat pocket."

Even though he was tied up, Daniel didn't want to take any chances. He trusted the man about as far he could throw him. Keeping the gun against Thoreson's nose, Daniel pulled the jacket open and removed a bag jangling with coins. He opened it and dumped the contents into his hand. "Hell, there's sixty dollars here. You wouldn't be cheating Miss Emmaline, now would you?"

"Man's gotta make a livin'."

Hell, even if she was making bad booze, she deserved more than the measly dollar a bottle he was paying her. "Where do you deliver it? You'd better not lie because I'm going to ask the same question of Emmaline."

"Woods."

Thoreson's answer nearly knocked him over. "The banker?"

Thoreson nodded. "I take it to the back of his bank."

Julia gasped. "But he's supposed to be an upstanding citizen."

"Yeah, right." Thoreson laughed. "If his wife or anyone else in town knew what he did besides bankin' they'd run him out of town. Hell, he owns most of the Badlands."

That was news to him. No wonder the guy acted like he owned the town, he practically did. "I need to get this money to Emmaline."

"What happens then?" Julia asked, watching the road again.

"We'll take the booze and Thoreson into town. We'll figure out if the booze is bad, then decide what to do about Emmaline and Woods." The only thing he didn't know was how to protect the booze while he retrieved Thoreson, Julia, and the horses.

He replaced the gag over Thoreson's mouth and made sure the ropes hadn't loosened. "Once I'm gone, pack up our gear and get

Thoreson's horse. It can't be too far from here. I'll pay Emmaline, hide the cart, and come back up here for you."

EMMALINE EMERGED FROM the woods when Daniel reappeared. "Got my money?"

Daniel handed her thirty coins he'd removed from the bag. "You live far from here?"

After making sure it was all there, Emmaline sidled up to Daniel. "Why? Wanna come visit me? I can show you a good time." She ran her fingers up his chest. "It won't cost you much, either."

Hell. He hoped Julia was too busy getting the horses to watch. He removed her hand. "No. I've got a girl. Simply want to make sure you get home all right."

Emmaline pouted, then took two steps back. "Figures. Don't matter where I live then. Tell Thoreson I'll see him next week."

"Wait," Daniel called out before she disappeared. "Where do I deliver the booze?"

"Woods. I don't know how Thoreson gets it to him."

At least he knew they were telling the truth. He picked out the trail she vanished down then tied a small piece of rope around a nearby branch so he could locate it later. Finding a safe place for them to come down from their camp, he pulled the cart to the side of the road and covered it with brush. Now came the hard part—getting a tied-up prisoner, a woman, along with three horses down the hill, the cart to town, and Thoreson to the jail. All without mishap. Good luck to him.

Chapter Twenty-Four

Five days later, Daniel sat in his stuffy office, leaning back in his chair, boots resting on the desk. He was exhausted. Julia and King sat in chairs across from him.

"I hear you solved the case," King said, lighting a cigar. "How'd you do that?"

He couldn't hold back a grin or the accompanying yawn. "Pure luck."

King shook out the match and tossed it in a dirty cup on the desk. "How so?"

"It was luck that Thoreson showed his face at our campsite before meeting Emmaline. Luck that I was able to get the bastard down the hill without breaking his or my neck. Luck that Julia was able to pull the cart behind her horse. Luck that Woods was out of town, so he didn't know who'd left the booze at his bank. Luck that I managed to get Thoreson to the jail without anyone seeing us. And luck that I found where Emmaline lived. Shit, her cabin was hidden so well in the woods I nearly walked into it before seeing it."

"It was more than luck, Daniel," Julia said, setting her small purse on his desk. "You worked hard on this case. You deserve more than what the saloon owners paid you."

King nodded. "I agree. How did you figure out the liquor was poisoned?"

Daniel dropped his feet to the floor and leaned his elbows on the desk. "Made Thoreson drink some."

"He drank poisoned booze without putting up a fight?"

"Hell, no. He was happy to drink it since he got it for free. The only one who knew it was poisoned was Emmaline."

Julia laughed. "It gave me great pleasure knowing he was sick for days. Serves him right."

"How sick did he get?"

"In my opinion, not sick enough after what he tried to do to Julia, but enough so he won't want to take a drink for a while. Besides, he'll be behind bars for a long time, unless the men who were poisoned get to him first."

"What about Emmaline and Woods?"

"We caught Woods selling the bootlegged booze to the Gem, Mollie's, plus a few other places in town. Even though he didn't know the liquor was bad, he did know it was made illegally, and was caught red-handed. We'll be checking into a few other of his activities, one of which is cheating his bank customers, but he'll be joining Thoreson behind bars."

"What'll happen to his bank?"

Daniel shrugged. "That's up to the courts, but there isn't enough money there to satisfy both his creditors and customers. I do feel bad for those who had used his bank and are now out all of their money." He picked up a piece of paper. "His wife had me draw up divorce papers. She's going back East to family."

King shook his head and blew a smoke ring into the air. "Besides his overbearing personality, I knew there was something about Woods rubbing me the wrong way. What about Emmaline?"

"Even though she was the one making the poisoned liquor, she's the one I feel most sorry for," Julia said.

King looked at the end of his dying cigar and took several puffs to restart the embers. "How so? People could have died because of her."

"She first worked at the Gem where she was so badly roughed up, she left for a job at Mollie Johnson's," Daniel said, setting down one piece of paper then picking up another. "She was beaten by one of the men. Mollie blamed Emmaline and kicked her out."

Julia went to the window overlooking the street. "Unfortunately, it wasn't only her customers treating her badly. I had a chance to talk with her before they took her away. You'd never believe she's only nineteen. When she was thirteen, her father used her then passed her to his brothers. She ran away from home and ended up in Deadwood, where men continued to use and abuse her. It was too much when Mollie fired her."

Daniel continued the story. "Evidently, one of the men at Mollie's had bragged about this cabin he'd built deep in the woods alongside a creek where he'd found gold. He was shot and killed in the street one night, so she knew the place would be deserted. It took her a few days to locate it, but when she did, she came up with a plan to get back at everyone who'd abused her."

Julia dropped the curtain she'd pulled aside and stood behind Daniel. "Her father and uncles had a still on their farm and sold liquor to the local taverns. Emmaline was part of the operation so knew how to set one up. Using the money she'd saved while working at Mollie's, she bought equipment in Lead to make the booze." She picked up Daniel's hat and plopped it on her head. "She'd learned about wild herbs from her grandmother, so it was easy to find poisonous ones and put them in the booze. It wasn't enough to kill anyone, only enough to make them sick. She was hoping the men would quit going to the saloons and they'd have to close down. Since Woods was one of the men who beat her, she hoped he'd be arrested."

King shook his head. "That's quite a story."

Daniel yawned again. "I'm just glad it's over."

"I understand you've received some inquiries from others to solve their problems," King said. "To think, I'm friends with a detective."

"I'm not joining the police, but maybe a private detective agency. I'll make more money that way. Money I'll need . . ." Damn, he almost said *to marry Julia*. Hell, he'd hadn't even asked her yet.

King raised an eyebrow at Daniel and grinned. "And what do you need money for?" He swept his hand around the room. "You have an office with a bedroom. What more could a man want?"

"Shut up, King." He stood. Time to change the subject. "It's almost lunch time. Shall we go, Julia?" He held out his elbow to her.

"Going to my place?" King asked.

"I don't know, can you keep your mouth shut?"

Slapping Daniel on the back, King laughed. "If you want."

"What's so funny?" Julia asked, a frown creasing her brow.

"Nothing, my dear. King's being a jerk."

Chapter Twenty-Five

September 19, 1879

In the week since the meeting in Daniel's office, Julia had seen him only twice, both times in the company of others. With shaking hands, she folded the finished story and put it in an envelope. Daniel had found a publisher for her, warning her it could take months before she heard anything.

She shrugged and sealed the envelope. Didn't matter how long it took, they wouldn't want to publish it, anyway. Meanwhile, she'd continue to sew for Hattie, plus for the other women who'd started placing orders. Thankfully, Mrs. Woods had picked up and paid for the additional dresses Julia had altered before leaving town. It would have been irritating if she hadn't been paid for them.

Her initial opinion of Mrs. Woods when they'd traveled to Deadwood on the coach together was pure haughtiness. As the wife of a banker, she certainly thought she was better than Suzanna and her, and pretty much every other person in every town they passed through. Her husband's arrest had shaken her to her core. With circles under her eyes, hair disheveled, top buttoned incorrectly, and a few pounds lighter, she'd looked years older than when they'd arrived a few months ago. Why Suzanna had wanted to emulate the woman was beyond her.

Julia put the sealed envelope on the bench by the front door, so she'd remember it tomorrow when King came to take her shopping. With Daniel wrapped up in the final details of the case, he hadn't been as available as she'd like. But it was his job, and she had no right to complain.

It would be several days before she had to go back to Hattie's. The girls had been so happy with the day dresses she'd made they'd all ordered more. Did the girls want something prim and proper to get out of the business? One could only hope at least a few of them would find a man to overlook their histories.

She ran a finger over the lavender, yellow, pink, blue, and green ginghams delivered earlier this morning. Now that the story was ready to send, she needed to start cutting out the one for Dorrie. After Suzanna came home from school, she'd work on other orders she received from women in town.

Dorrie had requested a blue and yellow dress—yellow for the bodice and blue for the skirt, with trim to match. Not ever having done something like this, she was a bit nervous. But the customer was always right—even if they were wrong.

It didn't take long to cut the fabric, so she had plenty of time to start sewing the pieces together. Daydreaming about Daniel and thinking about the next children's story always helped to pass the time. The clock struck two at the same time a knock came at the door. The same young man who'd delivered the other note handed her an envelope.

Making sure the seal wasn't broken before tipping the delivery boy a penny was important. Back home the entire town had known about the death of a neighbor's husband in battle before she did because the deliveryman was nosy and broke the seal. People had begun arriving at the widow's house with dishes of food. Thinking it was a surprise party the poor woman had fainted at the real news.

Sitting down in case it was bad news, she broke the seal.

I need you tonight. Very important. In dire need of your help. Be here by 10. Earlier if possible. H

Julia let the note fall to her lap. Why on Earth would Hattie need her at the brothel tonight? Something had to be wrong. Unless she got Suzanna to bed earlier, it would be difficult to make ten o'clock, let alone earlier. But today was Friday. Suzanna was usually pretty tired by the end of the week and retired early. With a bit of luck, that would be the case tonight. She could use their trip to King's ranch tomorrow as an excuse to end the night early.

JULIA HAD NEVER VENTURED out on a Friday or Saturday night. Hattie had warned her it was too rowdy and dangerous, but here she was, trying to act like an old miner wandering down the back alleys of the Badlands.

Getting Julia to go to bed earlier had been easier than she'd thought. Recalling how easily she could make her sister yawn, after supper she had kept up a string of yawns until Suzanna couldn't keep her eyes open. By nine she was in bed, sound asleep.

Now, here she was half an hour later waiting for Dorrie to let her in. With few lanterns lit and more bottles and barrels than usual strewn in the alley, it was a bit treacherous to find her way. All she needed was to trip and break something.

"Psst, old man, hurry up," Dorrie called into the darkness.

Julia raced up the stairs after her.

"Go right in," she said, opening Hattie's door.

Hattie sat at her table applying makeup as if she didn't have a care in the world. Irritation stabbed at her. Was this a joke? Ready to give the madam a piece of her mind for sending such an urgent message, she stopped at the tears in Hattie's eyes. Julia dropped to her knees in front of her friend and clasped her hands. "What's wrong? What happened?"

"Three of the girls have taken ill. We don't know if Ivy will live through the night."

"Did they drink any liquor?" She was sure the batch they'd taken from Emmaline had been destroyed, but that didn't mean there weren't other bottles out there.

"I don't think so. My girls aren't allowed to drink on the job. Makes them lose control and unable to handle the men." Twisting a lace-edged handkerchief in her hands, Hattie stood. "Not only am I worried sick about them, but I don't have anyone to work the balcony tonight."

A bad feeling came over her. A very bad feeling. Dare she ask? "What does it have to do with me?"

Hattie shook her head. "No. I need you to act as a balcony girl tonight."

"What?" She jumped to her feet and yanked at Hattie's arm. "Are you crazy? I can't be a balcony girl. What if someone recognizes me? What if Suz finds out and loses her job? What if a man wants to be with me?" She slapped her decrepit bowler hat against her leg. "No."

"But, Julia. If we don't have someone out there tonight, Mollie will say I must be closing my house or something to make me look bad and take my customers away. Swearingen will jump on the bandwagon, too."

"If so many girls are sick, how will you be able to handle the men?"

"I never have all the girls working the rooms every evening. One works the balcony, and one has the night off. But with three sick, I'm desperately short of girls. I don't always take customers but will tonight." A tear rolled down her cheek. "Please, Julia. I need your help."

She'd done a lot for Hattie. The disguises made sure it was difficult to know who she was. She wasn't sure what a balcony girl did. "What would I have to do?"

Hattie clapped her hands. "So, you'll do it?"

"Not until you explain what it involves."

"All you have to do is sit or stand on the balcony and call out what we offer to entice the men into my building."

Julia's heart fell and stomach flipped. That was all? She might as well announce to all of Deadwood she was working at Hattie's, which would guarantee their downfall in the town. "I can't do that. What if Daniel or King recognize me? Suz and I might may as well pack up and leave town tomorrow."

"We'll disguise you so well, your sister wouldn't recognize you."

It wasn't her sister she was afraid of. Well, maybe it was. Suzanna would kill her. Not to mention Daniel. But if he were to realize what she was doing, he'd understand she was simply helping a friend—wouldn't he? He hadn't said he loved her, but he acted as if he liked her a lot and wanted to spend more time together. Didn't that count for something?

"We'll keep you in the shade making it harder to see you. Sometimes simply being on the balcony without saying anything works, too. The more elusive a woman is, the more it drives men crazy."

Julia fingered the thimble in her raggedy coat pocket. What would Granny, the woman she admired the most, do? She was known for helping the most downtrodden and those deemed unsuitable for proper society. Hattie was right. With proper disguise, no one would know who she was. Besides, who would expect her to be a balcony girl? The sister of the schoolteacher? A seamstress? Daniel's girl? The one who helped Daniel catch Emmaline, Thoreson, and Woods?

"All right, I'll help."

Hattie hugged her. "Thank you so much. I'll never forget you for this." She clapped her hands. "Dorrie, you can come in to help get Julia ready."

THIRTY MINUTES LATER, Julia stood before Hattie's mirror. Who was this woman looking back at her? Hair hanging loose to her waist. Rouge on her cheeks. Kohl on her eyes. Lashes made darker by soot from a lamp.

Her hair weighed heavy on her neck. "Except for my family, no one has ever seen my hair down."

"Now, that's a damn shame," Hattie said, sliding the strap of a sheer, white nightgown down Julia's shoulder. "You have beautiful hair."

"Thank you." Julia bit her bottom lip and tugged the strap back up. "I'm not sure I can do this." While the nightgown reached to her ankles, the top dipped low enough to expose the tops of her breasts. Hattie had made her remove her underclothes. Even through the material, her dark nipples were evident.

"You can do this, Julia." Standing behind her, Hattie eased the strap down again. "Remember, you're to entice the men in, not sit there like some cold, snooty society woman."

"There's no way I could look like one in this outfit."

Hattie led her to a large tapestry and pulled it aside, revealing a door Julia hadn't known existed. When opened, she realized the purpose of the tapestry was to keep the noise from Main Street out. Her nerves spiked. She stopped. What had she been thinking to agree to this?

"That's good. The men will think I've hired someone new." Hattie took a wooden chair from her room and set it by the edge of the balcony. Something rolled across the balcony floor and off the side. "Damn. I think I lost an earring." She shrugged. "Guess it's lost forever. There's no way I'm going to search for it that crowd."

"What if a man comes into the saloon to pay for me?" The thought brought bile to her throat. She was made for only one man and it was Daniel—he just didn't know it yet.

Hattie flapped a hand in the air. "Easy. I'll simply tell the men you're new and not ready to take customers yet. I'll announce when you are." She pressed Julia onto the chair. "Now, I want you to sit sideways, so only your profile can be seen."

Tugging the sagging strap into place, Julia obeyed.

"No, no, no. Think entice." Hattie yanked it further down her arm, nearly displaying her entire right breast then hiked a side of the nightgown to her knee. "Think sexy."

Even though the night air was warm, Julia shivered. She'd never been so exposed in her life. What did she know about being sexy?

"Don't worry about anyone knowing who you are," Hattie said, as if she'd read Julia's mind. "You're simply going to sit with your side to the street. Tip your head to your left shoulder. Expose your neck. Yes, like that."

What if Daniel saw her? Something stirred deep inside her. Would he think she was sexy?

Hattie lowered the strap. Warm air caressed Julia's back.

"Now, you don't have to say a word. All I want you to do is keep your face averted, but crook your finger over the railing."

"How will the men know to look up here?"

"For one thing, they're used to seeing my girls on the balcony." Hattie stepped back into her room then reappeared with a small bell in her hand. "With your left hand, ring the bell to gain their attention." She patted Julia's hair. "I can't thank you enough for helping me tonight. Are you ready?"

"No. How long will I have to be out here?"

"I'll have one of the girls come up when the saloon is full. With you out here, it shouldn't take long."

Julia's stomach rolled as if she'd eaten something bad. "What if one of the men should decide to climb up here?"

Hattie disappeared into the room, then stuck her head back out. "Frank will stand guard outside. I'll leave the door open so you can slip back in here if needed."

Before she knew it, she was alone, on a balcony normally used by prostitutes. *Here goes nothing.* She rang the bell and then crooked her finger over the railing, making sure to keep her head turned.

"Hell, Joe," someone called out. "Will ya look at that. Hattie must've gotten a new gal."

"Hey, baby, come closer so's we can get a good look at ya."

Not a chance. She rang the bell and crooked her finger again.

A whistle filled the air. "I'm tellin' Hattie I get first dibs on that one."

"Lower your top."

"Raise your skirt."

Is this what Hattie's girls had to put up with all the time? Those poor girls.

"All she's doing is ringing a bell and wiggling a finger at us."

"Yeah but get a gander at her leg. Whoo-whee. That's the sexiest thing I've ever seen."

The balcony wobbled.

Ring. Crook. Ring. Crook. At this rate she wouldn't be able to move her finger tomorrow.

"Hell, I'm not waiting for Hattie. I want a sample of those breasts. I'm going up there now."

"Men. Get away from that post. No one is going to climb the balcony."

Thankfully, Frank was watching.

"Go on in and talk with Hattie about the new balcony girl."

Grumbles floated up to her. Never in a million years would she believe a man could get excited over a woman crooking a finger at him. Maybe it was the way Hattie had arranged her nightgown. Men enjoyed women's legs and breasts? Who knew? She sure didn't.

But it wasn't going to happen at Hattie's, nor with men she didn't know. Only one man piqued her interest. One who should never, ever find out what she was doing.

DANIEL STOPPED BEHIND a group of men gazing up at Hattie's balcony. What was the madam up to now? The competition between brothels and saloons was intense. Had she found a new way to get men to come into her establishment? From where he was standing, all he could see was the shapely leg and bare shoulder of a woman. A bell rang. A hand appeared over the railing. The woman wiggled her finger as if begging the men to come to her. Not a word was spoken, which was unusual. Usually the balcony girls were loud. This new move by Hattie was sexy as hell.

He had to agree with the men muttering among themselves about not being able to see her face. Some called up to her. If it weren't for Frank standing guard at the front, at least one man would be climbing to the balcony to get to her. Hell, he might even follow.

The prostitute shifted. Long, blonde hair flowed down her back. As one, the crowd groaned in appreciation. Everyone was almost certainly thinking the same thing—what would it feel like having those silky strands flowing over his naked body.

A man came out from the saloon. "Hattie says she's new and not ready for customers yet, but if'n you put your name on a list, she'll let us know when the girl is available."

The words were barely out of his mouth when the men surged forward through the doors. He had to give the woman credit for knowing how to lure the men into her place. He had no intention of putting his name on a list, but a drink would feel good right about now. It would also be fun watching the men fall over themselves getting their names on the list.

Something shiny on the boardwalk caught his eye. It wasn't a gold nugget. If someone had lost a piece this size, they'd be on their hands and knees searching for it. Ignoring the men pushing at each other, he stepped onto the boardwalk and picked it up.

Holding the item in his hand, he backed off the walkway and peered up at the woman on the balcony. It couldn't be. He opened his palm. How had Julia's thimble ended up down here? The bigger question was if Julia was up there, what the hell was she doing at Hattie's working as a balcony girl?

His heart sank. Dare he call up to her? Should he pretend he hadn't found the thimble? Maybe she'd given it to one of Hattie's girls? Which didn't make sense, either. It was a treasured item. When, how, and why would she have encountered the prostitutes?

With most of the men inside, Main Street was momentarily quiet. He had to know. "Julia," he whispered.

The finger stopped. The woman withdrew her hand. That could only mean one thing—the woman he was falling for was playing him for a fool. He knew she needed money, but to become a lady of the evening? Shit.

He and King were picking the sisters up tomorrow morning, so Julia couldn't be sleeping here. Could she? The only thing to do was wait for her in the back alley, since she would never leave through the saloon. But maybe she would. Since it was evident he didn't know her at all, there was no way he could predict where she'd leave from.

POCKETING THE THIMBLE, he crossed the street, not bothering to look back up at the balcony, afraid of what he might see. No longer thirsty for a drink or to listen to the men talk about the new girl, he climbed the stairs to his office. After removing his shoes, he lay back on the bed, tossing the thimble between his hands.

"Damn it all to hell." He threw the thimble across the room where it pinged into his water pitcher. To think he was considering spending the rest of his life with her. Saving his money so he could afford a better place for her—them. He didn't care if men shouldn't cry. His eyes burned with unshed tears. He'd briefly considered confronting her in the alley, because she would probably go home that way. With his current mood, waiting for tomorrow would be wiser.

He wasn't prone to violence, but as angry as he was at her deception, no court in the country would convict him if he harmed her. No, better to wait until tomorrow morning when they picked up the sisters.

Rolling over to his side, he curled up into a ball and stared at the wall through tear-filled eyes. He'd never trust a woman again.

Chapter Twenty-Six

"Hurry up, Suz," Julia called out the next day as she tied her bonnet. "Daniel and King will be here soon."

"Hold your horses. You're acting as if it's your first date with him."

Besides the anticipation of spending the day with Daniel, she was relieved to have made it through last night.

Like Hattie had predicted, the ordeal was over in an hour. The madam had come upstairs to tell Julia she could leave. After donning her prospector costume, Hattie had hugged her before placing a bag of coins in her hand. The bag was heavier than ever. She hadn't expected to get paid, but she wasn't about to turn the money down.

By the time she'd made it home, it was almost one-thirty. She stuffed the coins in her old worn-out boots where she kept her sewing proceeds. Hattie had been happy with the turn out and, even though a success, said she wouldn't call on Julia to do it again. She didn't think her nerves could handle it another time—especially since she thought someone had whispered her name.

Expecting someone to charge through Hattie's room to the porch to take her to task, every creaking board or loud voice spiked her nerves to the point where she could hardly breathe. After a while, when no one did, she chalked it up to her nervous imagination. To top it off, she couldn't find Granny's thimble. She knew she'd taken it with her for good luck the previous night. She hadn't noticed it was missing until halfway home. Then it was too late to return to the brothel and retrieve it. Besides, without Dorrie to open the back door for her, there was no way to enter, and she wasn't about to use the front door.

"Are they here, yet?" Suzanna asked, coming into the room, setting her overnight bag by the front door. "It's been a while since I've seen King. Spending time at his ranch again will be fun."

"I agree. I haven't seen much of Daniel since we caught Mingus, Emmaline, and Mr. Woods."

Voices sounded outside their door. Before they could knock, Suzanna threw it open. King smiled and pulled Suzanna into a hug. Daniel stood in the doorway, his eyebrows so deeply furrowed they nearly met above his nose. His lips were tightly closed. Fingering the lace at her collar, she took a step back. Was he angry? If he was, why?

"We need to talk," he said through clenched teeth.

"All right." When she approached the door, he stepped back. Was it her imagination or had he purposely kept from touching her? Her heart sank. What was going on? Wait, maybe he was serious because he was going to ask her to marry him, a question known to make men nervous.

She refrained from giggling and skipping to the back yard. "Is this all right?" she asked when they reached the garden.

"Fine."

His curt answer scared her. Surely, he should be down on one knee by now, instead of keeping his hands in his pockets and scowling more than before. He withdrew one hand and held it out, palm up.

Shock spread through her body. She couldn't breathe, couldn't think. "Where did you find it?" She reached out to take her grandmother's thimble, but he closed his hand around it.

"Where do you think I found it, Miss Lindstrom?"

Since she'd had it when she went to Hattie's, the answer was obvious. He'd been in Hattie's room. The idea crushed any feelings she may have had for him. "I thought you didn't spend time with prostitutes."

"What?" His voice came out in a squeal. "What are you talking about? Unlike someone I thought I knew *I* wasn't at Hattie's last night." With his hands clasped behind his back, he paced before her. "I was walking down the street last night when a bunch of men were raving about Hattie's new balcony girl. She didn't show her face, merely rang a bell and crooked her finger. Every man wanted that woman. Some even tried to climb to the balcony to get to her."

It was worse than she thought. He'd seen her. Now what should she do? "It isn't what you think, Daniel."

"No? What am I supposed to think, when the woman I have—or should I say *had* feelings for— the woman who I thought was an innocent, is earning money on her back?"

Julia retreated a step when Daniel stopped and stood before her. She didn't think so, but as angry as he was, would he hit her? "It's not like that. You have to listen to me."

"And here I was so careful to keep your reputation safe. Is Suzanna in on this, too?"

"What? No." She rubbed her forehead. "I mean there is no *this*. It was . . ."

"I don't want to hear what it was." He resumed his pacing. "How many men have you been with?" He stopped and raised a hand. "No. Don't tell me." He removed his hat and threw it on the ground. "I had plans for us. Plans for our future, when all along you've been playing me for a fool."

"No, Daniel."

"Don't call me Daniel. It's Mr. Iverson to you. In fact, I don't ever want to hear either name coming from you again."

Julia jerked him around to face her. "You have to listen to me."

"That's where you're wrong," he said, yanking his arm free. "I never want to see you again." He tossed the thimble at her feet, stormed off then turned back.

Hope filled her chest. Had he changed his mind?

"The only thing I'll believe is that Suzanna is truly an innocent, so don't worry, I won't spread the word about what a whore you are." Then he was gone.

Too shocked for words, she sank to the ground and covered her face with her hands. What was she going to do now?

"Julia, what's wrong? Where did Daniel go?"

Julia peeked through her fingers. Two pairs of shoes stood before her. King hadn't left with Daniel. He knelt in front of her.

"Tell us what happened? I've never seen Daniel so angry." He rested an arm on his bent knee. "The only thing he said on the way here was that he would never trust a woman again. You can tell us, Julia."

"I can't. It's too awful."

Suzanna sat beside her and took her hands. "It can't be that bad. What did you fight about?"

"You'll hate me." A sob grew in her chest. She hiccoughed. "You'll never want to be my sister again."

"That would never happen, Julia."

"I wouldn't be too sure about that."

King peeked beneath her bonnet. "Let us decide how bad it is."

Where to start? She took a deep breath. From the beginning was the best. "You know how I was trying to find sewing jobs?"

"Yes," Suzanna said, patting her hands. "And you seem to be making money at it."

"Well . . ."

Other than a few gasps from Suzanna and a chuckle or two from King, neither interrupted as she told her story.

"A cowboy? You dressed as a cowboy?" Suzanna asked when Julia paused.

"Is that all you can say?"

King sat on the ground and stretched out his legs. "I'd say you're one brave woman, Julia Lindstrom. Daniel is an idiot for not letting you tell your side of the story."

"Really?"

He nodded. "That's not to say I wouldn't be angry if I'd found Suz had done what you did. But since you weren't caught and were only trying to help Hattie to earn some extra money, I'd say yes, he's an idiot."

Suzanna whisked an ant from her dress. "Weren't you worried about your reputation if someone recognized you?" Her voice rose. "I could have lost my job if you'd been caught."

"Don't you think I know that? I was petrified, but we needed the money, and Hattie pays well." Didn't Suzanna understand how she felt about not helping with finances? "I was frightened with every step I took down the dark alley."

Did Suzanna's deep sigh mean she wouldn't forgive her? Losing her as a sister would be like losing a part of herself. More than likely worse than losing Daniel.

"How did I not know you were sewing the fancy clothes for Hattie?" Suzanna's question held less sharpness than before. Was that a good sign?

Julia shrugged. "It wasn't easy. I'd start sewing as soon as you left for school. Since you couldn't leave the kids alone, I knew I was safe all day. I gave myself an hour before school was done to clean up and work on the book. Of course, I always waited until you were asleep to slip out."

"But to be with *those* women." Suzanna shuddered. "They're . . . They're . . ."

Now her sister had gone too far, making them sound as if the prostitutes were lesser women than they were. Heat rose to her face. "I'll have you know *those* women aren't so different from us. They are nice women. They have the same dreams we do, but because of circumstances, they ended up earning a living the way they do. It wouldn't take much for either one of us to end up as prostitutes. I enjoy talking with them. Hattie treats them as a mother would, yet given the chance, they would leave, marry, and have a passel of kids."

Julia took a deep breath. "They are more friendly than the so-called society women you're so concerned about meeting." She pointed a finger at Suzanna. "Don't you ever forget where we came from. Dirt poor farm girls."

"She has a point, Suzanna," King said, finally speaking up. "While I don't frequent the upstairs of the brothels, I've heard Hattie has a kind heart. She's helped a lot of people in this town when they were down on their luck. That's more than I can say for those living on the other side of the Badlands."

What a relief to have King take her side. "Did you know Hattie survived the Chicago fire?"

King shook his head. "I had no idea."

"She was deserted by her boyfriend at a brothel. That's how she started working as a prostitute." A tear rolled down her cheek as she retold Hattie's story.

Suzanna sniffed. "I had no idea."

"That's why we can't jump to conclusions about people, Suzanna. We never know what they've been through."

"Wise advice," King said, jumping to his feet, lending the girls a hand. "The question is what to do about Daniel. You know he loves you. That's why he was so upset and jumped to the wrong conclusion about you."

Julia brushed off the back of her skirt and removed her bonnet. Looked as if she wasn't going anywhere this weekend. "I guess I can understand how he thought what he did, but he could have at least given me a chance to explain."

"Do you want me to talk to him?" King walked between them to the house.

"No. If he wants to believe the worst of me, then so be it." A sob built in her chest, but she tamped it down. There was no way she was going to cry in front of King.

"What are you going to do now?" King asked.

"Yes," Suzanna said. "You can't keep sewing for Hattie."

"Why not? It's good money. We need to buy wood for the winter and you two . . ." she waggled a finger between King and Suzanna.

Suzanna blushed. "Us two, what?"

"Never mind." She wasn't about to say when they get married. What if King had no intention of marrying Suzanna? How embarrassing if she said they were. "I can't continue to live here without contributing my share, and I can't afford to live alone."

"But what if Daniel blabs to everyone?" Suzanna asked, tucking her hand in the crook of King's elbow.

"He said he wouldn't. I believe him."

They stopped outside the front door. "I have a suggestion, if you want it."

"Short of saying I should become one of Hattie's girls for real, I'll listen to any ideas."

"Good. Suzanna, do you have some of your delicious lemonade?" King asked, moving the rocking chairs into the shade. "Have a seat."

Confused and concerned about his somber demeanor, she did as he asked, while King took a spot on the front step. When Suzanna gave them a glass of lemonade, she sat in the other chair.

"From what you said, someone leaves fabric in the bushes. Right?"

Julia nodded. "We couldn't call each other, or the operator would know. Before long everyone would know I was talking to a madam. I couldn't take the chance."

"Then when they're ready, you put the finished clothing in the same place for someone to pick up."

"That's right."

"Then you disguise yourself, go out after Suzanna is asleep, and venture down the back alley to Hattie's place. Dorrie meets you, takes you to Hattie's room, where you fit their dresses, and get more orders."

"That's about it."

Suzanna sucked in a breath. "I still can't believe you ventured out on your own after dark. I'd be so scared."

"Believe me, I was. Usually I had no problems, but once two drunks stopped me."

"Oh, my." Suzanna slapped a hand to her chest. "What did you do?"

"Nothing. They thought I was just a young pup and went on their way."

"May I continue?" King asked. "I'm not sure how often you've done this, but eventually you're going to get caught. So, how about I act as the go-between?"

Suzanna tipped her head to the side. "What do you mean by that?"

"Instead of using the bushes to transport the clothing, why don't I simply deliver them to you? There's no reason Hattie can't call me and tell me when something is ready. I can call her to tell her I'm dropping off the finished goods."

"What about fitting the girls?"

They were silent for a minute until Suzanna snapped her fingers.

"What if you keep your disguises but King escorts you to Hattie's? If someone stops you, you could pretend to be mute and let him do the talking."

"I don't know . . ."

King smiled, his eyes shining at Suzanna. "I think that's a fantastic idea."

Why would King help her? It was Suzanna he was infatuated with. Wait. He's probably doing it to protect her sister's good name. She mentally shook her head. Who cared what his motives were—as long as she could keep sewing for Hattie.

"You'd do that for me?"

"I'd do it for both of you." King patted Suzanna's hand.

By the gleam in his eyes, he wanted to do more. "I don't know what to say."

"Oh, for heaven's sake, Julia, say yes."

If it was at all possible, Suzanna's eyes glowed more than King's. If those two weren't in love, she'd eat her best bonnet. For a short time, she thought she was, too. Well, she still was, but it was over for them. Her heart clenched. A sob built. There was no way should would get over him today, but the major question was, would she ever.

Chapter Twenty-Seven

September 25, 1879

Daniel trudged up the stairs to his office. One week. One week of pain. One week of heartbreak since he'd found out about Julia working for Hattie. He unlocked the door to his rooms, tossed his hat on the desk, removed his coat, and sat on the chair. A bottle of whiskey and empty glass remained on his desk from last night after using the liquor to ease his anguish.

His hand shook as he poured a glass of the amber liquid. Six days since he'd confronted Julia with her deceit. Six nights of drinking himself into a stupor so he could sleep. Six days and nights of pure hell. He drank the whiskey down in one gulp, then poured another, and chugged it down before recapping the bottle. The temptation to throw the bottle across the room was strong, but then he'd have a headache and a mess to clean up.

Hell, who was he kidding, thinking getting drunk would cure what ailed him. To torture himself, each night he stood outside Hattie's, waiting for Julia to sit on the balcony, only to be disappointed when one of the other girls appeared. Each night, he was torn between being glad she hadn't made an appearance and sad she hadn't. At least he would have gotten a glimpse of her.

He wasn't the only one upset. Each night Frank explained to the men that the new gal wasn't ready, yet. The list of names to be with her grew. He told the crowd that when she was ready, Hattie would put all the names in a hat. The name drawn first would get to spend the night with the mysterious woman.

How was Hattie going to explain to the men that a new girl didn't exist? Or had Julia decided to join forces with the madam? He reached for the bottle again then jerked back. No. Even though he'd seen her with his own eyes, he still had trouble imagining Julia working in a brothel. Since he'd never guessed she'd enter a brothel or talk with a prostitute, let alone take part in the activities there, what the hell did he know? He slammed the glass on the table. Drinking the past week hadn't done anything more than give him a headache and upset stomach the next day, so what was the point? It didn't help him sleep, either.

Without removing his boots, he lay on his bed and threw an arm over his eyes. Not for the first time, he wondered if he should have let Julia explain herself. Maybe there was a reason for what she did. Without telling him what had happened after he'd left the sisters' house, King had called him an idiot. Maybe he was, but there was no way he could be with a woman who'd lie to or keep secrets from him, not to mention being a whore.

Biting back the anger that had become part of his life, he rolled to his side and fell asleep.

SHOUTING, SCREAMS, and bells ringing jerked him from a dream of kissing Julia. He peeled his eyes open. He rubbed them with the back of his hand and squinted across the room. The room was hazy, making the lantern light barely visible. Smoke? He coughed and sank to the floor.

Voices yelled from the street. "Fire! Fire! The town's on fire."

Shit. It had to be bad if there was smoke in his room. As he stood an explosion rocked the building, sending him flying to the floor. What the hell? It sounded like cannons going off. Had they gone to war again while he was sleeping? He crawled across the floor, grasped the doorknob, and twisted. Nothing. He jerked the knob. Stuck.

Damn landlord. The angry, swirling smoke thickened. He needed to get out of here before he couldn't see or breathe, stuck doorknob or not.

He kicked at the door. Luckily, he'd left his boots on. On the third kick, the door crashed open. There'd be hell to pay when his landlord saw the damage. Taking the steps three at a time, he got to the street in record time. People were running toward the hill, carrying whatever they could hold in their arms. Horses ran wild down the street. Over on Sherman Street, flames shot into the air, making the night sky glow. From what he could tell, the fire was heading toward downtown.

King ran down the street toward him. Soot covered his face. "The fire set off kegs of gunpowder at Jensen and Bliss' Hardware Store."

The old miner Daniel had seen on and off ran up alongside King. Gone was the stooped back. His hat was absent, revealing blonde hair draped over his shoulder. Daniel did a double take at the miner. Long, blonde hair? His face was as dirty as always, but beneath the grime, womanly features became apparent.

"Julia?"

She nodded.

"What the hell are you doing here dressed in those old clothes?"

King glanced over his shoulder. "There's no time to question her. Right now, we need to help people from the buildings and up the hill."

"I'll go to Hattie's and help them get out."

Daniel captured her elbow. "You'll do no such thing. Go back to your house. The fire isn't headed toward it."

Julia yanked her arm from his hand. "I'll do no such thing, Daniel Iverson. You can't tell me what to do." Without another glance, she ran toward Hattie's.

"Damn woman," he muttered, chasing after her.

"You got that right," King said, racing behind him. "A damn *fine* woman."

Daniel had no idea fire roared. In a fireplace, flames snapped and crackled cheerfully, but the fire hot on their heels snarled and growled like a hundred bears being attacked by thousands of bees. A woman, dressed in nothing but a sheer nightgown, screamed as she raced past them, a cat wrapped in her arms.

"Head to the hills," he shouted after her, praying all the other residents of the town would make it to safety.

The heat seemed to sear through his clothing. Taking a chance, he looked over his shoulder. Flames were devouring buildings three doors away. How was anyone going to get out alive? He and King threw open the doors to Hattie's as Julia disappeared up the stairs. Shit. Now he not only had to help the women, but make sure Julia was safe, too. Already windows were bursting from the heat.

When they reached the second floor, Julia had already pounded on the first two doors to the right of the stairway.

"You follow Julia, I'll take these rooms." King nodded in the opposite direction. "Fire! Get out now," he yelled, pounding on the first door.

Hattie's girls popped from their rooms holding thin wrappers to their chests, some followed by men wearing nothing but their long johns.

In front of him, Julia coughed, still yelling for the women to get out. "Run! Fire! The entire town's on fire!" She shoved two of the girls toward the back stairs.

"Hattie," a woman he recalled was Dorrie, shouted. "You have to get Hattie out of here. She took something to help her sleep."

"We'll get her out, Dorrie. Help the other girls. You don't have much time to get to the hills before the entire town is gone."

He pounded on a few more doors, making sure the inhabitants escaped, barely registering that one of the emerging men owned the haberdashery, was married, and had five children.

"Hattie! Wake up! The town's on fire." Julia beat on the last door and tried the doorknob. "It's locked. Hattie!" She turned to him. "You have to help me get her out."

Like he'd done in his room, Daniel kicked at the door, sending splinters of wood flying.

"She's not going to be happy about us breaking her door down," Julia said, entering the darkened room.

The scent of lilacs mixed with smoke hit him when he raced behind Julia to the still form beneath a pile of blankets.

Julia shook the woman. "Hattie," she coughed. "Hattie, wake up."

Daniel pushed Julia to the side, threw back the blankets, and scooped Hattie into his arms. The woman didn't weigh more than a bird, making his task easier. The window shattered. Cinders struck the drapes, instantly setting them on fire.

"Toss a blanket over her," he shouted over the increasing roar. Fire raged outside the window, lighting up the city like it was high noon. "Put one over your head, too, then let's get out of here."

Making sure Julia was in front of him, they ran down the smoke-filled hallway. "Where's the back stairs?"

"Here," Julia called then disappeared into the darkness.

"It figures she'd know where to go," he muttered to himself, hoisting the limp Hattie over his shoulder, giving him a free hand to follow the railing down the stairs.

"This way," Julia yelled, emerging from the building as a large beam swung down from above, blocking the stairwell behind them. She seized his hand.

With all the smoke, it was difficult to follow the shadows of people charging up the hill. At the top, out of breath, eyes stinging and legs burning, he lay Hattie on the ground. The smoke stung his nose. Would he ever be able to stand the smell of smoke again?

"What the hell?" Hattie whispered, her eyes fluttering open. "What am I doing outside?"

Julia sat beside her. Tears made muddy rivers down her sooty face. "The town is on fire." She stared in the direction of the school-house. "The school looks safe. I hope Suzanna is."

Daniel eased himself to the ground. He rested his elbows on his raised knees. Around him people cried, calling for friends or loved ones. Had everyone gotten out? Down below, the fire raged, consuming building after building like a starving monster. Buildings men had purposely burned as a firebreak hadn't stopped the con-flagration. Like children playing hopscotch, the blaze skipped from building to building, eating everything in its path.

King squatted in front of Hattie. "Is everyone accounted for?"

"I . . . I don't know."

Julia stood and brushed off the seat of her pants, which was ridiculous to Daniel. As dirty and smoky as her clothes were, the sight of her being careful of the back of her pants made him chuckle. Another explosion rocked the ground.

"Must be the Colin's place. He had barrels of gunpowder on hand."

"I see Dorrie with Ivy. I'll send them over here and search for the others."

He should help her, really, he should, but he wasn't sure if his legs would hold him up if he stood.

"I'm going to head to Suzanna's to make sure she's all right," King said, rising to his feet.

"How're you going to do that with the entire town burning?"

"I'll follow the top of the hill. When I'm above their place, I'll head down. I need to make sure she's safe."

"What about your place and Leona?"

A tear made white streaks down King's face as he gazed at the inferno below. "Thankfully, Leona was in Lead visiting friends and my guests got out safely." He shook his head. "And there's not a damn thing I can do about the building. It's gone." With those last words, he disappeared among the people waiting out the firestorm.

Daniel recalled the fear spiking through him when Julia showed up with King. Why had she been with his friend? Were they fooling both Suzanna and him? His heart clenched.

The people around him cried out as one when three buildings on the Badlands side of Main Street, including a bank, collapsed.

"What will we do?" a woman said, sobbing into her hands.

"We'll rebuild, that's what," an old timer answered. "Not much else we can do."

Yeah, what else could they do? But if the banks were destroyed, where would the money come from? The fire raged, leaving nothing but blackened piles of smoldering wood and the empty shells of the few buildings in town built with bricks. Where had his building been? Like everyone else stranded on the hillside, he had nothing but the smoke-encrusted clothes on his back.

Before he had a chance to say anything to her, Julia left Dorrie and Ivy beside Hattie, then disappeared into the hazy night without a glance at him. To the east above the hill where the new cemetery was located, the early morning sun poked through the smoke-filled sky. How long since the fire first started?

"Thank you for saving my life, Daniel," Hattie said, sitting up, wrapping the blanket around her shoulders.

Daniel picked up a twig, broke it into pieces, and tossed them one-by-one to the ground. "You should thank Julia. She's the one who insisted we save you and your girls." Was he proud of what she'd done, or angry Julia knew the place so well, she'd known exactly where to go?

"You're wrong about her, you know."

"Am I now?" He glanced over his shoulder at the madam. "Seems as if the facts speak for themselves."

Hattie let out a breath. "Facts you are unaware of. She is the sweetest, most caring, innocent woman I've ever had the pleasure to call my friend."

"*Innocent?*" He flicked a twig into the air. "Yeah, right."

"You listen to me, young man," Hattie smacked him on the arm. "Never once since she started sewing for me did she go downstairs. Never once did she meet or entertain men. All she did was become our friends when everyone else crossed the street if we dared to leave the brothel. She never judged us, but listened to our stories, our dreams."

"What about being a balcony girl?"

Hattie chuckled. "She told me you'd seen her. Crushed her heart the way you treated her."

"Crushed *her* heart? Hell, when I figured out who was up on the balcony, I nearly threw up. I wanted to kill all those men drooling over her."

"What she did was help a friend. I didn't have anyone to go out there that night. I couldn't let Swearingen, Molly Johnson, or the other brothel owners figure out I was short-handed. All I did was send a note to Julia telling her I needed help." Hattie leaned back on her arms and stared at the sky with red-rimmed eyes. "Without questioning what I needed, she came."

"I bet she loved the idea of acting as one of your girls on the balcony." His sarcasm would more than likely earn him another smack from Hattie. He flinched at the glare she threw at him. Yep, she certainly would give him a good one.

"Stop judging her, you ass. It took a lot of convincing to get her to go out there. She was so nervous someone would find out who she was, but doing as I said, she played her part well."

"You can say that again."

"Dammit, Iverson. Aren't you listening?" She whacked him again. "I told you she never saw or talked to a man when she came to the brothel. She needed to earn some money to help Suzanna with expenses. She's an excellent seamstress, but mending didn't make enough money."

The crowd moaned when two more buildings collapsed. It wouldn't be long before there would be nothing left to feed the fire—then nothing left of Deadwood.

"If you'd given her a chance to explain, instead of accusing her of awful things she'd never done you'd still be together."

"I was going to ask her to marry me."

Whack. "Then talk to her. Explain that you were an ass for not listening to her. If you didn't love her, your heart wouldn't be broken. You wouldn't be drinking every night."

Daniel jerked his head in her direction. "How do you know about that?"

"Humph. For all that we're in competition with each other, the saloon and brothel owners keep track of our customers and talk. Besides, the men in this town are worse gossips than the women." She tapped him on the arm. "And I'll tell you one more thing."

Was it something else to make him look like a fool? "What's that?"

"Someone attempted to blackmail her."

"What? Who?" What else could she have been going through that he didn't know about?

"And instead of going to the man she has strong feelings for, she came to me." Hattie smacked him on the arm. "Even though you've helped us in the past, she knew damn well what you'd think if you found out she was sewing clothes for a bunch of prostitutes. Was she right?"

"Yes." Shame nearly choked him worse than the smoky air. He would have turned his back on her just as he had before finding out the truth about her being on the balcony. "When was this?"

"A few weeks back. I told her I'd take care of it."

Daniel wiped an arm across his burning eyes. "And did you?"

Hattie nodded. "Somehow Mollie Johnson got wind of what she was doing. Mollie hates my guts and figured Julia would come running to me to pay the blackmail. She was right. Julia did come to me, but so, so wrong in thinking I would pay any kind of money to that nasty woman. I set her straight."

"What did you do?"

"Never you mind what I did." She tugged the blanket tighter to her neck. "Let's just say Mollie won't be bothering Julia, my girls, nor me anymore."

"Does Julia know?"

"She knows I took care of the matter, but not how I did it."

He didn't know what to say. In the back of his mind, he'd worried he hadn't given Julia a chance to defend herself, and now to learn about the blackmail? Guilt was a tough thing to admit and swallow.

"What are you going to do, besides watch our town burn to the ground?"

"Find Julia."

"Good boy." She pressed her foot against him. "What are you waiting for? Christmas?" she added when he hesitated.

Good question. What was he waiting for? There was never a good time to eat crow. His stomach rumbled. "I hear ya," he muttered, leaving Hattie.

Chapter Twenty-Eight

Julia was bone-achingly tired. After locating two more of Hattie's girls and sending them back to the madam, she continued her search among the throngs of survivors, the majority of whom had nothing more than the clothes on their backs.

As she wound her way through soot-covered, coughing, crying citizens, she was stopped more times than she could count.

"I'm thirsty. Do you have water?"

"I'm burned. Can you help me?"

"What are we going to do?"

"Have you seen my brother/son/husband/wife/daughter?"

Who did they think she was—Molly Pitcher or Florence Nightingale? Couldn't they tell she had nothing more than they did? She glanced toward the school. It and their house seemed to have suffered no damage. So, yes, she did have more than others but how was she supposed to get water or clothes for them? Walk through the fire?

"Julia?"

Even raspy from smoke, Daniel's voice was recognizable. Her heart lurched. What did he want?

"Julia?" he asked again, standing beside her. "Can we talk?"

She shrugged. "I thought you said everything you wanted to say to me and didn't ever want to see me again. Why should we talk now?" She sank to the ground and crossed her legs. "Go away, Daniel."

Daniel sat beside her. She edged away. "I'm sorry I didn't give you a chance to tell your side of the story. I was an ass."

"Yes, you were. But would it have made any difference? You had your mind set that I was working at Hattie's brothel. What changed?"

"Hattie explained it all to me."

"Oh, so believe her, but not me. You are an ass. Supposedly you cared for me. You sure had a strange way of showing it."

He sighed. "I'm so, so sorry. I shouldn't have jumped to conclusions."

Julia twisted her body to face him. "Just what was it about me that made you think I'd become a prostitute? Was it the way I walked? Talked? Flirted with dozens of men?"

"No."

"Then what? I never gave you any cause to think ill of me." She fisted her hands to keep from slapping him. "Please, tell me."

"You're absolutely right. You've done nothing to make me think you were one of Hattie's girls. But when I found your thimble below the balcony, I figured out who the woman was that all the men were drooling over and making lewd comments about. I was so jealous, I wanted to hurt someone."

"Did you?"

Daniel shook his head. "No. I started drinking instead."

Drinking? It was so unlike the man she'd come to love. Yep she still was in love with the idiot. Or maybe she was the idiot. "Oh, Daniel. You didn't."

"Yep, but I stopped. Couldn't handle the hangovers." His toneless laugh was barely audible. "It didn't help my broken heart anyway."

Hope filled her. Had he been as heart-broken as she?

"I was going to ask you to marry me."

If he had asked her before he found out about being a balcony girl, she would have said yes. But now? Probably not. She couldn't marry someone who didn't trust her.

Daniel took her hands in his. "Aren't you going to say anything?"

"Like what?"

"Like, yes."

The man was delusional. "You expect me to say yes after believing I was a prostitute?"

He shoved his fingers through his hair. "Put that way, no."

As much as she believed he was sorry and wanted to say yes, she wasn't about to let him off the hook so easily. She peered down at the town. The spreading flames seemed to have slowed down. Without much left to feed it, the fire was dying a slow death. Embers glowed in a few places. Smoke still spiraled into the air, but the majority of the fire was over. The sun rose over the peak of the hills on the other side of town, giving everyone of better view of the devastation.

Daniel nudged her. "What're you thinking?"

"I'm thinking I need to go back to Hattie and the girls. They'll need my help. Good-bye, Daniel."

COULD A MAN'S HEART break twice in a week? Julia didn't look back as she drifted into the crowd. Hell, did he expect her to fall into his arms after saying he was sorry? Wishful thinking on his part. He'd give her a few days to calm down and approach her again. Her beauty, intelligence, and, most of all, strength, were too good to let go.

Hell, she'd done what she needed to do to survive and did it without sacrificing her morals. In her place, he might have done the same thing. Even though he had helped some of the prostitutes for free, it was different for a man. It wasn't right, but a man's reputation wouldn't be ruined by being in contact with ladies of the evening. In his mind, this wasn't fair.

He stood. Right now, the town needed able-bodied men to rebuild. His heart may be broken, but his body wasn't.

Chapter Twenty-Nine

Daniel walked among the cold embers, hoping to find something—anything—of his office and belongings. But, like everyone else, the fire had devoured everything in its path. Not surprisingly, the town was already coming to life. Only three days after the fire and several saloon owners had already erected tents, slapped boards across oak barrels, and opened for business.

Surprisingly, only one person had perished, a deaf man who hadn't heard the bells ringing. Over three hundred buildings were destroyed. The town fathers were discussing how to better prepare the town in case of another fire. It was ordered that all buildings were to be made from bricks, not the haphazard wood constructions of the past. There was also talk of assuring the buildings be rebuilt in a more organized manner. Deadwood would rise again, bigger and better. He wanted to be part of its regrowth.

Already the citizens were asking for his legal advice. Mrs. Ellsner, from the Empire Bakery where the fire had started, needed his help to keep from going to jail—if they still had one. It wasn't her fault a lamp had fallen off a table and caught the canvas-covered walls on fire. Or that the hose company had lost their equipment in the flames and couldn't help.

His toe hit something hard. Scraping back the still-warm ashes, he came up with his old blue, metal cash box. Although scorched, it was still intact. Most of the blue had flaked off. He'd locked it the day before the fire. The box didn't contain much, since he kept most of his money in the bank, but it would help when goods came in to replace those lost. Thankfully the vaults the banks used had survived the fire, or the citizens of the town would be in worse straits than they were now.

Keeping busy would keep his mind off Julia. Word was they'd opened not only the schoolhouse for shelter, but their home, too. Too bad those 'upstanding' citizens who still had their homes didn't follow suit. The selfishness of some of the rich never ceased to amaze him.

With his cash box tucked under his arm, he headed toward King's now empty lot.

"Were you able to salvage anything?" he asked his friend, who was shoveling ash into a wagon. Where the hell was the town going to put all the debris?

"The stoves are intact." He pointed his shovel toward a pile at the corner of his lot. "Most of the plates, cups, and silverware. They'll all need a good scrubbing. It seems anything made from ceramic like sinks survived. All the beds, dressers, tables, and anything else made of wood were burned. I have no idea where to start."

"We're here to help." Julia's voice sent shivers down his spine. How he'd missed her.

Suzanna stood next to Julia, a rake in one hand and bucket in another. "Tell us what to do."

With handkerchiefs tying back their hair, old rubber boots rising to their shins, and skirts tucked into their waistbands to keep from getting dirty, they looked like a couple of girls no older than twelve.

"Well?" Julia said, directing her question to King.

"Not that I'm not appreciative, but shouldn't you be helping those staying on the school property? When I left this morning, more tents were going up."

"There are enough people to help," Suzanna said. "Besides, we were getting tired of all the whining and crying from some of the women. You'd think they could get off their lazy backsides to help out."

Shaking her head, Julia leaned on the handle of her rake. "After we found some of our things stolen from the house, the sheriff kicked them out. There's been a lot of looting, so he asked General Sturgis of Fort Mead to send in soldiers to protect property not damaged by the fire. After he left two men to protect the house and school, we hightailed it out of there."

King rubbed the back of his neck. "I'm still digging for anything that's useable. You could help while Daniel and I fill the cart with junk." He jerked a thumb over his shoulder. "I have a pile started over there."

AFTER AN HOUR OF WORKING, Leona arrived with her friends: two men and two women. Along with their tools and backs, they brought food with the wagonload of supplies. With four more pairs of hands, it didn't take long for the lot to be cleared.

"They've set aside an open stretch of land south of town for debris," King said, hitching a mule to the wagon. "I'm not sure what they're going to do with it, but that's the least of our problems."

"We brought some large tents we can set up as a kitchen," Leona said, walking to the wagonful of supplies. If we can get them up today, the dishes, pots and pans washed, and stoves scrubbed tomorrow, we should be able to start cooking by the following day."

"That's wonderful, Leona," Julia said, wiping an arm across her face.

After spending the afternoon keeping his eyes off her, he couldn't resist any longer. Her hands were filthy. Strands of hair had escaped her handkerchief and trailed down her cheeks. Smudges of soot covered her skirt as well as streaks on her nose, forehead, and chin. The temptation to wipe her face clean was strong, but never having been

in love before, he didn't know how to treat a woman as angry as bees
being evicted from their hives. It might be wiser to leave her alone.

"We can take these things back to our house to wash tonight," Julia said.

Peeling his eyes from her face was difficult but the grunts from Leona's friends as they attempted to haul the canvas tents from the wagon, said it was time to get back to work.

"WELL, I'LL BE DAMNED," King said from behind Daniel a few hours later when he returned from emptying the wagon. "How'd you get those tents up?"

"See those dirty women over there?"

"It's hard to tell, but do you mean Suzanna, Julia, Leona, and her friends?"

Daniel rocked back on his heels, careful not to fall backward on his tired, aching legs. "Yep. They labored like work horses to get the tents in place."

"You're kidding."

"Nope. I guess growing up on a farm helped them build some muscles." Daniel wiped a forearm over his forehead. "Too bad you weren't here to see it."

"Yeah." King shook his head. "Hell, if there was a restaurant around, I'd buy everyone supper."

Daniel had to chuckle at King's comment. Right now, the closest restaurant was in Lead. "Speaking of food," he glanced at the sun low in the sky, "we should quit for the day. Everyone's exhausted. We can load whatever needs to be washed into the wagon and haul them to Julia and Suzanna's."

King nodded. "Sounds fine with me. You going to stay with me tonight?"

"I don't know."

"A tent has to be better than wherever you've been sleeping the past few nights."

The idea of heading up into the hills and bedding down with only a quilt someone had thrown at him didn't appeal in the least. He glanced at Julia. Would it be worse than being so close to her and not being able to touch her?

"Hell, man. Swallow your pride. Get on your knees. Beg for forgiveness again."

Easy for King to say. Suzanna had him so high on a pedestal, he'd break every bone in his body if he fell. A deep rumble echoed through the valley. He eyed the sky. Dark, angry clouds were inching their way closer to Deadwood. Did he really want to sleep out in the rain?

"All right. Let's get things packed before it rains and we're mired in muddy debris to our waists."

GOODNESS, SHE WAS TIRED. At home she would have been able to work this hard and still have energy to stay up to read. She must have lost some of her stamina only doing gardening, sewing, and writing her children's books. Was there one spot on her body that didn't hurt or wasn't covered in dirt? Where was a water trough when it was needed?

"Let's load up what needs to be washed and get back to the schoolhouse before the skies open up," King said.

Julia took in the sky. How had she missed how dark it was getting? Would they make it back before they were drenched? With the roads so muddy, it would be like walking through cold molasses.

Groans and a few swear words filled the air as their group stood and loaded the salvaged goods. As dirty as she was, maybe getting caught in the rain wouldn't be so bad. At least it would wash them off.

Daniel's hand brushed hers when he hooked his fingers in the handles of the pots she handed him. Desire skittered through her. Even dirty and smelling of the ash he'd rummaged through all day, he was still as desirable as ever. It wouldn't be long before she'd be on her knees begging for him to take her back.

When everything they'd found was loaded in the wagon, the group made their way around piles of rubble, roaming horses, pigs, chickens, shells of brick buildings, and men throwing up tents wherever they could find an open spot.

By the time they arrived at the schoolhouse and makeshift tent camp, rolling clouds loomed overhead. Thunder rumbled a warning. Men scrambled to put up the additional tents that had arrived while they were working at King's.

King stopped the mule by the door to their house. A guard stood in front of the door, a rifle hooked across his arms.

"What do you want? This is a private home."

"It's us, Julia and Suzanna. We live here."

The guard stepped closer and peered down at them. "Sorry, with all the dirt on your face, I didn't recognize you."

"That's understandable." She unlocked the door, wrinkling her nose at the scent of smoke that had seeped into the building. The sight of her bed through the open bedroom door made her want to weep. How long before she'd be able to find comfort there?

Suzanna dropped to the couch. "In case we don't get their tent up, I invited Leona and her friends, the girls, anyway, to stay in the house tonight. If it's all right, Leona can bunk with you. May with me. Jill said she'd sleep on the couch. She's the shortest, so it makes sense."

Julia shrugged and suppressed a yawn. "Fine. Fine. Aren't the men putting up tents?"

"They're helping put up the ones that arrived today." Suzanna shook her head. "I can't believe how inept some people are—especially the women. You'd think between them, they'd figure it out themselves instead of waiting for help."

"What about the stuff from King's?"

"He said to leave it in the wagon to let the rain wash some of it off."

Julia rolled her sleeves to her elbows. "Well, let's get to it, then."

"My garden," Julia yelled when they rounded the corner of the house. The fence had been torn down. Several cows chewed on corn stalks while a young boy tugged beans from their plants. A woman yanked peas off vines, while another pulled up her radishes. "What in heaven's name do you think you're doing?"

"We need food." The woman said. "Since you're too uppity to offer up food from your house, we're taking what we need."

Julia slapped her hands at her waist. How dare the woman call her uppity, when Julia had seen her cross the street to avoid Hattie and her girls. "I'll have you know I've given away all we own since the fire. I don't have anything left."

The woman sniffed and stuck her nose in the air. "I just bet you did. If I went into your house, how much would I find hidden?"

Fear spiked its talons down her back. In their hunger would they attack the house looking for food?

"I'm telling you there's nothing left. The people of Lead and other towns near here are bringing food and other necessities to town."

"I haven't seen anything."

"They've been bringing it to downtown." If she'd get off her lazy rear end, she'd know that.

"Well, that doesn't help me any, now does it." The woman pushed past Julia, nearly knocking her to the ground.

Raised voices came from the area where at least twenty tents had been put up.

"I insist you help me before those those heathens," a female yelled, the haughtiness in her voice familiar.

Mrs. Woods? What was she doing here? Hadn't she left town?

"I'm telling you, Mrs. Woods, we're getting tents up as fast as we can." Daniel held a tent pole in his hand. "These ladies asked for help first."

"Ladies my backside. They're no ladies." She pointed a finger at Hattie and her girls. "They're, they're . . . a blight to polite society and shouldn't be seen with the rest of us."

Why, that horrid woman. Before she could take a step to confront her, Daniel set down the pole and stood nose to nose with Mrs. Woods.

"Back off. These *blights on society* as you call them, have been helping other people. Tending to the sick. Making fires. They also gave up their blankets for people." He flicked a hand at the quilt around Mrs. Woods shoulders. "Where do you think this came from? I don't see you giving it away to help the children." He pointed a finger into her nose. "And they did it all before taking care of themselves. All I've seen you do is sit on your fat ass and make demands. Well, *lady*, you're on your own."

"But . . . but . . ." She flinched as a roll of thunder crossed the sky. "It's going to rain."

Daniel turned his back on her and picked up the pole. "Well, then, unless you get your tent up, you're going to get wet. I don't know what you're doing back in town, anyway."

Mrs. Woods puffed out her chest. "I came back to gather the rest of my belongings, which," she dabbed a handkerchief at her eyes, "are all gone. I have nothing left."

"Hell, Mrs. Woods," Daniel gripped the pole until his knuckles were white. "Neither does anyone else. You know what I have left?" She shook her head. "This." Daniel swept a hand down his body. "The damn clothes on my back. Just like her, her, her, and her." He pointed to Hattie and her girls. "Yet, they've managed to not sit around expecting to be waited on. They *chose* to take care of others. C'mon, ladies, let's get this tent up before we get soaked."

Mrs. Woods picked up a corner of a tent laying at her feet then let it go. Julia's estimation of Daniel grew until her chest nearly burst. Without saying a word, Julia took a pole preparing to help with Hattie's tent.

When the first fat, heavy, drops of rain spattered down on them, they'd nearly put up all the tents. Mrs. Woods sat where they'd left her, crying into her hands. Silly woman. While everyone ran inside their tents, taking whatever belongings they'd found, Hattie stood in front of Mrs. Woods.

"You're welcome to stay with us tonight."

"What?" Mrs. Woods peered up at the madam. "You're asking me to stay with you after what I said?"

"Right now, it doesn't matter who you are, what you do, or where you came from." Hattie held a hand to the woman. "We're all in the same predicament. Come, join us."

Something wet streamed down Julia's face and it wasn't rain. One more time, Hattie had shown her strength and kindness.

Mrs. Woods stood. "All right." She handed Hattie the quilt. "I believe this is yours."

Hattie handed it back. "We can share."

Julia swallowed around the lump in her throat. Maybe Mrs. Woods learned something today. The women disappeared as the skies opened. Instead of rushing into the house, she stood in the rain, arms open wide, letting the surprisingly warm water rinse her body and soul.

"It's been a long time since we've played in the rain, hasn't it," Suzanna said, bumping Julia in the side. The rain came down in torrents, pounding on the tents, making it difficult to see them. "But I think we'd better get inside before we get struck by lightning."

Hooking their arms together, they giggled and jumped through puddles as they had as children.

THE RAIN BEAT ON THEIR roof for an hour, giving them a chance to dry off. Leona and her friends were staying the night, so Julia had given the ladies nightgowns to change into. Leona was a whiz in the kitchen, managing to make scrambled eggs tasting as if they'd been made in a fancy French kitchen—not that Julia would know what that would be like, yet they were some of the best eggs to hit her taste buds.

Instead of putting on her nightgown, Julia changed into clean clothes and sat at the kitchen table.

"Why aren't you ready for bed?" Suzanna asked while the girls chatted in the living room.

"Now that the rain has stopped, I want to go for a walk."

"Hoping to bump into Daniel?"

Julia hid a smile. "No." Liar. "I overheard King say he was going to do a turn as a guard, so I should be safe." Actually, it was Daniel she heard, something she wasn't going to admit to her sister. "I've heard there is still some stealing going on. I can't imagine people taking advantage of the fire like that."

Suzanna smacked her hand on the table. "I know. It makes me so damn mad."

"Suzanna Marie Lindstrom! You swore."

"Sometimes the only way I can express myself is by swearing. I only do it when no one is around." She grinned, then took a chair across from Julia. "There are days I have to bite my lip to keep from cussing at some of the kids."

"I thought you loved teaching."

"I do, although some of those kids could test the strength of a saint. What's hard is they can be so funny and inappropriate I have a hard time keeping from laughing. Little stinkers."

Julia toyed with a fork left on the table. "I suppose school will stay closed for a while."

Suzanna nodded. "Until people can get their homes rebuilt, we'll stay closed. It's a good thing we were open through the summer or we'd really be behind." She patted Julia's hand. "Worried about not having any sewing jobs?"

"No. I was paid well and put the money aside. I may give some of it back to Hattie so she can rebuild."

"That would be a wonderful gesture. At least the board is going to continue to pay me while we're closed."

Julia stood and stretched her arms above her head. "Well, I'm going to go for a walk before I go to bed."

Suzanna winked. "Say hello to Daniel for me."

THE RAIN SUPPRESSED the over-powering scent of burned wood, oil, rubber, leather, and other items Julia couldn't identify, leaving the air fresh and clear. For the first time in days, Julia's lungs didn't fill with smoke when she took a deep breath. The downtown was doubtless nothing more than a big mud and ash puddle now, yet at least the air was breathable.

Julia passed the school building. She wasn't looking for Daniel. Really, she wasn't. She paused. Who was she kidding? Of course, she was. Seeing him stand up for Hattie against Mrs. Woods had been a thing of beauty. There was no way she could hide her feelings from him any longer. Ignoring him was hurting her more than him, anyway.

A figure stood at the end of the driveway. Her heart skipped a beat until she realized the person was too short to be Daniel. She walked back toward the house. She didn't blame him for being upset with her, but it still irritated her that he hadn't given her a chance to explain.

A man leaned against the side of the house. He turned. Daniel. Legs shaking, she took one step. Then another, and another, until she stood before him.

"What are you doing out here, Julia?"

"I wanted a breath of fresh air. I figured the rain would have cleared up the smoke."

Daniel sucked in a deep breath, then glanced down at her. "It is refreshing, isn't it?" He frowned. "Is that the only reason you're out here?"

"No. I wanted to talk to you."

"Oh, yeah?" He folded his arms across his chest as if protecting his heart.

"Yeah. I missed you."

"I missed you, too." He tucked a loose strand of hair behind her ear. "And I'm so, so sorry I didn't give you a chance to explain. I let fear, anger, and jealousy take over my brain."

Julia leaned into him. "Jealousy?"

He nodded. "Yeah. Knowing it was you up on the balcony letting all those men drool over you drove me crazy. I'm the only one who should have been drooling over you. I will if you give me another chance."

Julia didn't say anything. Should she?

Daniel placed his hands on her shoulders. "Look, I know I was an ass. I know it's not fair women can't do or say what they want, when they want. My mother was every bit as strong as my father, helping him in his business. He said she was one of the smartest partners he ever had. It's wrong that it's a man's world. I'm not sure what we can do to change that. Maybe someday our children will be the ones to change the world."

Children. Her heart swelled. "Like giving the women the right to vote? The right to do any job she wishes? The right to not to have to depend on a man to make a living?"

"When we have daughters, I'll help fight for it."

Well, that was surprising. Most men didn't believe women could be equal to men, but with Daniel as their father, anything was possible. "Promise?"

Daniel nodded. "So, if I ask you to marry me again, what will you say?"

"Will you not jump to conclusions?"

"Yes."

"Will you help raise our children or dump the job on me?"

"Together. We'll raise our children together. My father and uncles have been known to change a diaper or two."

Her lips trembled to keep from smiling. "Will you let me make my own decisions?"

"Yes."

"If I ask, will you help me make those decisions?"

"Of course. Isn't that what partners are for?" He kissed her forehead. "I know plenty of couples who work side-by-side. My parents. Colin and Sadie Haywood. Believe it or not, the blacksmith and his wife."

"My parents."

"See? We simply need to find our places—together—as partners."

This time she couldn't hold back a grin. This was the man made for her. The one she was meant to spend the rest of her life with. She leaned up on her tiptoes as if to give him a kiss, then stepped back and held out her hand. "Partners?"

Daniel shook her hand, then wrapped her in a hug. He was her home. Her love. Her partner.

"Partners. Partners for life," he whispered in her ear.

Julia smiled into his shoulder. And this time she knew he wasn't jumping to conclusions. Partners for life.

Excerpt from
The School Marm
The Darlings of Deadwood - Suzanna

King Winson slogged through the mud, avoiding horses, oxen-driven wagons, and drunks. Even though it was only ten in the morning, there were plenty of all of three. Mud splattered on his already filthy clothes. With the spring thaw, water from the hills congregated in Deadwood's main street.

He scraped his hand over the week-old, scruffy hair on his face. He needed a shave, a bath, and clean clothes before he went to meet the weekly stagecoach set to arrive, he glanced at the town clock hanging near the bank, in an hour.

As he plodded his way across the street to King's Inn, his restaurant and hotel, he avoided a particularly large pile of ox dung. A horse raced down the street, slinging mud in every direction.

"Stagecoach is a-comin'," the man yelled, slapping his hat against the horse's hindquarters.

With his foot in the air to sidestep the horse droppings, King couldn't move in time to get out of the way. Why was the arrival of the stagecoach garnering such excitement when it had been coming to Deadwood for three years?

As the horse passed, its tail whipped across King's face. Arms flailing, foot waving in the air, King's leg went out from beneath him. Rump first, he landed in the pile of manure he'd been trying to avoid.

Someone falling in the street was not an uncommon occurrence, so luckily no one paid any attention. No one, except for his best friend, Daniel Iverson.

"Well, don't just stand there laughing like a hyena, help me up." The mud was slippery, slimy, and disgusting. Without anything to grip to pull himself up, he kept tumbling back into the mire.

"Catch." From his place on the wooden sidewalk Dan tossed one end of a rope. "I'll pull you up."

There was no way he was going to let his friend reel him in like a floundering fish. "Just hold on to it." His hands, slick with goo, tugged on the rope.

"Wait," Dan said. "You're going to pull me in. I'll tie it to a post."

King eyed the rickety post holding up an equally rickety overhang. The way buildings were being thrown up and with the gold tunnels meandering beneath the town, he wouldn't be surprised if he pulled the entire building down, with the entire block falling like a row of dominos.

With a deep breath, he pulled himself toward his friend. The mud sucked at his boots threatening to draw them off with each step until he made it to the boardwalk. He fell to his back, catching his breath as Dan laughed.

"Shut up, big guy. It could be you next."

Dan adjusted his string tie and straightened his immaculate blue vest. "Hey, don't you have the stagecoach to meet?"

King stood and wiped his filthy clothes. His boots were full, his pockets drenched, his beard encrusted, and the brim of his hat turned down, nearly covering his eyes.

"You'd better get cleaned up, before Mrs. Woods arrives." His friend tapped a finger against his smirking lip. "If the stage is almost here, you won't have time to clean up proper." Dan's smile suggested only one thing. "You know what you have to do, don't you?"

Knock his friend into the street? "Yes, I know what I have to do." Ignoring stares, he clomped toward the nearest horse trough. He removed his boots and poured the goo onto the street. With a grimace, he tossed them into the water, then, taking off his hat, climbed in. After dunking his head several times, he crawled out, stepped back onto the boardwalk, and shook himself like a dog.

A shout came from up the street. Darn. The stagecoach was here. He tugged his boots over his feet, slapped on his hat, and walked toward the stopping place. A hand halted him.

"You should let me escort Mrs. Woods," Dan said, stepping in front of his friend. "You look like someone who spent a week hunting game for his restaurant and then fell in the mud. If there are any other women on the stage, you can help them."

Even though they'd probably be women for the whorehouses in the Badlands, he supposed it was better than nothing. The rate of women to men was skewed toward men. Any new women in town were welcomed.

The stagecoach turned the last corner into town. Charlie pulled back on the reins. Josiah strained back on the brake. The coach slowed. A shout came from a tavern to King's left. The doors creaked open. He caught a blur from the corner of his eye. A blur that became a brick wall as it hit King in the side. A blur that tossed him over the side of the boardwalk and back into the mud.

SUZANNA CLUTCHED HER bonnet, the perspiration in her hands wrinkling the fabric. The driver had taken them down the winding, twisting mountainside at breakneck speed, sending her fellow passengers bobbing, weaving, and bouncing against each other. The small lunch they'd had hours ago was creeping its way up her throat.

Saliva pooled in her mouth. She swallowed deeply and patted her damp face with her handkerchief. The breeze from the open windows wasn't helping. Mrs. Woods even looked a little green around the gills. A lady like her doesn't throw up, does she?

With one last turn, the horses slowed. A massive sigh of relief filled the inside of the coach as the driver urged the horses on. Taking a deep, cleansing breath, Suzanna peered around her sister and out the window at the passing scenery.

This was Deadwood? Where were the fancy houses? The cobblestone streets? The society ladies shopping? The paved sidewalks?

This was... She bit her bottom lip and gripped the small bag containing her meager coins. This was chaos. People, mostly men dressed in clothes that had seen better days, milled around on the raised, wooden sidewalk. Straggly beards, worn-out boots, cigars hanging between their lips, and hats looking as if they'd been dragged by oxen.

The buildings they passed weren't much better. Had anyone even measured before slapping them up in a slapdash way? At least most of the towns they'd traveled through had some type of order to their main streets. These buildings weren't even in a straight row, and some of the boards used in construction still had tree bark on them. Signs of various sizes and shapes hung haphazardly, as if a drunk had put them up.

Julia grabbed her hand. "Oh, my. I believe there are Chinese people here. Look at their strange clothes."

Chinese? In Deadwood? Several children dressed in pants and tunics stopped to stare beneath a sign reading, *Hong Fee, Washing, Ironing.*

Before they stopped, Mr. Silverstone opened his door and stepped into the mud. He reached into the coach. "Here, Miss, give me your hand."

Suzanna peered down her nose at his dirty nails. No way was she going to touch him. The other door opened, and a wide plank board was placed between the coach and some wooden steps leading to a boardwalk. At least they wouldn't have to slog through the mud.

A handsome man, dressed in a crisp white shirt beneath a blue brocade vest, stepped onto the board and held out his hand. Was he rich?

"Mrs. Woods, I presume? I'm Dan Iverson. I can take you to your husband."

Mrs. Woods tittered. Women that age tittered? But she didn't blame the woman as she felt like giggling herself. Oh, my, he was good-looking. Holding her hand in the crook of his arm, Mr. Iverson guided Mrs. Woods down the platform.

She and Julia waited for him to return. He would, wouldn't he? No gentleman would allow two single women to leave the stagecoach unescorted. After a minute, Julia stepped through the door.

"What are you doing?" Suzanna grabbed her arm.

"I'm not going to sit here and wait for some man to help us. We traveled here on our own, we can find lodging for the night on our own."

Her sister was probably right. The sooner they found a place to stay, freshen up and rest, the better. Tomorrow she'd meet with the people who hired her. Making a good impression was vital.

Julia was already on the boardwalk when someone reached inside. "Miss? If you'll give me your hand, I'll help you down the ramp."

The man's deep, raspy voice sent shivers down her spine. Not scary or creepy shivers like Mr. Silverstone produced. But something new and delicious, like heading into a new adventure. Holding her bonnet in one hand, she placed the other in his. Tingles spread up her arm. Her face flushed. Was she getting sick? That was all she needed in a strange town.

Lifting her skirt daintily like Mrs. Woods, she stepped from the coach, expecting someone handsome and gentlemanly. Instead, her eyes beheld the dirtiest, muddiest, most disreputable person she'd ever seen. The sides of his hat, which he hadn't bothered to remove, dripped water. With the amount of mud or whatever that covered him, it was difficult to tell the color of his shoulder-length hair. The ends of a scruffy beard were matted together, while any skin not covered in facial hair looked as if he'd taken a bath in the middle of the street. His clothes didn't look or smell any better.

She yanked her fingers from his.

"Miss?"

"Thank you, but I believe I can walk on my own." With her nose in the air, she stepped past the man. As she reached the end of the plank, a cat ran past, followed by a mangy dog. The dog rubbed against her skirt. She tottered backward on her heeled boots. Her bonnet flew from her hand. She arms flailed like a windmill.

"Miss!" the man yelled, grabbing her arm as two more dogs, barking as if they'd treed a raccoon, charged past.

The first one rammed into her legs, the second into the man. She clutched his arm to regain her balance. He grasped her other arm. Her heels teetered on the wooden edge.

"Hold..." The man's words were lost as they tumbled over the side.

The mud, as she landed on her back, was soft. Gooshy, wet, and soft. Not like the man who landed on top of her, pushing her farther into the goo. Someone laughed. She opened one eye and, through muddy eyelashes, peered over the man's shoulder.

Several people gathered on the boardwalk, pointing and snickering. More followed, including children she'd probably be teaching. Soon, the entire crowd was laughing. Tears pooled in her eyes.

"Get off me, you big oaf." She pushed against his broad chest. "People are staring."

The man raised up on his hands and looked down at her with the bright, blue eyes, like the sky on a bright summer's day. Her heart skipped a beat, and something fluttered in her stomach. She was definitely getting sick. Nothing else could explain it.

She closed her eyes and opened them again. Mud stuck in the creases of his frown. "Get up. You're embarrassing me." Pushing against him was like trying to move a boulder the size of a house. "Please."

The man blinked, then, shoving against the ground, stood, extending his hand. "I'm so sorry this happened. Those d—" He cleared his throat. "I mean it's the darn dogs' fault."

Getting herself up was going to be a problem. Ignoring his mud-encrusted hand, she pressed her palms behind her and pushed upward, only to have her hands slip. She could do this.

"Show's over folks." Mr. Iverson, without a speck of dirt on him, shooed the gawkers away until only her sister and one other, older gentleman were left.

After the third attempt at extracting herself, the big oaf leaned down and put his hands on either side of her waist. She slapped his hands. "What do you think you're doing, you lout? Get your hands off me."

"Miss, I'm only trying to help you out of this mess."

Before she had another chance to smack his hands away, he drew her up, the mud slurping and sucking at her clothes. As if she weighed nothing more than a mouse, he lifted her onto the boardwalk, his large hands spanning her waist. Her hair came loose from its bun, the long strands clinging to her blouse. She wiped at a muddy strand stuck to her face. Mr. Iverson, Julia, and the older man took a step back when she shook out her skirt.

The disreputable lug plopped his even more disreputable hat on his head. Maybe if she knew the man, which she positively did not want to, she would laugh at his grubby appearance.

"Are you all right?" Julia asked, holding shaking fingers to her mouth.

Was her sister hiding a smile? She better not be. Suzanna narrowed her eyes and fisted her hands at her waist. This was a disaster. Could things get any worse?

The elderly gentleman stepped forward. "Miss Suzanna Lindstrom?"

Suzanna raised her chin. How could this man possibly know her name? "Yes."

"Oliver Ogden at your service." He clicked his heels and gave a small bow like he was greeting royalty rather than a schoolteacher covered from head to toe in muck.

Suzanna took a step backward. Oh. No. It couldn't be. But it was. It was the man who had written and offered her a job. Probably witnessed the entire fiasco created by the imbecile standing beside her. Could the ground just swallow her up now? Wait, it almost did. She struck out her hand, then pulled it back, wiping her fingers on her skirt, which was ridiculous. Mud wiping on mud only created more mud.

"I'm, uh, pleased to meet you."

Mr. Ogden gaze swept her from head to toe. "I believe I'll allow you to freshen up a bit. I'll see you in the morning in front of King's Restaurant." With that, he tipped his hat and strode down the sidewalk.

About the Author:

Tina Susedik is an award-winning, multi-published author in both fiction and non-fiction. She is published in history, military, romantic mystery, erotic romance, and children's books, with twenty-eight books to her credit. Her books are in both print and eBook format. She lives in northern Wisconsin with her husband of forty-six years. She also writes as Anita Kidesu. Tina hosts a radio show, "Your Book Garden," where she interviews authors of all genres.

Where to find Tina:

Twitter: https://twitter.com/TinaSusedik
Website: www.tina-susedik.com
Facebook: https://www.facebook.com/TinaSusedikAuthor/
http://www.pinterest.com/tinasusedik/
Goodreads: https://www.goodreads.com/photo/author/1754353.Tina_Susedik
Newsletter: http://tinasusedik.us11.list-manage.com/subscribe?u=874ff86e3f10f756a138fbc3a&id=1cfdf516fc[1]

Books by Tina Susedik
Riding for Love
All I want for Christmas is a Soul Mate - Anthology
My Sexy Valentine
Sizzle in the Snow
Never With a Rich Man

---

1. https://l.facebook.com/l.php?u=http%3A%2F%2Ftinasusedik.us11.list-manage.com%2Fsubscribe%3Fu%3D874ff86e3f10f756a138fbc3a%26id%3D1cfdf516fc&h=ATNA-jGtIpC7Tz8vdC3sYYLhcCiMepWFUb2h2JGkoXHipuBjGtBon-oPOJNT8ryII0xPdQdtB-Jp01wQoYRyT_JC_6CvbgLOMSr4-8PMAEG_1Syqofne1NDlmYxT_RnORX3jB9VQ

The Trail to Love: The Soul Mate Tree Collective
Missing My Heart – A Chandler County Mystery
Missing Innocence – A Chandler County Mystery
A Photograph of Love – Hell Yeah!
Love With a Side of Crazy – Hell Yeah!
The School Marm – Wild Deadwood Tales Anthology
The Home Front – Destiny Whispers Anthology

Writing as Anita Kidesu

South Seas Seduction
Surprise Me
Surprise Me Again
Double the Surprise

Children's Books by Tina Susedik

Uncle Bill's Farm
The Adventures of Peanut and Casey on Uncle Bill's Farm
The Hat Peddler

Made in the USA
Middletown, DE
26 April 2022